PROLOGUE

It's hot in the trunk of the car. Ike Thoreau gasps, feels like he can't breathe. He calls for help with a dry and burning throat. He headbutts the lid, his arms bound behind his back with what feel like cable ties. There's a bag over his head. The bag doesn't help with the heat. Makes him feel hotter. Sweat gets in his eyes. His legs are free, though, and he uses them to kick out. The car is moving. He doubts they're still in Kirkwood. Doubts there's anyone out there can hear him.

They must've been waiting for him. He'd just got home when it happened. Just pulled up and parked his car after another late night at the offices of the *Cullingworth County Times*, trying to tell a story seemingly no one wants to hear. It was dark. He wasn't looking around, wasn't checking the streets, because why would he be? Despite everything, despite what he's been looking into, what he's found out, he never thought he was in any danger.

They came from behind. He still doesn't know where they parked their car, where they lay in wait for him to approach his front door. He had his keys out, was looking down, when he heard the footsteps. They came so fast he didn't have a chance to turn around. They body-checked him from behind, banged his forehead off his front door, one of them – he thinks there were two, thinks there *are* two – snuck in a kidney shot; then they dragged a bag down over his head. A burlap sack. It blocked out the world. Then he was dragged to the car, given another kidney shot every time he faltered. If he dragged his feet or made himself heavy, he was dealt a kick in the ass, a slap in the back of the head, anything to keep him moving. On the way, his arms were pulled back. His hands were clasped together, his wrists bound.

The two men were strong. Ike is not. Ike is tall, but he's rail thin, has never put on the mass his father promised him always came to Thoreau men later in life, when they hit their thirties. He's thirty-three now. He has a horrible feeling he might not make it to thirty-four.

When they bundled him into the car, they struck him in the back of the head. He doesn't know what they used, but it was hard. He thinks it was more than just a fist. The narrow lens of the world within his burlap sack began to spin. His eyeballs swam. He went dizzy. Thinks he blacked out for a bit; he isn't sure how long. Everything has happened so fast. As soon as he came round, he started hollering, started thrashing.

The car moves steadily. It doesn't slow. No one tries to pull them over, to stop them. No one has heard his cries. Ike settles. Gulps. Breathes hard. The fibers of the sack get drawn into his mouth when he sucks in air. He coughs and splutters, and that makes things worse. The only sound, other than the engine and his ragged breathing, is the beating of his heart. It gets louder, deafening in his ears, until it's all he can hear.

WRONG TURN

A TOM ROLLINS THRILLER

PAUL HEATLEY

INKUBATOR
BOOKS

For Aidan

Then the car stops.

Ike freezes. After a journey in which he was so desperate for breath, he finds himself holding it in. Grits his teeth. Braces himself.

Car doors open and close. They're coming to the back of the car. They're coming to him. Ike wants to play it cool. He knows they'll have heard his screams, heard his thrashing, but now, as they come for him, as they look upon him, he's going to be tough. He won't give them the satisfaction of seeing him weak.

As the trunk opens, a whimper escapes him.

Two pairs of strong arms reach into his blind world, announce themselves by sound and touch. They haul him bodily from the car, drag him round the vehicle, the bag still over his head.

"Please," Ike says. "What's this about – come on, *please*, take the bag off, please. I don't even – what's this all about?"

His desire to be strong, to be cool, to be tough, it has faded quickly away. Now, all he wants is to end this night alive.

Only when he's in front of the car, forced down to his knees, is the sack removed from his head. The head-lights are on behind him, casting his shadow long across the desert floor. Something scuttles away at the furthest reaches of the light. Somewhere, far away, a coyote howls.

Ike understands. He hasn't been kidnapped, brought out to the desert, and forced down to his knees with the headlights of a car behind him just to talk.

"Please," Ike says, still begging. He doesn't see what else he can do. "I don't understand – is this because of –?"

"Will you just shut your fuckin' *mouth*," one of the men says, tired of the pleading. "*Christ*."

Something connects in Ike's terrified brain. The voice. There is a familiarity in it. He knows it. He knows the man talking. "I know you," he says. "I know who –"

Something connects with Ike's skull, now. It's hard, and it's cold, and Ike knows it is a gun. He trembles; he cries out; he almost pisses his pants. Tears roll down his face. He starts sobbing. He doesn't care.

"You just don't know when to fuckin' *stop*, do you?" the voice, the familiar voice, says. The gun clicks. Ike doesn't understand what it means, doesn't know much about guns, but he knows it can't be anything good.

Ike starts shaking his head, begging again, between sobs now, his only recourse. "I won't print the story," he says, tasting snot. "I promise I won't print the story. I won't print it, I won't. I'll delete it. I'll delete the whole thing. I won't print it –"

"Jesus Christ, will you shut him up already?" says the other man, the one who hasn't spoken yet. Ike isn't listening as closely now, but if he were, he reckons he probably would have recognized it, too.

"Gladly," the first man says.

"I'll delete the story. I won't print the story, I swear, I swear, I –"

"Damn right you won't." He pulls the trigger.

1

Tom Rollins is on his way to Mexico. To Guaymas. He's in Texas currently, heading for the border. The urn containing the ashes of Alejandra Flores, of her and his brother's unborn child, are to his right in the footwell of the passenger seat. Safely tucked in so it doesn't roll. Tom won't let it out of his sight.

It's a long way to go to Guaymas, but he doesn't have the radio on. He doesn't want music. Right now, he isn't listening to anything but the wind that whips by past his open window. His thoughts are focused, and he wants to keep them that way. All the way to Mexico. The pendant that hangs from his rearview mirror, the skull-faced visage of Santa Muerte, dances in the warm breeze that blows through. He glances at it, just once, and it brings remembrances that tighten his white-knuckled grip on the steering wheel, make his eyes flicker to the urn one more time.

The car is a Ford, dark blue in color. He bought it cheap, in cash, from a dealership back in New Mexico a couple of days ago. A week after he last saw his father, his stepmother, his brother. Anthony, his baby brother, was trying to take a swing at him at the time. They had differing views as to what should be done with Alejandra's ashes. Tom knows – *knows* – that she wanted to be taken back to Mexico, to be spread on her home soil. Anthony disagreed. Anthony wanted to go against her wishes, to keep her atop his mantelpiece or on his windowsill like some kind of ornament.

Tom took the urn. He knows it's the right thing to do. He has to honor her. If his brother won't, he will. More than that – though he won't admit it out loud – it is Anthony's fault she is dead. Tom feels this, feels the bitterness that comes with this knowledge. She died because of Anthony. Because of the trouble he got himself into, and then because he couldn't keep her safe.

Tom's eyes go to the Santa Muerte pendant watching over him. He remembers Alejandra's words when she gave it to him.

She'll keep you safe.

In war. She was to keep him safe while he was overseas, in a desert hell, taking shots from insurgents. She did her job. Tom is still alive. He's still safe, relatively.

Alejandra needed Santa Muerte, not him. Alejandra needed to be kept safe. Needed to be kept alive.

Tom stayed low after he took the urn. Got rid of the car he'd been driving, traveled on foot to a cheap motel in the middle of nowhere. A lot of people were looking for him. The CIA, for a start. Tom went AWOL from his black ops squad, and they weren't happy about that. Now, after recent events, certain illicit elements of the FBI are looking for him, too.

Senator Seth Goldberg, however, has said on television that he'd like to shake the hand of the man who saved his and his family's lives, and those of his entire congregation, not to mention everyone else present in that part of Dallas that day.

His brother is probably looking, too. Hot on his trail, though he should have found the trail quickly went cold. Tom stayed in that motel for a week before he bought the Ford, then stayed there another couple of nights before continuing on his journey. Anthony will not find him; Tom is confident of that. Tom was always the one who paid more attention to their father's after-school lessons in survivalism – in tracking and in covering one's tracks. His time in the army only further compounded his existing knowledge. Anthony has never been in the army. He's barely held a job. He's been in jail, but that's hardly the same thing.

It's hot in Texas. It's hot in New Mexico, too, where he has spent most of his time recently, but it's a different kind of heat here. Oppressive. Dry. Almost as soon as he crossed the border, his shirt clung to his back with sweat. He glanced in the mirror and saw beads pop on his forehead. The open window doesn't help, but it's better than keeping it up. It wasn't like this in Dallas. Tom is keeping his distance from Dallas. His face might still be fresh in people's minds there, even with his newly grown beard and his hair longer than it's ever been before.

He spent yesterday in Lubbock, with Cindy 'Shriek' Vaughan. She didn't sound surprised to hear from him when he called to tell her he was coming. "Would you believe I've been expecting this call?" she said.

Tom went to her apartment.

"I like the new look," she said, letting him in. "Very hirsute."

Tom grunted. "I'm sure you can guess why."

"Oh, I've been reading all about your recent

exploits," she said, smiling. "Should I be hailing you as a national hero, Mr. Rollins? Seems everyone else is."

"Not everyone," he said. "That's why I'm here."

Cindy went to her computer, sat down with one leg tucked under herself. "I figured."

"You said, last time, that you can forge documents, create new identities."

"I'm not sure I said that second part."

"I read between the lines. I watched you work. I have faith in your abilities."

"Flattery will get you everywhere, Mr. Rollins." She winked at him. "What're we talking here – new driver's license? Passport?"

"Yes, and yes."

"You're going overseas?"

"I'm crossing a border."

Distracted suddenly from these memories, Tom sees something up ahead. Cars parked in the middle of the road. Flashing lights. Looks like an accident. So far his journey has been uneventful, the road mostly devoid of other vehicles. He slows in preparation.

When he gets close enough, he can see what's happened. A crash. Looks like two cars were racing each other, both of them pointing the same way, the direction Tom is going in. The one on the wrong side of the road has sideswiped the other while overtaking. Tom sees the passenger-side wheel has popped, causing the driver to lose control, to swerve across the road, hit the other, cause his front end to buckle. There are skid marks on the road where the two cars, entangled, have dragged each other forward, the drivers' feet slammed down on the brakes.

The Highway Patrol is present. Tom can see them on either side of the crash, one on the left and one on the right, directing traffic. On the opposite side of the crash, there are two other cars waiting to get by. The road is blocked, and they have to go onto the desert, directed by the patrolman waving them on.

The drivers of both cars are unharmed. Tom spots them standing way off to one side, sheepish, heads bowed and hands clasped, while another of the patrolmen admonishes them, questions them, takes their details. It could have been worse, Tom knows. There could be blood baking on the asphalt right now.

Tom gets close. There is a plain black baseball cap on the passenger seat. He brushes the hair back off his forehead, pulls the cap on. He's already wearing sunglasses. Wants to cover as much of his face as possible.

The patrolman directing traffic on Tom's side motions him to stop, points where to go. When he sees Tom's window is open, he calls, "Take your time – it's rough there."

Tom nods, drops a gear, makes his way slowly round the crash. The uneven surface below rocks him side to side. Stones scrape the bottom of his car. He can hear sand thrown up by his spinning wheels. He goes slower. Hits a big rock, judging by the almighty thud he hears underneath, from the front, throwing him forward. Tom grits his teeth, expels air through flaring nostrils, is glad to get off the desert sand and crawl back up onto the road. The patrolman on the other side, seeing him emerge, tips the brim of his hat, salutes him. Tom raises a hand to wave in response. He drives on. Puts distance between himself and the crash scene.

It's far behind him when the knocking starts. Tom isn't sure he hears it at first. Thinks it might just be something carrying on the wind. But then he starts to feel it, the way the car jerks in his grip. The way it shudders. The knocking gets louder.

Tom remembers the thud as he circled the crash,

briefly crossed the desert. *"Shit."* Whatever it is, he's going to have to check it. There's no way he's going to make it another seven hundred miles with something knocking under the hood of his car.

There's a sign for the next town. He has to turn off for it. Brenton, ten miles. This is not a detour he wants to take, but it is necessary. He manages to make it eight before smoke starts billowing out from the front of the car, from under the hood, obscuring his view through the windscreen. The engine dies.

Tom pulls to the side of the road, doesn't attempt to restart the engine. It would only cause more damage. He takes a deep breath, remains calm. Gets out of the car. It is no cooler outside than it is in. The smoke, at least, is settling. It is not billowing out as it was.

Hands on hips, he looks up and down the road. There are no cars coming. He wipes the sweat from his face, flicks it onto the road, half-expecting it to sizzle. He waits until the smoke dies to a faint rising wisp, and still nothing has passed him. Nothing he can wave down, nothing to give him a tow.

In the distance, through the haze in the air, he thinks he can see Brenton. It's not too far. He could leave the car, just pick up a new one, but it looks like a small place, doubts it has a dealership. There's bound to be a garage in Brenton, though. Somewhere that can fix him back up, send him on his way.

Tom kicks a stone off the road. "Well, *fuck.*"

He reaches into the car, releases the handbrake, takes it out of gear, and starts pushing.

2

Sally Blevins owns the one and only hotel in Brenton. She inherited it from her father. It's nothing flashy. Crispin Blevins had high hopes for it when he first bought the building. These hopes did not come to fruition. Much like the rest of the town, it's fallen into disrepair. It's occupied almost exclusively by meth heads, and feels more like a halfway house than a hotel most days.

Right now, one of those meth heads is leaning on the counter behind which Sally sits, talking her ear off. Darby White is her longest-staying guest. He doesn't have anywhere else to go, has lost everything he had to his addiction. She thinks he's high right now. He talks speedily, has the animated quality he always gets when he's had a hit or two, his eyebrows moving up and down like they have a life of their own.

"You know the mayor's running for governor, right? Hey, Sally, you know that, right? You know he's running for governor?"

Sally is looking past his bouncing body, through the

small lobby to the window at the side of the open door, thinking about being somewhere else. Anywhere.

"Hey, hey, *Sally* – Sally, you there? You home? Anyone home?" Darby starts waving his hand in front of her face, starts laughing to himself, giggling, like he's just said something funny.

She has no doubts, now. He's high.

"Yes, Darby," she says. "I'm aware that the mayor is running for governor."

"'Cause you seen all the posters up, right?"

"Those, and other reasons."

"Well, listen, okay, listen, some guys were around this morning, looking to put up a fresh batch of those posters, I reckon, because the election is soon, right, real soon, but they didn't like the look of old Brenton, so they paid me to put em up for them – twenty bucks, twenty bucks, just like that." He clicks his fingers. "Twenty bucks for a morning's work. Not bad, huh? Twenty bucks."

"Uh-huh." Sally turns her eyes from the window, lays them upon him. "You think about using any of that twenty bucks to pay your bill?"

At this, there is finally a hesitation in Darby's rolling speech. He stands on the spot, though he continues to move, as if he's vibrating, his eyes flicker to the side, trying to come up with a good enough excuse. "*Uh...*" He runs his tongue round the inside of his mouth, over his ruined teeth, probes the gaps where some of them have fallen out.

Sally waves it off. "Guess I'll just keep your tab rolling, huh? You at least save any of it for food?"

Darby lights up at this. "Oh yeah, oh yeah, totally! First thing I did, I got myself a candy bar."

Sally raises her eyebrows. "Nutritious."

"Yup, you bet. Keeps me going, uh-huh. Had peanut

butter in it. All the protein a grown boy needs." He winks.

Outside, she hears a car pull up to the sidewalk in front of the hotel, parking in what little shade is out there. Two doors open, close. There is talking. Sally recognises one of the voices as her sister's.

"You ain't gotta come in, Dean," Anna is saying. "You can just stay out here if you wanna. It ain't like we're gonna be talkin' about anything that's of interest to you."

"Sit in the car and cook like a dog?" Dean says. "No thank you, Miss."

"You ain't gotta stay in the car. There's a bench there. Or you can go to the bar, get a drink."

"I'm coming in, Anna."

They reach the open door. Anna steps in first, smiles and waves at her sister behind the counter. "Sally," she says. "Hope you don't mind me dropping by like this. Just felt like getting off the ranch, thought I'd stop by and see you."

Sally returns the smile, though she's not pleased to see Dean Slade with her, babysitting, like she's not a fully grown woman and can't be permitted to do her own thing in her own time. "You ain't gotta announce yourself for me, Anna," Sally says. She stands, waves for her sister to come round to her so they can hug.

Darby remains leaning on the counter until he realizes Dean is hard-eyeing him. Sally watches over her sister's shoulder. Sees how Darby continues to vibrate on the spot, until Dean finally says, "Think you oughtta give the two ladies a little space, Darby?"

Darby jumps at the sound of his voice, at his command. "Sure thing," he says. He forces himself to smile at Dean as he slinks past him. His open mouth is painful to look at. He goes outside, takes his usual spot on the bench in front of the hotel, lights a cigarette.

Sally and Anna break their embrace, take seats. "It's a little cooler back here," Sally says. "Got the air con." She pats the top of the nearby unit.

"I'm glad of it," Anna says, holding her hands out to it like it's a roaring fire on a frozen day. "Dean refuses to put it on in his car."

"Eats fuel," Dean says, standing by the door, leaning into the frame. He winks at Sally, knowing she won't be happy to see him here.

Dean Slade is the best friend of Earl McQuade. Earl is Anna's boyfriend. Earl doesn't like letting Anna out of his sight. Sally had thought when Anna moved out to the ranch with him he would have finally eased off a little, but no. Anna isn't permitted to go anywhere without an escort, not even to visit her sister.

Sally has inherited their father's dislike of the McQuades with greater fervor than Anna ever did. Sometimes, Sally feels like her disdain has to make up for the two of them. If Crispin Blevins knew his little girl, his littlest girl, was living with a McQuade, he'd be turning in his grave.

Sally and Earl first started dating in high school. Crispin was still alive then, and she kept it hidden from him. Kept it secret from Sally, too. She probably thought their forbidden love was Shakespearean, like Romeo and Juliet. Loved the thrill of it, the sneaking around, as much – if not more – than the person she was actually sneaking to see.

After Crispin's heart gave out on him and he died, Earl's true colors became a little clearer, even to Anna. He became possessive, seeing nothing now that could stop him from having what he wanted. He became jealous, too. It was the jealousy Anna disliked most, the jealousy that had chased away all of her male friends, because none of them wanted to mess with someone whose last name was McQuade. She broke up with Earl, more than once, but he was persistent as well as possessive, and he wouldn't take no for an answer – still won't – until Anna just gave up and moved in with him.

Sally knows this is not all Anna has given up on. She has a suspicion that Anna is using drugs, to help her tolerate her new living arrangements and this relationship she finds herself trapped in. It's meth, most likely. It's probably easy to come across at the ranch. Earl is likely giving it to her himself. Anna's teeth are fine, still straight and pearly white, but her skin looks tight and tired, pinched at the corners of her eyes. Whatever it is, whatever she's using, Anna won't admit to it. Sally has tried to ask, and was met with vehement denials.

They make small talk, each asks the other how they are, while Dean makes sure to stand within earshot, eavesdropping. Sally can just imagine Earl telling him to listen in on their conversation, to make sure Anna isn't trying to run out on him, plotting with her older sister.

As much as Sally would like it to, silently wills it to, the subject never comes up. Anna never raises it. Anna has resigned herself to her life, suffering for choices and mistakes she made when she was too young to know any better, and believed she was in love with the first boy to tell her he felt the same way.

Sally does not believe her sister is happy out there. *Will not* believe it. She can see it in Anna's tired, browbeaten eyes. This isn't love. It's one of the furthest things from it. It's ownership. It's captivity.

Another car pulls up out front. Sally hears Dean suck air through his teeth. She looks up, sees a Cullingworth County Sheriff's Department cruiser park right in front of the door. Right in front of Dean. Deputy Daniel

Murphy gets out of the car, puts his hat on his head, dips the brim to both Darby and Dean.

Anna peers over the counter. "Looks like everyone's coming to visit you today, huh?"

"Sure feels that way," Sally says.

"You and Daniel had an argument or somethin'?"

Sally raises an eyebrow. "No. Why'd you say that?"

Anna laughs. "'Cause you should see the look on your face right now. It's all right to be pleased to see him, y'know. I won't think you're any less of a badass." She nudges her with her elbow, giggles some more.

Sally gets to her feet, though doesn't step round the counter. Dean blocks Daniel's way, doesn't make a move to step aside. "Afternoon, Deputy," he says.

"Afternoon, Dean," Daniel says. "Far from home, ain't you?"

"Anna needed a ride to see her sister, and you know me. Always happy to oblige a lady whenever I can."

"Mm. I'm sure. Think I've heard that about you, Dean, once upon a time."

"More than likely. My gentlemanly behavior is renowned. What brings you to the fair town of Brenton, Deputy?"

"Why, the scenery, of course." Daniel looks up into Dean's face, smiles, waits for him to move. Dean is slow about it, but he finally steps aside, motions that the way is clear for Daniel to enter.

Daniel steps into the lobby, comes to the counter. He's smiling at Sally. He takes off his hat, sets it down. "How you doin' today?"

"I'm fine," Sally says. "How're you?"

"Hot." He grins, nods at Anna. "I didn't know you'd have company."

"Don't mind me," Anna says, chewing on a lock of hair and spinning side to side in her swivel chair.

Sally ignores her sister. "What can I do for you, Daniel?"

"I was just passing by, figured I'd stop in and say hello."

"When're you gonna take my sister on another date, Deputy Dan?" Anna says. "Been a while since the last one now, hasn't it?"

"Well, I wonder that myself," Daniel says. "I keep waiting for her to be free."

"Then you're gonna be waiting a long time," Anna says. "You've gotta take the initiative, man. You're gonna have to drag her away from this place."

Sally stands very still, rolls her eyes. "If only there were someone here to share the burden with me," she says.

Anna doesn't respond to this. Just keeps swivelling in her chair, grinning at Daniel.

"Ignore her," Sally says. "You try to drag me out, I won't thank you for it."

"Wouldn't dream of it," Daniel says.

"Such a gent."

"I take tips from Dean," Daniel says, knowing Dean will be listening in.

"Your shift nearly over?"

"I got another couple of hours on the clock, then it's done." He checks back over his shoulder, leans forward across the counter, lowers his voice so only Sally can hear. "What *are* my chances of a date?"

"Slim. My help has quit."

"Again?"

"Yup. This all you came by for?"

"No, but your sister got me thinking I should try my luck." He winks at her. "I'm on my way to see Frank," he says, his voice returning to its normal volume. "He ain't been in for a few days now, and he ain't answering his phone, either."

"He ain't just sick?" Sally says.

"That's what the sheriff thinks, but no one else has heard from him. Ain't like Frank to not be in touch."

Daniel turns, still leaning on the counter. He faces Dean. "How about you, Dean? You heard anything from Frank?"

Dean glances over, shrugs. "Frank Aynsley?"

"Deputy Frank Aynsley, that's right – I know you and your buddies are familiar with him."

"Ain't denying it."

"Uh-huh. You heard anything from him? Maybe about him?"

Dean shrugs again. "Should I have?"

Sally watches the back-and-forth between the two of them, feeling like there is a subtext, an insinuation. If Daniel is implying something, that perhaps Dean, or Earl, had anything to do with Frank's sudden silence, Dean's remaining calm about it, not letting it get to him, giving nothing away. He leans against the wall next to the door, lethargic. Scratches his jaw. Turns his head and spits out onto the sidewalk through the open door.

"I'm just curious," Daniel says. "Like I said, you and your buddies know him well."

"Didn't you say the sheriff said he called in sick?"

"I did. But that was a while ago now, nearly a week, and he ain't responded to anyone's messages or calls checking in on him, making sure he's all right."

Dean holds out his hands. "I don't know what you expect me to say. I sure hope he's all right, Daniel."

Before Daniel can say anything else, Darby comes rushing up to the door. He's more animated than he was earlier, talking to Sally and telling her about his twenty bucks. "Come take a look at this, guys." He's waving at them to follow him outside.

No one moves. They all look at him. Dean, closest to the door, is the first to go. He steps outside, looking doubtful that whatever has caught Darby's eye is going to be of any interest to him, but then he bursts out laughing. "Aw, man," he says. "Looks like someone new is rolling into town."

Darby starts to laugh, too, following Dean's lead.

Sally looks at Daniel, then at Anna, then the three of them go to see what's so funny. Sally and Daniel make it to the door. Anna watches from the window. "What's happening?" she says.

Sally steps out onto the sidewalk, shields her eyes with her hand. From down the road, coming into town, just passing by the bar, a man comes. He's pushing his car. As he gets closer, she can see that his shirt is off, tucked into the back of his jeans. He wears a baseball cap backwards to keep the hair out of his face. His forehead glistens with beads of sweat, and the muscles of his thickly corded torso are slick with it.

Dean is laughing still. "How far do you think he's had to push that thing?"

There are others out on the streets of Brenton and hovering in their doorways, watching the stranger come into town, pushing his car through the center of it. They stop and stare, talk among themselves. Some of them laugh, like Dean. None offer to help.

"Don't you think you should go give him a hand?" Sally says, turning to Daniel.

Daniel puts his hat back on. "Suppose I'd best," he says.

"Just leave him, man, just leave him," Dean says, but Daniel ignores him, steps off the sidewalk and onto the road, makes his way over to the stranger pushing his car.

"Back inside," Sally says to the rest of them. She can't make the whole town go back in, make them stop staring at the unfortunate stranger like he's some sideshow attraction, but she can at least clear up her small corner of it. "Come on, everyone. You too, Darby. Get back on up to your room."

3

The first thing Tom notices about Brenton is that it's a shithole.

Most of the buildings he passes, the ones that used to be businesses – or perhaps still are, it's hard to tell – have their windows boarded up, their doors barred shut. Weeds grow through the cracks in the sidewalks. He passes a car with four flat tires, dumped at the side of the road, rust eating up its frame. He starts wondering if there's a garage here at all. If maybe he's pushed his car these last two miles in this sweltering heat all for nothing.

The people don't look much better than the town. They appear in similar states of disrepair. Many of them are pale, ill looking, like vampires, except he knows they're more than likely meth heads. In a few of the smiling, laughing mouths, amused at his predicament, he spots rotten, blackened, and missing teeth.

He makes it halfway through the town when, out of the corner of his eye, over the top of his car, he notices someone approaching. When he looks, he sees it's a cop.

Tom doesn't slow. Looks straight ahead, keeps going. He's not doing anything wrong.

"Give you a hand?" the cop says.

Tom doesn't answer the question. Instead, he asks, "There a garage around here?"

"Sure." The cop goes to the back of the car, starts pushing. Tom feels the weight of the car lighten, feels it moving again with a pace it hasn't had since he first started. "You keep steering. I'll direct you. You just wanna take a left at the corner there."

The garage isn't far from where the cop joins him. They stop the car right outside its open doors, can hear the mechanic inside whizzing an air gun, the thunderous rattle of it putting a wheel back on a vehicle. Tom grabs his shirt from where it's tucked into his waistband, pulls it back on. The cop is looking at him expectantly. "Thanks for the help," Tom says. "Appreciate it."

"Sure thing. You need anything else?"

"No, I'm good. I got it from here."

The cop nods. "Mechanic's called Lonnie, though everyone just calls him Lon. Don't let him try'n fleece you, okay? Ain't many people round here still got their cars, and the ones who do are wise to him, so he tends to crank up the prices for out-of-towners."

Tom nods. "Got it."

The cop tips his hat, then turns round and heads off to the corner again.

Tom watches him go, waits until he's round the corner and out of sight, then turns and goes into the garage. The cop didn't recognize him. Either has never seen a picture of him, or the beard and hair were enough to throw him off. This far out of the way, Tom doubts they'll have seen his face. Even if they have, they won't be expecting him to pass through, and he'll have been quickly forgotten, like any other number of bulletins they've seen over the years. Chances are some of the people around here won't know anything at all about what went down in Dallas, and that includes the cops.

The radio is turned up loud. It's tuned to a classic rock station, and the mechanic – Lon – is singing along with Led Zeppelin, doing his best to hit all the high notes as he lowers a car from the ramp. Lon has long hair tied loosely back, and his blue overalls are stained almost black with oil and grease. Something hangs from the corner of his mouth; he occasionally pauses in his singing to draw from it, blow the smoke out. Tom can smell the smoke. It's not a cigarette.

"Hey."

Lon spins, eyes wide. He spits the joint out, crushes it underfoot. "Oh, hey, hi, hello there." He smiles. His teeth have bits of food in them, but they at least don't look like they're about to fall out. "Help you with somethin'?"

"Car's broke down." Tom tilts his body so Lon can see past him, can see the car parked outside.

Lon sees the car, raises his eyebrows. He leaves the lowering ramp, the wheels still hovering a few inches from the floor, and heads out to take a closer look. He walks around it, like he's expecting the damage to be on the outside, easy to spot.

"I'm in a rush," Tom says.

Lon stops walking at the front, looks it over. "What's wrong with it?"

Tom explains what happened. How he's had to push it the two miles from outside town to get it to here.

"They should never have waved you onto the desert, Jesus Christ," Lon says, shaking his head.

Tom is inclined to agree.

"Well, let's pop the hood, and I'll take a look."

The hood open, Lon produces a flashlight from the breast pocket of his overalls. Tom notices, as he pulls it out, that there are a few more tightly rolled joints in there, too. One of them almost falls out as he brings the flashlight free.

Lon leans inside, takes a look around. "Radiator's burst," he says, straightening up. "Hate to tell ya, it's gonna take a while to get a replacement here. I'll go order it right now, but we're still lookin' at a couple of days."

Tom sucks air through his front teeth. "Nothin' you can do to repair it?"

"You musta hit some big rocks, man. You take a look at it for yourself if you wanna – there's nothin' I can do about that."

Tom remembers what the cop said about Lon's tendency to fleece outsiders, leans inside, peers down into the gap at the front of the engine. He can't see much, but what little he can looks bad. He grits his teeth, realizing he is stuck in the town. *"Fuck,"* he says.

"Fuck indeed, my man," Lon says.

"There no way to speed things up?"

"You in a rush to get somewhere?"

"Yes."

"Then I'm sorry to break it to you, but no. Nothin' I can do but order the part and change it once it gets here."

"Shit. Then I guess I'm stuck here." Tom looks round, up and down the road. "There a hotel or a motel or somethin'?"

Lon points. "Take a right on the corner there, and it's the biggest building on the left. You can't miss it, one of the only ones not boarded up."

Tom reaches inside the car, pulls his rucksack from

the passenger seat and the Santa Muerte pendant from the mirror. He pockets the pendant.

"You got a number or somethin'?" Lon says. "I can call you once it's done."

Tom slings his rucksack over his shoulder. "You won't need to call me," he says. "I'll come by and check. Every day."

He hands over the car keys, holding Lon's eye as he does so, then follows the mechanic's directions to the hotel. As he gets closer, he notices the cop's cruiser is parked out front of it. There's a guy sitting on a bench nearby, smoking a cigarette. He smiles at Tom. Tom ignores him.

A man and a woman are leaving the hotel as he approaches. The man sees Tom, and his face splits into a big grin. He starts chuckling. "Oh, hey, man, bad luck about your car, right?"

Tom grunts. "Yeah."

"Sure was a hell of a sight to see you come pushing it down the road like that." The man laughs.

"Leave him be, Dean," the woman says. "It wasn't all that funny."

"Oh, I don't know about that," Dean says. "It looked pretty damn funny to me!"

The woman grabs Dean by the arm, starts dragging him away, toward a car parked in the shade.

Tom shrugs the encounter off. It's nothing. It's not worth it. He steps inside the hotel and finds the cop who helped him push the car to the garage leaning against the counter, talking to the woman on the other side of it. The cop turns, smiles at him. "You get it dealt with?"

"Radiator's bust," Tom says.

"Damn."

"Yeah."

"How long's it gonna take to fix?"

"Coupla days."

"So you're stuck in town?"

"Looks that way."

"Appears you've got yourself a new guest, Sally," the cop says to the woman behind the counter.

The woman, Sally, doesn't respond. She looks at Tom, says, "That right?"

"Don't have much choice," Tom says.

She beckons him forward. The cop gets out of the way. Tom notices the small lobby of the hotel is, thankfully, cooler than outside, sees the small air-conditioning unit behind the counter.

"Thirty bucks a night," Sally says.

"Okay," Tom says. "I'll pay for the one, then take the rest as they come. That all right?"

Sally shrugs. She doesn't care how he wants to do it. "Whatever pleases you."

Tom pays cash. Sally slides the key across to him.

"Third floor," she says. "Right at the top of the staircase, you can't miss it."

Tom takes the key, nods at the cop again, then heads through the door at the side of the lobby, to the stairs.

4

First thing Tom does when he reaches the room is check it over. It's very basic – a bed, a television set atop a chest of drawers at the foot of the bed, a small table in the corner by the window, and a bathroom. He glances in the bathroom and is pleased to see there is a shower. He looks out the window and can see the town below, the road he pushed his car along.

He hasn't taken his bag off his back yet. He drops it onto the bed, goes back to the window. Checks points of escape, should they be needed. He pulls the window open, can hear voices in the street below. Ignores them. Pokes his head out, looks up and down, counts floors. Seven of them. Then he looks left to right. No fire escape. As he came up the stairs, he saw at the end of the hall was a door marked as such, figures it must be on the side of the building. Can't be reached from his window. This isn't ideal, but there's nothing he can do about it. Looking down, gauging the height, he supposes the fall wouldn't kill him, but it'd probably shatter his ankles, break his leg.

He pulls his head back inside the room, closes the

window. There is no air conditioning, and it is hot, but the open window doesn't make much difference.

On his way up to the room, he'd passed a few of the hotel's other occupants. They look as bad as the people on the street. They all looked like junkies, bar one who sat on the flight leading up to the next floor, his head held in his hands, who just looked depressed and down on his luck. Tom supposes there is a thin line that separated this man from the junkies, and it is potentially only a matter of time before he joins their ranks.

Above the television, there is a long mirror. It's full length, but it's cut off at waist height by the chest of drawers. Tom can see the wiring in the back of the television in it. He wonders if many people want to lie back on the bed and watch themselves while they are watching television.

He opens his bag, reaches inside, into one of the pockets, and takes out his one and only picture of Alejandra. He looks at it for a moment, keeps his jaw clenched, ignores any pangs he might feel upon its study. It's the two of them, standing out on the porch where she lived in back in Harrow with Anthony. Anthony took the picture. Tom has an arm around her shoulder. Alejandra has an arm around his waist, his lower back, and the other across the front of his stomach, clasping her other hand. They're both smiling. Tom is looking down at Alejandra, she is looking into the camera. Her hair hangs loose and long, down past her shoulders. A lock of it is across her cheek. Tom tucks the photograph into the mirror's frame, where she can smile over him while he sleeps. He inserts it so he is not visible in the picture, hidden away. Only Alejandra is shown. He clutches the Santa Muerte emblem pendant in his pocket, then turns away. He does not take the urn, her ashes, from his bag. Leaves it there, safe.

Tom has to get to Guaymas. He has to get there, for her.

Being stuck here, in a town he has never heard of, will eat him alive. This is not a diversion that he needs. He can feel himself growing antsy already. Needs to distract himself. Has no interest in turning on the television. He kills time with some push-ups and sit-ups, feels the sweat running down his body in the hot room. After, he takes a cool shower, then takes a seat at the desk by the window. He reaches into his bag again and pulls out his Beretta M9. Disassembles it on the desk, cleans it, puts it back together. He can do it fast, but he takes his time. Just wants to keep his hands and mind occupied. He makes sure to put the gun back in his bag when he's done, to tuck it safely down the side next to his clothes, where he can grab it with ease if need be.

The room begins to darken. It finally starts to cool, though he can tell it will still be a warm night. He looks outside, and it's dusk. There aren't many people in the street, and the ones he does see are going to the bar, the only place that looks open. He realizes he hasn't eaten since this morning, and the realization makes him hungry. He grabs his jacket and leaves the room in search of food.

Outside, another of the hotel's guests is leaning on the banister, talking to someone on the floor below. Tom sees that the door of the room next to his is open, and assumes this is his neighbor. The man turns at the sound of Tom's exit, at him locking his door, and he smiles like he wants to talk. "Oh, hey, man," he says. "How you doin'? You good? Name's Darby, Darby White, looks like we're neighbors, huh?"

Tom grunts, just to be polite.

Darby is undeterred. "What're you in town for, man?

Just passing through, I bet, right? Say, what happened to your car?"

Tom has no interest in talking to junkies. Knows that if this guy is high right now, he'll talk his ear off. Decides to ignore him, walks by him, down the stairs, keeps going until he reaches the lobby.

Sally is there still. She sits behind her desk, which is lower than the counter. She's reading a book. Tom almost walks straight past, then stops himself and turns back to her. She looks up when she realizes he's looking at her. "Help you, Tom?"

Tom raises an eyebrow. "Didn't tell you my name."

"No, but you had to sign yourself in. I ain't gonna lie, somethin' tells me *Smith* ain't really your last name. I took a guess on callin' you 'Tom,' but I can see from your reaction that part is true, at least."

"Who says I'm not really a Smith?"

Sally shrugs. "I've been doing this a long time. Smith is one step up from an M. Mouse or a D. Duck. You wanna take a look through the sign-in book, see for yourself?"

"I'll take your word for it," Tom says. "How long *have* you been doing this?"

"Since my dad died. This hotel used to be his. Now it's mine."

"A hotel is quite an inheritance."

"It's all he had to leave."

"You didn't consider selling it?"

She snorts. "Who would wanna buy it? You seen this place?"

Tom gets the feeling the hotel, perhaps Brenton in general, could be a bone of contention for her. She sees he's wearing his jacket, changes the subject. "Going somewhere?"

"I got hungry," Tom says. "Maybe you can help me

out, actually. There a diner round here, or a grocery store?"

"Ain't no diners in Brenton, not anymore." She checks the time. "And the store just closed ten minutes ago."

"Well, hell, bad timing. Anywhere else does food?"

"Ain't a service I provide, I'm afraid – room and a bed, that's what I offer. Only other place open at this time is the bar. It does sandwiches, but I wouldn't recommend going over there, especially not so close to it being dark."

"Why not?"

"It just ain't the kind of place where a stranger is going to be made to feel welcome."

Tom is unperturbed. "That don't bother me none. Your shift ain't over yet?"

"Oh, no, it never ends, my friend. Hotel life is *for* life."

"That sounds rough."

"Well, I *had* cover, but he's called in sick, or else he's not coming back – I'm not totally sure just yet. Whenever I hire someone new, they come in for a couple of days and nights, full of enthusiasm, desperate to impress; then they start making excuses for missing shifts before they finally just tell me they're not coming back. I guess that's what I get for hiring outside of Brenton, but the pool of potential round here is pretty damn shallow. I'm sure you've noticed."

"I didn't wanna say anything negative about a place where I'm a guest, and only just arrived at that."

"Oh, please, negative away. You've been here long enough to make an assumption – one quick glance is usually all it takes to see what we're all about. Anything you could say ain't anything we haven't already heard before, and nothing we haven't already said about ourselves."

"If you ain't getting off, when do you plan on sleeping?"

She circles her finger in the air, indicating the rooms above her, the inhabitants. "They don't need me every second of the night. Besides, Darby usually tries to help out. He'll man the desk, make sure there's nothing that needs my attention, and if there is, he'll come and get me. I won't be far. We're still a few hours off that point yet, though."

Tom remembers the man on the landing, outside his room, his neighbor. The smoker on the bench from when he first approached the hotel. "I think I've met your man Darby," he says. "You trust him to watch out for you?"

"Sure. I mean, what is there for him to steal? Besides, I trust him a lot more than the rest of the tweakers."

Tom frowns. "Is that wise?"

"Darby knows if he tried to fuck with me, I'd put him out on the street. He doesn't have anywhere else to go, so he's not going to take that risk. I'm the one bridge he hasn't burned."

"Speaking of tweakers," Tom says, "I couldn't help but notice most of your clientele seem to fall into that category."

Sally looks at him like she's waiting for him to make his point. When he doesn't follow through, she says, "You already said you took a look at the town; why do you sound so confused about it now?"

"It looks like there's a problem."

"Oh, there's a problem all right, more than one, but we don't have all night, and I don't have the inclination to go into them."

"Fair enough." Tom looks toward the front door, still

propped open. It's almost dark outside now. "Well, I'm gonna go get something to eat."

"Good luck to you," Sally says. "Remember – keep your expectations *low*. I said they do sandwiches. I didn't say they do *good* sandwiches."

"I'll keep that in mind." Tom leaves the hotel, crosses the road. The night air is still warm, though it is not as stifling as it was during the day. He takes a deep breath, goes into the bar.

T om has a corner booth in the bar. Everyone looked at him when he first walked in, like they were in some old Western movie, but for the most part, they seem to be ignoring him now. They sometimes glance his way, whisper among themselves, but by and large they leave him be.

He eats a ham and lettuce sandwich, sips on a soda. He took Sally's advice and kept his expectations low, and so far the sandwich isn't too bad, which surprises him, as the bar is a dive.

He's been in worse places, but this – which he couldn't help but notice has the confident namelessness of being the only bar in town, nothing but a neon sign above the open door that flickers and says *BAR* – is definitely in the top five. There's nothing in the way of decoration, and this is a lack of pretension that Tom can admire, but there's nothing in the way of care, either. The walls look like they've been in need of a fresh coat of paint for more than a decade. They're cracked and peeling, and the wall beside him has been picked at, the paint removed until only the grey concrete below is showing.

A row of booths lines the wall, at which Tom occupies the corner, and there are a few tables in the middle of the floor. There's no pool table, but there is a dart board. A couple of men are playing a game, but instead of aiming for numbers, they've pinned one of the many posters Tom has seen around the town, imploring the people of Cullingworth County to elect their very own Mayor Lyle Smithson to governor of Texas. There's a date for the upcoming election, and it's less than a week off. The mayor's handsome face smiles back at the two men peppering him with holes. Tom saw that there were two kinds of posters: the ones that were sun-bleached and tattered and had obviously been there for a long time, and a fresh batch that look as if they were just put up this morning. The one they take aim at on the dart board is one of the newer ones.

There is no music playing, nothing to hear but the low murmuring of gathered voices, and a couple of loud ones in the booth at the end, opposite to him, next to the door. He ignores them for the most part, but he can't help but see that the occupants, two young men, are clearly drug dealers and make no secret of the fact. The bartender polishes glasses, serves his customers, makes like he doesn't notice they're there, despite their noise-making, their raucous laughter, their unconcealed offering of their goods, and admonishments for short payments – "Make it last this time, huh? I know what you're like, man, smoke it all up, then you ain't got nothin' left 'til your next welfare check clears. You really wanna have to wait that long?"

"Motherfucker, it's short, and if it's short you get *half*, don't try and get one past on me, y'hear? I'll break your fuckin' ass in two."

"Ah, Joey, my man! This guy right here, this fuckin' guy, honestly, he's my best fuckin' customer – swear to God, if I had kids, this guy alone would be putting em through college!"

Tom sits at the corner of his booth, watches them work. They're selling meth. Tom isn't surprised. He sees the exchanging of cash for small clear baggies of broken crystals. They make no attempt to hide what they're doing. Tom assumes this is a regular, probably daily and nightly, occurrence.

The meth heads are obsequious to the dealers, take their abuse, their mockery, their bullying, the way they lord themselves over them because they know the tweakers can't do a damn thing about it. They just keep their heads bowed, nod along, force painful-looking smiles, like it's all done in good fun, like they're in on the joke, like being called a "pathetic, filthy, junkie motherfucker" is just an everyday fact of life that they have resigned themselves to. Tom supposes it is, but if he were in their position, he still wouldn't like to hear someone saying it to him.

He can't help but feel part of the dealers' performances are for his benefit. Like they're doing it just to show off for the stranger they earlier saw enter the bar, giving him a good look at the power they hold in this town. How they so fearlessly flaunt it. Perhaps they think he might be interested in their wares, and they're giving him a good show in case he feels nervous about coming over and enquiring.

Tom looks away, does his best to ignore them. He doesn't care. This isn't his problem. He's going to finish his sandwich and his soda; then he's going to go back to his hotel room. Tomorrow, he will go and check in with Lon and keep checking in on him until the part arrives, and then make sure that Lon prioritizes this job over any other. The sooner he can get out of here, back on the road to Mexico, the better.

Darby enters the bar. Tom doesn't notice him at first, doesn't look up until he hears the two dealers raising their voices to him, clearly pissed off. "We told you last time, man, don't try and pull this fucking shit with us!" They're loud, louder than they've been with anyone else. Tom watches the exchange.

Darby presents himself to them meekly, talks quietly, so low that Tom has to strain to hear what he is saying. "It's just a one-off, I swear – ask Matty; he'll tell you. I was flush this morning. I can pay, I *can*. This is just a one-off, come on, man. I'm coming down, I can feel it. I need this, just one-off, get me right – check with Matty, check with him. He'll tell you –"

"Damn it, shut up!" One of the dealers slams his hand down on the table, causes Darby to jump almost a full foot off the floor. "We don't wanna fuckin' hear it! You either come to us with cash, or you don't come at all. We made this fuckin' clear the last time. We're sick of your shit."

The other dealer looks as mad as the first, says, "What did we tell you last time you were short, Darby? What'd we tell you would happen next time you came crawling round here with empty pockets?"

Darby opens his mouth, but before he can say anything more, the dealer who slammed his hand down jumps out of the booth, up to his feet, slaps Darby hard around the back of the head, then shoves him hard, so he falls on his ass. The rest of the bar is silent. They're watching. A couple of men at the bar keep their backs turned, sip their drinks, pretend it's not happening.

The dealer is looming over Darby, looks like he's not

done, like he's either going to start kicking or drag him out of the bar.

Tom knows he shouldn't say anything. Knows he should just mind his business, wait for his car to get fixed, and then get the hell out of here. He knows this is what he should do.

He knows this.

He knows –

He puts his sandwich down and clears his throat. Does it loud enough to get the dealer's attention, get his ears to prick up, then says, "That's enough."

The dealer wheels on him, his eyes narrowed. He pauses, sizes Tom up. "What'd you say?"

Tom repeats himself. "That's enough, big man. You don't have anything else to prove with a guy half your size and coming down. Let him walk out of here on his own two feet. You can give him that much."

The dealer hesitates, his eyes locked with Tom's. The other dealer remains in the booth, but leans out to see the stranger, hear what he's saying, to size him up himself.

The first dealer decides against starting anything. He takes a step towards his booth, turns back to Darby. "Get the fuck outta here," he says.

Darby scurries back up to his feet, shoots a grateful look to Tom, then hurriedly exits. The dealer shoots Tom a look too – it's anything but grateful – then he sits down. The patrons of the bar go back to their low-volume mumblings. Tom returns to his sandwich. He'll finish it; then he'll leave. Last time he was in a bar, minding his business like this, he got dragged into a fight he shouldn't have risen to. He doesn't want to do that again. Doesn't want any trouble, not here. He'll go back to his hotel room, he'll wait for his car to be fixed, and if he's got to be stuck here another day or two, he'll be sure to reach the grocery store before it closes next time.

Before he can finish, only a couple of mouthfuls left, a face he recognizes enters the bar. The guy he saw earlier with the woman, the asshole making all the jokes about him pushing his car – Dean. He's with someone else now. Not the woman. Another guy, same age as Dean, he'd guess. Thin guy with a ratlike face, dark hair brushed to one side. Together, the two of them go straight to the bar, get a couple of beers; then they go to the booth with the two dealers. Tom can't help but watch.

The two dealers are pleased to see them, speak their names. "Earl, my man! How you doin'? Dean, looking good, bud." As it transpires, Dean and Earl are not here to buy. They're here to be paid. The dealer, the one who decided to back down from Tom, hands them a roll of cash. They're dirty notes, and Tom can almost smell them from his end of the row. Dean and Earl slide into the booth with them, settling in for the night.

The four of them lower their heads at the insistence of the dealer who slapped Darby round. Tom notices in his peripheral vision how Earl and Dean start glancing back at him. Sees how Dean's eyes widen with recognition, how he quickly lowers his head with excitement and starts whispering animatedly.

Tom finishes his sandwich, drains his soda, and gets up to leave. He doesn't want any hassle.

Earl stops him as he passes. "Hey, man, what's your rush?"

Dean perks up in his seat. "Hey there, buddy. How you been? Your car fixed yet?"

Tom doesn't respond to Dean. "I'm done," he says to Earl.

"Hmm, that so?" Earl rests his chin in his hand. "I

don't think you're done just yet. I think you can hang out a little while longer."

"No, I don't think I will," Tom says, and starts for the door.

This response catches Earl by surprise. He jumps to get out of the booth, to rush in front of Tom and block his way. Dean joins him, his face plastered with a punchable smirk. "Slow down there, partner," Dean says. "You didn't hear what my buddy said? You ain't leaving just yet, so cool your heels."

The two dealers are out of the booth now, too. They stand behind Tom, the four of them boxing him in.

"What's Darby to you?" Earl says, making his best tough-guy face, narrowing his eyes and jutting his jaw. With his ratty features, Tom has to try hard not to laugh.

"Nothing," Tom says.

"Nothin'? Then why're you hassling my boys, huh?"

"Because your boys are a couple of asshole bullies."

Earl laughs. "Well, *yeah*. Why you think I hired them? Damn, man, I understand you ain't from round here, right? Am I gonna have to clue you in on how things work here in Brenton? Am I gonna have to pull the old *Do you know who I am?* I mean, I know you don't, but I'd sure as hell like to let you know."

Tom feels like Earl has rehearsed this line. Again, he feels like he has to stop himself from laughing. He doesn't want trouble; he just wants to leave. He stands his ground and grits his teeth and doesn't say anything, no matter how hard Earl tries to get a rise out of him.

"Damn, Dean, you weren't kidding about this guy – fuckin' no sense of humor, huh?"

"Truth be told," Dean says, "I'm starting to think he might be one of them retards. Look how he's just standing there. He even blinked in a while?"

"Naw, man, you're right, I don't think he has. Shit, buddy, are you retarded? Hey, maybe you're one of them, what're they called..." He starts clicking his fingers, trying to remember.

"Autistic," one of the dealers offers.

Earl snaps his fingers again. "*Autistic*, that's the one! That what you are, man? You autistic?"

Tom doesn't answer. Waits for them to get bored. He doesn't think they'll try anything. They're bullies, nothing more. They're all posture and talk; they won't do a thing.

"Naw, he's nothin' so fancy," Dean says. "He's just a retard. Just look at him. You can see it."

Earl nods. "I'm starting to think you're right, Dean. Nothin' fancy about this motherfucker. Just a stray, don't understand where he is and too dumb to keep his fuckin' mouth shut when he ought to." He starts looking Tom up and down, like he's trying to find something new he can exploit. His eyes almost return to Tom's face, but they stop just below, focus on his neck, on the Santa Muerte pendant Tom is wearing as a necklace. Earl starts to grin. "What's this?" he says. He starts reaching out for it, wanting to take a closer look.

Tom pulls back so he can't touch it.

"Oh my," Earl says. "Little touchy about a piece of jewelry, ain't we? That's all right, I don't gotta touch. I'll just lean in for a closer look." He leans forward. Tom grits his teeth harder, tells himself to stay calm, to let it slide. It doesn't matter. Fuck these guys and fuck this town. None of them matter. He just needs to –

Then Dean asks, "So what is it?"

And Earl says, "I dunno, man, just some kinda spic-lookin' knick-knack –"

Then Tom headbutts him.

"What the fuck –!" Before Dean can add anything else to this sentiment, Tom jabs him in the eyes. He spins, moves fast before the two dealers behind him can react, kicks the one that earlier sized him up in the balls and punches the other straight in the face, puts him down. Caught him right in the jaw, knocked him out cold. He turns back to the other, hands clasped between his legs, hooks an arm round the back of his head, and drives his face down into his rising knee.

He turns back to Dean, who has stumbled backward almost out the door, his hands at his face, rubbing his teary eyes. Tom reaches out, takes a handful of his hair, drags him closer and smashes him across the face with the point of his elbow. Blood sprays from Dean's mouth, and he falls flat on his ass. Tom kicks him in the chest, puts him down.

Earl remains still on his knees. He's bleeding from his nose, where Tom's forehead connected. There is a deep gash across the bridge of it. Earl's right hand covers his face, his left arm is up, outstretched, begging off. The blood covers his mouth, his teeth.

Darby steps back inside, alerted by the scuffle. He looks round, down at the fallen men. He looks at Tom. "You do this?" Tom doesn't respond. Darby whistles through his teeth. "Oh, man, you shouldn't have done this."

Earl has scurried back on his knees, is up against the wall. He starts motioning to the rest of the room. "Any of you motherfuckers ever wanna get well again, you'd better beat this son of a bitch's ass down! Right now! *Right fucking now!*"

Tom turns. The other bar patrons are all looking at him. They're hesitant, but they come forward, doing as Earl says. There are about eight of them. Not many, but more than enough. The two forerunners, the biggest guys in the bar, look at each other.

"*Now*, damn it!" Earl says, almost screaming, flecks of blood spraying from his mouth.

The patrons look at each other again, shrug, no other choice, *fuck it*, and they charge en masse.

Tom stands his ground.

6

D aniel Murphy, off duty, in his regular clothes and driving his own car, travels back to Brenton. Like most of the sheriff's department, he lives in Kirkwood, though some of them live in neighboring Elliston, but he spends more of his time in Brenton than the rest of them. Most of the force has written it off as a lost cause, a town that can't be saved, just another one of many countless others all across the states of America. People know about it; they just don't talk about it, turn a blind eye. They're just grateful it's not in their town.

Sally said she'll be working all night. He parks outside the hotel, thinking she'd appreciate some company. He steps inside, a six-pack of beers in one hand, and smiles at her.

Sally looks up over the top of her desk, does a double take like she was just expecting one of the many junkies who reside in her hotel. "You came back," she says.

"I did," Daniel says, tearing two cans from the pack

and handing one to her across the counter. "Pleased to see me?"

Sally shrugs one shoulder. "I mean, I suppose." She marks her place in the book she was reading and puts it to one side, takes the beer.

She's joking. At least, Daniel thinks she's joking. Hopes she's joking. She always plays things so cool, it's often hard to tell whether it's just her dry sense of humor coming through or if she's actually unhappy about something.

"Is this to do with what Anna said?" Sally says.

"What do you mean?"

She holds up the can of beer. "Are you bringing the dates to me now?"

"I just thought you might like some company." He glances down at her desk. Other than the book, there's not much else there. An empty cup of coffee and a couple of bills. "How's your night going?" He glances round the empty lobby. "Looks slow."

"It's always slow. It's the nights it's busy are the exceptions."

Daniel takes a drink, looks at the four remaining beers. "Y'know," he says, "I don't have to hang round if you don't want me to. I don't wanna impose. I just thought, maybe, y'know, you might like to see me. And I wanted to see you." They've been dating, off and on, for almost a full year now, and Daniel still isn't entirely sure whether Sally likes him all that much. "But, y'know, if you've got more important things to do, like sit in the shadows and brood, I completely understand."

She smirks at this. Daniel is pleased. "Did you manage to see your buddy today?" she says.

"Frank?"

"Yeah."

Daniel shakes his head. "No. I went by his house, but there was no answer."

"His car there?"

"Yeah. I mean, it sure looked like he was home. Curtains were all closed, though, so I couldn't see anything through the windows."

"He married? Got a girlfriend or somethin'?"

"He's not married, and as far as I'm aware, he ain't seeing anyone at the minute, but Frank's always been a kinda private guy, so it wouldn't surprise me if he was seeing someone and just hadn't let any of us know."

"Strange you can't get in touch with him, though. Strange he ain't answering his door, either."

Daniel nods along, strokes his jaw. He needs a shave. The stubble scrapes his fingertips.

"You worried?"

"I wasn't, but I'm kinda starting to."

"Maybe you should've tried to force the door."

"I'm starting to think so, too. I checked under the floor mat, see if there was a spare key or anything, checked the top of the doorframe, too, but there wasn't. Couple more days, and me and a couple of the boys from the station are probably gonna go round and kick that door down."

"You wanna leave it that long?"

"Not particularly, but you gotta give a private man his privacy."

"Someone's been sick this long, it's liable to be something serious."

Daniel sighs. "Yeah," he says. He opens his mouth to add more, but before he can, Darby comes bursting into the lobby. He stops himself, almost skids across the floor, takes a deep breath, and starts walking to the stairwell.

Sally watches him with a raised eyebrow. "Something wrong, Darby?"

He turns his head a little, about to speak, pauses when he sees the man in the jeans and shirt is Daniel, unaccustomed to seeing him out of uniform. Darby bites his lips, top and bottom, looks toward the open door back the way he came, deliberating something.

"Darby?" Sally says.

"Uh," Darby says, scratching his chest through his ragged T-shirt. "Listen, man," he says, addressing Daniel, "you ain't heard this from me, all right? But there's a fight broke out at the bar. You better go over there and break it up, else they're likely to kill him." Darby shakes his head. "I told him he shouldn't have done that."

"Who?" Daniel says. "Done what?"

Darby enters the stairwell without answering. They hear him hurry up the stairs to his room.

Daniel and Sally look at each other, then Daniel heads for the door. Even from down the road, he can hear the commotion inside the bar, the yelling and cursing. He pulls out his phone and calls in backup, then starts down toward the bar. Behind him, Sally stands in her doorway, arms crossed, watching.

By the time Daniel comes on the scene, Earl and Dean and a couple of their boys, flanked by others who Daniel imagines are bar patrons caught up in it all, are outside, sheltering. They're all bloodied, beat up.

"What's going on here?" Daniel says. No sooner do the words leave his mouth than a man comes flying out the door, as if thrown. He hits the ground flat on his back, raises his head a little like he's going to try to get back up. He promptly stops, surrenders, groans as he lets his head drop to the ground.

The noise from inside the bar has quietened. The scuffle seems to be at an end.

Earl turns to Daniel. "He's a fucking wild man," he says, blood running down his face from a nasty gash on his nose. "You got backup comin'? You're gonna have to get this sumbitch under control."

A figure emerges in the doorway. He looks like he has taken a few shots, but nowhere near what he has dealt out.

"That's him!" Earl says. "Get the fuckin' cuffs on him!"

Daniel realizes he recognizes the man stepping out. Saw him earlier in the day. Helped him push his car round to Lonnie's garage. The man's eyes meet his; he stops. They both stare at each other. The man wipes blood from his knuckles off on his jeans. "What happened?" Daniel says.

Earl speaks, as if he were the one being addressed. "This motherfucker came looking for trouble – he starts trying to pick a fight with us, we try to calm him down, but he just wouldn't take no for an answer."

"You can see what he's done," Dean says, rubbing his reddened eyes. He points at the fallen man Daniel saw fly from the bar. "This guy's outta control, Daniel. You need to get him locked up before he trashes the whole damn town."

Daniel is familiar with Earl and his buddies. He has his doubts as to their version of events.

Earl picks up on his doubt. "*What?*" he says. "You don't wanna take my word for it?" He grabs the nearest patron, an older guy with a beard and a swelling eye and split lip, who isn't part of his regular crew but cowers with them. Earl drags him forward. "Tell him what happened!"

"He, uh, this guy here." He points at the man in the

bar's doorway, the man who hasn't moved since he first stepped out and saw Daniel, "He, uh, he came in the bar here and just started swinging on Earl and his pals. Don't rightly know what he was looking to accomplish. A few of us tried to pull him off, and he started in on us."

A few of the gathered nod and grunt agreements, but Daniel sees how Earl shoots them looks first, encourages their participation.

The crowd is too big, and Daniel has heard enough. He needs to clear the sidewalk. "All right," he says. "Everyone back inside, and quick about it, before I start checking pockets."

The stranger from out of town understands this instruction is not intended for him. He steps aside, his eyes never leaving Daniel.

The patrons file dutifully back inside, limping and groaning as they go. Someone has to help up the man thrown out moments before, put an arm over his shoulder and draw him inside. Earl and his boys make to follow them, but Daniel stops Earl. "Not you," he says. "I got a few more questions."

The three with Earl hold back with him, but Earl motions for two of them to go inside. Dean stays.

Daniel is unsurprised. His right-hand man, the two of them joined at the hip, and when they're not at the hip, it's usually because Dean is out keeping an eye on Anna. Daniel dreads to think what goes on out at the ranch, what Anna allows herself to be subjected to.

"The two of you just stand over there, all right?" he says. "Don't go anywhere."

"Wouldn't dream of it, Daniel," Earl says.

Daniel takes a step closer to the man. "Didn't get your name earlier, buddy."

The stranger doesn't respond.

"Hey, buddy, you hear me?"

"Tom," he says.

Daniel realizes Sally has come over, is standing by his shoulder. "Tom?" she says.

"He already told you? I got the impression he really didn't wanna tell me."

"He had to sign in."

Daniel grunts.

Sally looks at Earl and Dean, raises an eyebrow. They both grin at her. Sally curls her lip with disdain, then crosses the road back to her hotel.

"You remember me from earlier, don't you, Tom?" Daniel says. "I helped you with your car."

Tom clears his throat, turns his head to the side, spits. "I remember you."

"You wanna give me your version of what happened here?"

Tom wipes the back of a scraped-knuckle hand across his mouth, dabs at his nostrils where there is some blood. He cuts his eyes at Earl and Dean, runs his tongue around his mouth, over his teeth. "Figure it's best I just keep my mouth shut for now."

"You sure about that?" Daniel says.

Before Tom can say anything else, the night lights up, the flashing lights of the backup Daniel called for. Daniel turns to them, waves them over. He turns back to Tom. "If you wanna say somethin', anythin' at all, now's the time, friend."

Tom reverts to his former silence. Says nothing. Looks to the side, away from the newly arrived cruiser, away from Earl and Dean.

The deputies get out of the cruiser. Daniel knows them. Lloyd Taylor and David Johnson. "What we got here?" Lloyd says, looking the scene over. Earl catches their eye, each of them, grins at them.

Daniel explains to them what has happened, what he has been told. He sighs as he does so. If Tom refuses to say anything, no matter how much Daniel doubts the story, he has to go off what Earl and his buddies have said happened.

"Well, sure looks like the new guy came out the better for it," David says, laughing.

Earl's grin falters at this. David notices, and his laugh quickly stops. Daniel sees this happen.

Lloyd and David step to Tom, read him his rights, cuff him.

Earl steps forward, but waits until Tom's arms are bound behind his back. "Hey, buddy, hold up."

Daniel tries to stop him, but Dean gets in his way, blocks him. Daniel pushes him to one side, but it's too late. Earl grabs a necklace Daniel hadn't noticed Tom was wearing, yanks it from his neck.

"Don't worry, man," Earl says. "I'll keep hold of this for you – I'll look after it real good. You ain't gotta worry about a thing." Earl pockets it.

Tom surges forward, looking like he's ready to tear Earl's throat out with his teeth. Lloyd and David both have to grab him, restrain him. "Easy there, big fella," Lloyd says, showing his teeth as he struggles to hold Tom back.

Earl remains close, taunting him, sticking his tongue out and swinging it side to side. "Told ya, man, don't worry about it."

Daniel gets between them both, puts a hand on Tom's chest and shoves Earl back with the other. "Back off," he says. "Stay back."

He turns back to Tom. "Calm down, buddy. You gotta calm down, or else you're gonna land yourself in more trouble than you already are."

Tom settles back, much to the visible relief of Lloyd

and David. They keep hold of an arm each, though, just to be safe. His eyes are on Earl, boring through him. Daniel does not like the look he sees in them.

Another cruiser pulls up, summoned by Daniel's call. It pulls to a stop behind the first one.

"You gotta say somethin' to me, man," Daniel says. He steps close to Tom, speaks so only he can hear. "You don't say anythin', then it's all their word over yours. Hey – Tom, you hear me? You hear what I'm telling you?"

Tom does not look away from Earl. "Yeah," he says. "I hear you."

7

T om is in jail.

The cruiser brought him through to the sheriff's department in Kirkwood after the fight in the bar. Even in the dark he could see the differences between Kirkwood and Brenton.

Kirkwood, for a start, is clean. Far cleaner than Brenton. There were no weeds growing through the cracks in the pavement here – nor, for that matter, were there any cracks. The windows were not boarded over, the doors were not barred. It was late, but had there been any people out on the streets, Tom is sure they would have looked healthy. They'd have had all their teeth.

He noticed, too, that here the seemingly ubiquitous posters for the mayor's run were more plentiful and remained in pristine condition. They weren't being torn down and used for dart practice.

Tom has slept a little. It's morning now, and he woke to find some blood dried and cracking on his face, the taste of it in his mouth. Most of it isn't his. He hopes all that he can taste is, though. He went to the sink next to the toilet, splashed cold water over his wounds and cleaned himself off.

Now he sits on the bench, waiting for what comes next. His body aches a little, from the few hours of sleep he managed to snatch lying on the narrow bench. His face, save for a few stinging cuts and tender bruises, feels fine.

His personal belongings have been taken away. That doesn't bother him. It's the Santa Muerte pendant that eats at him. Knowing where it is, who has it. He feels uncomfortable without it. Feels almost naked without it on his person in some way, whether around his neck or in his pocket. He balls his fists on his thighs and tries not to think about it. Pining will not help anything. It'll just make him feel worse, make him more agitated. Thinking of Earl, of what he will do to him, will not help, either, but it gives him something to focus on.

To pass the time, he reads the graffiti etched into the wall, wonders what it was scraped in with. Fingernails? Keys that were missed in the pat-down? The messages make little sense to him – threats to particular people, a couple of phone numbers that promise good sex, and many, many declarations of people who previously occupied this cell, determined to leave a piece of themselves behind, even if it's just their names.

Tom is alone in the cell. He's glad. Last thing he'd want would be a still-high tweaker talking his ear off, or one coming down, writhing in the center of the floor, sure they're about to die. There is another cell directly opposite, separated only by bars, and this too is empty.

The door leading into the room opens, and Tom looks up. One of the deputies comes through. It's not Daniel. Tom hasn't seen him since outside the bar, since he was taken away. From the backseat of the cruiser, he'd seen him crossing the road, going over to the hotel, while the new cops on the scene from the second cruiser took over questioning Earl and Dean, except it hadn't much looked like they were questioning them. Looked a lot to Tom like they were all joking together, having a good laugh at something. Most likely at his expense.

The deputy takes Tom out of the cell, into an interrogation room, cuffs him to the table, and leaves him alone. Tom waits, looks at the table below him. Sees that people have attempted to scratch messages here, too, though with less success. He studies himself in the two-way mirror opposite, sees for the first time the effects of the fight. There is minimal bruising, and the swelling isn't so bad; it looks like it's already going down. Tom didn't take many hits in the bar. They were sloppy fighters, charging in without any thought for defense. Tom only took a few shots, and most of those were dealt by emaciated junkie fists likely suffering a comedown. They did little damage, and he's always been a fast healer. He's sure these scant markings will be cleared before long.

The door opens, and a man steps inside. He's tall, and his back is ramrod straight, though he wears an easy smile as he approaches the table. His salt-and-pepper hair is combed straight back, and at a guess, Tom would figure him to be in his mid-fifties, though he still looks strong. His body is firm, his jaw is hard, and his hands, as he rests them upon the table, look like they've seen their fair share of trouble. He wears a sheriff's badge, and his name tag reads Sheriff Larry Collins. "Morning," he says, still smiling. "How you feeling?"

Tom shrugs. "Been worse."

"I hear that more than you'd think." The sheriff leans back in his chair, appraises Tom with cool blue eyes. "Figured I'd wait until the morning before I spoke to you, give you a chance to sober up."

"I wasn't drunk."

"Sure sounds like you were. I don't know many men would pick a fight with an entire bar."

Tom doesn't refute this. There's no point. It's the word of Earl and his buddies – and all their customers – against his, and there are far more of them.

The sheriff leans forward again, holds himself up on his elbows. "I ran a quick background check on you, Mr. Smith. Or do you prefer Tom?"

Tom shrugs. "Either's fine."

"Tom it is, then." Larry winks. "Looks like you're largely a Boy Scout, Mr. Smith. I don't see any other infractions on your record, nothin' so much as a traffic violation. Got me scratching my head why you'd come to my town and start trouble."

Tom folds his arms.

Larry grins at this. He keeps his tone conversational, almost friendly, but Tom can detect an edge beneath him. "You trying to hard-ass me, kid?"

Tom decides the best way to play it with this small-town sheriff is respectful. "No, sir."

"You sure about that? 'Cause the way you got your arms crossed, the way you're looking at me, I've seen it a million times by now, kid. You think it's ever thrown me off, even once?"

"I don't think there's much could throw you off, sir."

Larry laughs at this. "You ain't wrong, kid." He drums his fingers on the table. "You got somethin' about you, Tom. I've seen it before. Military?"

Tom made sure, when Cindy created his new identity, that it didn't say anything about any time served in the army. These details are too easily traced and too close to his reality. "No, sir. Can't say I've ever served."

Larry drums his fingers again, turns his head, and

regards Tom like he isn't sure he believes him. "Your daddy in the army?"

"He might've been. I never knew him." Again, another detail in the history of Tom Smith, the persona Cindy has created for him.

He wasn't happy about the name she chose. Looked at her with a raised eyebrow, said *Smith? Really?* Easy to remember, was Cindy's reasoning. *You know how many Tom Smiths are out there? You know how many files would have to be waded through, you ever get yourself into trouble?* She looked at him. *Just keep yourself out of trouble, though, all right?*

Tom studied the documents she'd made, memorized every facet of them. If the sheriff is trying to catch him out on any of the details, he will not succeed.

"Surprises me," Larry says. "Usually I've got a good gauge for this kinda thing."

"Were you in the military?" Tom says.

"No. I went straight into law enforcement when I got outta school, but I had a lot of friends went off to war. You remind me of some of them – the ones who came back, that is."

"Should I take this comparison as a compliment?"

The sheriff's smile does not fade, but what he says next does not sound particularly friendly. "Take it any way you like."

The sheriff doesn't say anything immediately after. He watches Tom across the table, their eyes locked. Tom knows he should probably defer, should look away, but he doesn't. He's never backed down, and even now, when he knows he is not Tom Rollins, he is Tom Smith, he cannot break old habits so easily.

The sheriff speaks first, that same conversational tone he's held all the way through, though his eyes are narrowed now, and he tilts his head a little. "There's somethin' familiar about you, Mr. Smith. Somethin' real familiar. We met before?"

Tom stays calm. "I think I'd remember if we had."

"You ever been by this way before?"

"No."

"Hmm. There's somethin' there, somethin' I just can't quite put my finger on."

"Maybe I've just got one of those faces," Tom says.

"Could be. Could be you're just reminding me of somebody else. Gonna eat at me, though. Gonna bother me that I can't put my finger on it." The sheriff shakes his head. "What's your line of work, Tom Smith?"

"Nothing, at the minute," Tom says, relieved that the sheriff is moving the conversation along. It could just be that Tom reminds the sheriff of someone else, but there's also the risk that Larry saw what happened in Dallas, that he saw the picture of Tom's face that was flashed all over the news, head shaved and beardless. "Between jobs. I usedta work on cars, but I lost that position, things being what they are."

"So what you doing with yourself now?"

"Just driving. Seeing the country. I saved up my money for a long time, I figure I've got a right to use some of it before I need to find a way to make myself some more."

The sheriff nods along. "Well, I don't see anything wrong with that. Nothin' wrong with saving your money so you can take a ride and a good long look at this great country of ours. After all, that's what we work for, ain't it?"

"I certainly think so."

"All right, then." The sheriff drums his fingers once more on the tabletop. "Earl has decided not to press charges for last night, and you should consider yourself lucky for that. It's real hard to travel freely and see the country when you've got an assault charge pending."

Tom sits silent, not sure how the sheriff expects him to react to this.

"You'll be free to go this afternoon, but be sure to behave yourself, y'hear?" Larry gets to his feet. "You cause any more trouble, and it won't be Earl McQuade and whether he wants to press charges you'll have to worry about." He stops by the door, looks Tom over again. "I'll send in one of my deputies to escort you back to your cell. Try to keep your nose clean for the next few hours, huh?" He taps his nose, winks at Tom, then leaves.

8

After talking with Sally the night before, Daniel has decided against waiting the two days to see if Frank will either get in touch or return to work. Now he's heading out to his place again, worried.

He's not alone. His friend and fellow deputy Mark Colt rides with him in the passenger seat of the cruiser. "I don't feel too good about busting his door down," Mark says. "Frank's gonna be pissed at us, finds we've damaged his home."

"We'll pay for it," Daniel says. "And we'll only bust the door down if we absolutely have to. But right now, I'd rather know he's all right than worry about upsetting him over a broken door."

"You can't pick the lock or nothin'?"

Daniel looks at Mark, raises an eyebrow. "What has ever given you the impression that I might be able to pick a lock? I'm a lawman, Mark. How dare you insinuate such a thing."

Mark grins. "You're gonna try it first though, right?"

"I mean, I'll give it a *try*," Daniel says. "Hell, you can

give it a try if you want, but I ain't got high hopes for our chances of success."

"Maybe we should've brought along one of the Brenton meth heads with us," Mark says. "I'd bet my bottom dollar they all know a thing or two about pickin' locks."

"We don't need to go give them any excuse to be bad," Daniel says. "And besides, Frank wouldn't be happy we let a tweaker, likely to tell all his tweaker friends, know where he lives."

They'd told the sheriff what they planned on doing before they left the station. Larry sat behind his desk, leaned back in his chair, and raised his hands. "Can't you just let the man be? He ain't had a single sick day in all the years I've known him; somethin' like this was bound to creep up on him eventually. He told me it felt like the flu. That shit can really knock you on your ass. It ain't no surprise to me he ain't been in touch with anyone since."

"It's been a long time now, though, sir," Daniel said. "It would just put my – and I think a lot of the boys' – mind to rest to know he was all right, that he hasn't… hurt himself or somethin'."

Larry shrugged. "Suit yourself," he said. "When you see him, send him my regards – and that I told y'all to let him rest."

Daniel and Mark reach his street, pull up outside his house.

"Car's here," Mark says.

"Mm," Daniel says. "Was there last time I came by, too."

"And he didn't answer?"

"Didn't even twitch a curtain, so far as I could see."

They get out of the car, go to the front door, ring the bell, knock. They wait, though Daniel isn't expecting anyone to answer. He looks at Mark, raises his eyebrows.

"See what you mean," Mark says.

"I wasn't lying."

"Round the back?"

Mark nods, and they head down the side of the house and around to the back. Mark tries knocking again, rattling his knuckles against the glass, but Daniel is bent over, checking the lock. He has two hairpins in his pocket, borrowed from Sally. He gets down onto his knees, twisting the pins out of shape.

"Your own?" Mark says.

"They're borrowed. Though to be honest, I don't think she's gonna get them back." He holds them up, shows the way he's twisted one into a T shape by bending one of its legs in the middle, and has straightened the other clip out. "I ain't sure what these do exactly, but I don't think they'll do it again."

Mark stops knocking. "Don't look like he's gonna answer," he says. "Try your best."

"I will," Daniel says, "but just keep in mind this is my first time doing this, so be patient."

"Sure. That's what everyone calls me, Mr. Patient."

Daniel fiddles the clips around, feels and hears the occasional clicking, but it doesn't seem to take. "Fuckin' goddamnit...I'm just gonna smash this fuckin' door in a second."

"Give them here," Mark says. "I'll have a try."

Daniel hands him the clips, gets out of the way. Leans against the wall with his arms folded. As he gets comfortable, he notices one of Frank's neighbors is out in their backyard. She's hanging up sheets on her clothesline. They catch in the breeze, billow like a tent. Daniel goes over to the fence that divides the two yards.

It's chest high, and Daniel rests his arms on top of it. "Hello, ma'am."

The lady turns, sees a cop, and starts to smile. "Hello there," she says. She's in her late sixties, has a smile like everyone's favorite grandmother. "I'm not in trouble, am I?" She has a twinkle in her eye as she says this.

"I sure hope not," Daniel says. "We're friends of Frank's – just wondering if you've seen him lately?"

The lady steps over to the fence, looks at Mark at the door, trying to break in. Her eyes narrow. "Is he –?"

"We're worried about our friend," Daniel says. "Deputy Aynsley called in sick over a week ago, but no one's seen or heard from him since. I tried calling by yesterday, but he didn't answer the door, and it looks like he still ain't."

"Oh," the lady says.

"Do you remember the last time you saw him?"

She looks off to the side, thinks. "Can't say that I do," she says. "I just mind my business, keep myself to myself. Frank left early, he came back late most nights, so I can't say our paths crossed all that often."

"I don't suppose you happened to notice the last time his car left the driveway?"

"I'm sorry," the lady says. "I can't say I did. Oh!" Her eyes brighten all of a sudden. "I did see something! Now, remember, I keep myself to myself, but I heard something, and it was late, so I looked out my curtain, you understand. It was late at night, almost midnight, and when you start hearing things at that hour, you want to make sure no one's trying to break into your home."

Daniel nods. "That's understandable. I'd do the same."

"Well, I heard a car pull up, and I could hear all these voices, so I took a look outside. Frank came out of the house, was talking to them through their window, then he got into the back, and they drove off. That was that. Nothing particularly interesting, I'm afraid."

"You recognize the guys in the car?"

"Didn't see them."

"What about the car? That look familiar?"

The lady shakes her head. "No. Frank never got many visitors, not that I saw, anyway."

"And he went with them willingly?"

"Oh, yes. Seemed to know them. It wasn't like they were arguing or anything, they were just talking."

"That was the last time you saw him?"

"Yes, but for how late he went out, it was probably very early in the morning when they dropped him back off, and I would've been asleep."

"So you never saw them drop him back off?"

"No."

Daniel thinks about this. Behind him, he hears Mark announce, "A-*ha*!" and turns to see that he has gotten the back door open and is getting to his feet, looking very pleased with himself.

Daniel turns back to the lady. "Well, thanks for your time, ma'am. Hopefully we'll find Frank wrapped up in bed, and then we won't have anything else to worry about."

"Well, I sure hope that's the case," the lady says, then gets back to hanging her washing.

"The old girl have anything to tell?" Mark says once Daniel is close enough.

"Not really," Daniel says, leaving out the story of the late-night outing, not sure if it means anything. They step inside together, call out, "Frank? Frank, you home? It's just us – Daniel and Mark."

"Daniel Murphy and Mark Colt," Mark says, in case Frank is in need of clarification.

The back door has led them into the kitchen. It's as clean and ordered as Daniel would expect from a man like Frank. The counters are clear; the bin is not filled to overflowing. There is a small plastic container next to the bin with a few recyclable items inside.

"Should've put that out a couple of days ago," Mark says.

Daniel steps through into the living room. There is a smell in the air, a musty odor, as if the house has not been aired out in a while.

"What're you sniffing for?" Mark says. "What d'you smell?"

"Nothin'," Daniel says. "Frank? You home, buddy? Call out if you can hear us."

There's no answer.

There is no sign of disorder in the living room. They go through to the hallway, the foot of the stairs. Daniel leads the way. Mail has piled up on the floor mat before the front door. Mark hangs back a few paces, looking everything over. "This is the first time I've been in Frank's house," he says. "It looks...pretty much how I expected it to."

Daniel ignores him, starts going up the stairs. "Frank?"

When this call again receives no answer, he gives up on shouting. He finds himself taking his time on the stairs, feels his stomach tighten when a couple of them creak. There's a worry in him now, a fear of what he is going to find when he reaches the upstairs.

He looks left and right when he comes to the landing, and listens. Mark comes up the steps behind him, unaware of the noise he is making. Daniel steps onto the landing, pushes open the first door he comes to. A spare bedroom that has been converted into a gym. There is a weight bench in the middle, a barbell on top of it. One of the walls is mirrored, and there is a stack of dumbbells in front of it.

The next door is the bathroom. It's empty. There's only one door left.

"Must be the bedroom," he says.

"Uh-huh," Mark agrees.

Daniel goes to the door. He puts one hand on the handle, and the other unconsciously goes to the holster on his hip. He pushes the door open. The room is empty.

"The fuck?" Mark says.

Daniel steps inside. The bed is made.

Mark follows him into the room, looks left and right, even checks behind the door, as if he expects Frank to be hiding from them. He's not. There's no sign of him. "Well, shit. Where is he?"

Daniel goes to the wardrobe, checks inside. Doesn't look like there are any clothes missing; all the hangers are still occupied. He goes to the chest of drawers beside the bed and looks in there, too. Again, it doesn't seem like anything is missing.

"What're you looking for?" Mark says.

"If he ain't here, and he ain't at work, where is he?" Daniel says. "All his clothes are still here. It don't look like he's gone for a trip."

"Think we should call the sheriff?"

"Yeah," Daniel says. "Call him, tell him Frank ain't here, and there's no sign of where he might be. I'm gonna keep looking around."

"I don't think there's much to see."

"I'll feel better for taking a look."

"Sure." Mark goes back downstairs to call the sheriff.

Alone, Daniel gives the room a more thorough look-ing-over, though he has no idea what he might be searching for. Down on his knees, he checks under the bed. It's clear. He checks the drawers again, runs his hand along the back of them, behind the boxer shorts and socks, to see if there might be anything hidden there. There isn't.

He leaves the room, steps into the bathroom. It looks pristine, not the bathroom of a man who's been suffering with the flu for more than a week and likely shitting and vomiting at all hours of the day and night.

He goes into the spare room, the makeshift gym, though he doesn't expect to find anything here. However, glancing into the mirror, he spots the reflection of a desk, a closed laptop. Peering around the door, he sees it. There's a swivel chair, and he perches himself in it, opens up the laptop.

A slip of paper is pressed inside. Daniel picks it up. There's something written on it. It says 'Ike Thoreau', and underneath this is a phone number. Daniel pulls out his own, dials the number, but it goes straight to voicemail. Daniel decides against leaving a voice message just now, and then hears Mark coming back up the stairs. Daniel pockets the number.

"You find anything?" Mark says.

"His laptop." Daniel turns it on, but it's password protected, and 'password' in both upper and lower case doesn't unlock it. He puts the lid down, turns back to Mark. "What'd the sheriff say?"

"Asked if the house looks like a crime scene. And, I mean, I don't know about you, but it sure don't look like one to me."

"No," Daniel agrees.

"So he told us to leave it alone for now, wait and see if we hear anything from him in the next few days – could be he's got something personal going on, maybe out of town, and he's too embarrassed to tell us about it, so he's made up the excuse of being sick."

"So we ain't gonna do anything about it? Frank's missing."

"Not yet. Sheriff says we'll give it a few days, then if we still ain't heard anything and we still can't get in touch with him we'll have to put out a missing persons report."

"If he *is* missing," Daniel says, "then we're leaving it too long." He remembers the story the lady next door told him of seeing Frank getting into a car, seemingly with people he knew, and driving off into the night. He doesn't know if this comforts or worries him.

Mark holds out his hands. "Ain't nothin' more we can do, not right now. Sheriff says we've gotta get back out on patrol."

Daniel remains in the chair, looks to one side, worried for his friend.

"Come on, man," Mark says, seeing the look on his face. "Frank'll be fine. Whatever it is, he's a big boy, and he can look after himself."

"I suppose you're right about that," Daniel says, his eyes flickering toward the weight bench, thinking of how his shirt would strain at his chest and shoulders and arms. "Well," he says, getting to his feet, "I suppose we'd best do as the sheriff says."

They head back down the stairs, but Daniel can't shake the sinking feeling he has in the pit of his stomach. Like something bad has already happened, they just don't know about it yet. He's worried about Frank, and there's nothing he can do about that, and that just makes the feeling all the worse.

"I just thought," Mark says as they reach the back door. "Are we gonna have to lock it up behind ourselves again using that clip?"

9

Tom waits to be released. He's not alone now. Shares the cell with two big white guys who were brought in together a couple of hours before, along with a black guy who sits in the neighboring cell. The three of them sit together, the white guys with their backs to the black's cell.

Tom sits alone, opposite, arms folded. Looks to the side of the group, minding his business. They're not doing the same for him. Huddled, they glance in his direction, talk between themselves. Tom gets flashbacks to last night in the bar, the way Earl and his group had looked back at him, whispered about him.

The two guys in his cell are both big, but for different reasons. One of them is muscular; the other is fat. The muscular one turns to Tom, leans forward, clasps his hands, rests his elbows on his thighs. "How you doin'?"

They've been in the cell together for more than two hours, and this is the first any of them has attempted to talk to Tom. He doesn't think they suddenly want to be friends. "I'm fine," he says, goes back to staring off to the side, away from them.

The fat guy leans forward, clasps his hands, and rests his elbows on his thighs in a pale imitation of his muscular friend. He lifts his chin. "You been in a fight?"

Tom knows he's referring to the few bruises he sustained. When he takes too long to answer, the muscular guy says, "Barely looks like a bruise, man. Looks like a love tap. Looks like somethin' my bitch gives me when she sucks on my neck."

The fat guy laughs. To Tom, he says, "That what it is really, guy? Someone been sucking on your face?"

Tom turns to them now, gives them his full attention. He'd already looked them over when they were first put in the cell with him. Paid attention to the way the fat guy was short of breath after just a few steps, and the way his muscular pal rubbed his lower back as he sat down, more than likely a niggling side effect of all the weights he lifts day after day with potentially poor form. "Could be," Tom says. "Sure felt like love taps. Could've been that in the middle of it all, I had someone sucking on my face and I didn't realize."

The two of them laugh at him, and the black guy in the next cell joins in. He stays close to the bars, listens, watches Tom. His top lip curls up when he smiles, showing his teeth. Tom is sure it's supposed to look intimidating.

"You're a joker, huh?" the muscular guy says.

"No jokes," Tom says. "Just how it is. I look at you, I can see you've been in some fights, right? I'll bet you've come out of it wondering what the hell someone's been doing to you."

The three of them look at each other a moment, like they're thrown by Tom joking with them. They weren't expecting this kind of response. The muscular guy turns back first. "So you're in for fighting, huh?"

"That's right," Tom says.

"You win?"

Tom tilts his head side to side. "Well, I'm in here, and they're not, so I guess that depends on your perspective."

"You gonna ask us what we did?" the fat guy says.

Tom shrugs. He doesn't care. "You seem like the kind of guys who like to share. I'm sure y'all will get to it soon."

The black guy chuckles, pushes himself up from the bench and away from the bars. He starts pacing the floor. "We overstepped our boundaries, man," he says.

"It was your idea to try Elliston, man," the fat guy says.

"Well, I figured it was far enough away from Kirkwood," the black guy says.

"Shoulda stuck to Brenton," the muscular guy says. "That's what we were told."

"Yeah, well, we're gonna get a one-way trip back to Brenton once they figure we've learned our lesson," the black guy says.

Tom listens to them. Their statements make him curious, though they don't elaborate further. He doesn't ask. He's curious, but he tells himself it's not his business. Like the stuff in the bar with Darby, that wasn't his business, either, but he stuck his nose in, and now he's here. In this cell. He should have eaten his sandwich and gone back to his hotel room. Should be waiting for his car to be fixed. Instead, now when he gets out, he has business to attend to. He has to get the Santa Muerte pendant back, and he has to make Earl pay for taking something that doesn't belong to him. Something so important.

The muscular guy gets to his feet, starts pacing, following the black guy's lead. He stretches his arms out, flexes his chest. "Man, I'm bored as fuck," he says.

He twists side to side, then touches his toes in an effort to loosen up his lower back. Tom watches, he sees.

"Try doin' some more push-ups," the black guy says.

The fat guy crosses the cell, joins Tom on his bench, sits a little too close to him. "You ever been arrested before?" he says, breathing hard after crossing the short distance between benches.

"Sure," Tom says.

The muscular guy sits down on the other side of him, on his left, again too close. He takes a closer look at the bruises, so close Tom can feel his breath. The muscular guy is trying to make him uncomfortable.

"What you get arrested for before?" the fat guy says.

"Fighting," Tom says.

"You make a habit of it?"

"Sure sounds like it," Tom says.

The muscular guy reaches out a finger, reaches to touch one of the bruises on Tom's cheek. Tom tilts his face away from him. "Don't like being touched, huh?" the muscular guy says.

Opposite them, the black guy has stopped pacing in his cell. He hasn't sat back down. Instead, he rests one knee on the bench, leans into the bars, his arms dangling through them.

"I don't think we caught your name," the fat guy says.

"No," Tom says. "You didn't."

The fat guy laughs again. "Man, you've got some stick up your ass. Say, you ever been to prison before?"

Tom doesn't answer.

The muscular guy laughs now, too. "Plenty time to do a *lot* of push-ups in prison," he says.

"You know what we'd do to a pretty thing like you on the inside, we were feeling bored?" the fat guy says.

"Hell," the muscular guy says, "you know what we'd do to the likes of you just to pass the time?"

Tom understands what they're implying, and he doesn't care for it. They're leaning even closer to him now, their bodies pressed against his. If he doesn't make the first move, they will.

Tom gets off the bench, pushes himself up to his feet. He moves fast, before they realize what he's doing.

"Hey, c'mon, come and sit back down with us," the muscular guy says while the fat guy laughs.

Tom crosses the cell, goes to the black guy. The black guy stays where he is, arms dangling nonchalantly through the bars. "These two friends of yours?" Tom says.

The black guy still has that look on his face, that sneer, trying to look scary. "Two of my best," he says.

"You sure got some shitty friends," Tom says. He moves lightning fast, grabs the black guy by the wrists.

The black guy's eyes go wide; the sneer is wiped from his face. "Get the fuck off of me!"

In control, though still moving fast, Tom pushes him back, away from the bars, then pulls him forward, fast. The black guy's chest hits them hard, his face squeezed between them. With careful aim, Tom punches him in the center of his crushed face, right through the bars. The black guy goes down, flat on his back.

"Hey – what the fuck!" It's the fat guy, trying to get off the bench.

The muscular guy is already up, the bigger threat of the two. He swings a left, which Tom easily leans back from, then a right, which he ducks, travels through, then spins and slams both clasped fists into his lower back. The muscular guy cries out, goes down to his knees.

The fat guy is up now. He's already panting. Tom jabs him in the center of the face, busts his nose, sits him back down. He turns back to the muscular guy. Even with his back pain, he is still the bigger risk.

The muscular guy is using the bars to pull himself back upright. Tom gets behind him, grabs his head in both hands, pushes his face forward into the bars. Dizzies him. Drags him down to the ground and kicks him twice in the face, subdues him. The muscular guy is on his knees and his elbows. Tom kicks him hard in the chest, puts him onto his back.

The fat guy is cupping his face, blood pouring through his fingers. With his free arm, he takes a swing at Tom. Tom easily ducks it, leans forward, and gives him a quick jab to the chin. The fat guy stumbles back, hits the wall. It's all that keeps him propped up. He lets go of his face, uses both hands to try to find a grip on the wall. Tom cuts loose on him, peppering his body and face with quick, sharp punches. He probably could have just given him one or two, put him down, but when a man is threatening to rape him, he takes that kind of thing personally.

When he finally lets up, the fat guy slides down the wall, hits the ground, and rolls over onto his side.

The black guy in the neighboring cell is on the floor still, out cold.

The guards take their time responding to all the noise. Tom imagines they're content to let the animals they've caged tear each other apart for a little while before they attempt to calm and separate them. They enter only after everything has silenced, and when they do, Tom has already returned to his seat on the bench, folded his arms.

The two deputies look the scene in both cells over, then look at Tom. One of them laughs. "You punch him through the bars?" he says.

They cuff him and drag him back to the interrogation room. Tom doesn't resist. Now that he's cooling down, the adrenaline is leaving his system, he's annoyed at himself.

Shouldn't have done that, he thinks.

A bar fight, now a jail fight.

When the sheriff comes to see him, a half hour later, an eyebrow is raised, and he does not look impressed. "Just can't help yourself, can you, kid?"

Tom doesn't attempt to blame it on the other men. Doesn't say *They started it*. He's not a schoolboy, and it won't make any difference.

"Looks like we're gonna have to give you a few more days, cool you down," Larry says. He doesn't sit this time, remains standing on the opposite side of the desk, his stiff back making him look taller. "I'll take them two boys outta your cell, but they're just gonna be right next door, and if they say anything to hurt your feelings, you better just ignore them, hear me?"

Tom knows an answer is expected to this, so he nods.

The sheriff looks down at him for a moment longer, his mouth twisted. "You get out of here, I want you *gone*. First thing you do, get yourself out of Cullingworth County. It's a quiet place, a peaceful place, and we don't need a troublemaker like you comin' round and making things noisy for the rest of us. I don't care where you go next, but it better be far away from here. You understand me?"

Tom nods again.

The sheriff studies him, his mouth still twisted; then he leaves the room. Tom is left to sit alone a while longer, presumably to cool him down. But, at the same time, he reckons it's so the deputies have time to clean up the mess he's made in the two cells.

D aniel has heard about what Tom did to the other three inmates locked up with him. "You wanna see him?" Larry asks.

"Naw," Daniel says, "I'm good." The two of them aren't friends. He's just a guy he helped push his car one time.

Daniel told the sheriff what he thought happened the night of the bar fight. Earl and his boys, and the occupants of the bar, all claimed Tom started it, but Daniel has his doubts. Knows better to believe every man in the room when Earl or one of his boys is in that room, too. Too many of the people of Brenton have a sickness, and Earl and his father are the only ones with the cure.

At least, that's what Daniel and others think. They've never been able to prove it, but it's commonly believed the McQuades are the ones responsible for the meth problem in the town of Brenton. Whether they cook it or distribute it, or both, Daniel is sure they're involved. It certainly seems that way when everyone is so eager to bow and scrape for them, rush around at their beck and call, never stand against them. It hasn't gone unnoticed, the difference between Brenton and seemingly every other town in Cullingworth County.

Daniel knows where McQuade ranch is, though, and he's driven by it enough times, both on and off the clock, and he's never seen any evidence of them cooking there. If they are responsible, they do it elsewhere. If they solely deal in distribution, well, they have that big old barn that's not being used for anything else to store it in.

Regardless of what happened between them and Tom at the bar, the sheriff's department is required to follow the rules. Daniel's hands are tied, and he can't work off hunches. More than that, Tom hasn't done himself any favors by beating up his cellmates. Three on one (though admittedly one of the three was on the other side of the bars) certainly makes it appear he likes having the odds against him.

One hunch that Daniel *is* working on, however, is the worry that something might have happened to Frank Aynsley. He's tried to call Ike Thoreau's number a couple more times, but there's still no answer. Through to voicemail every time, and every time Daniel decides against leaving one. Instead, he looks up who Ike Thoreau might be, and is intrigued by what he finds.

Ike is a reporter for the *Cullingworth County Times*, located right here in Kirkwood. Ike himself lives in town, on the outskirts. Daniel goes by his house, but much like at Frank's, there is no answer when he knocks. Also like Frank's, there is a car, which Daniel assumes to be Ike's, parked out front. The curtains, however, are open. When he peers inside, he sees an open pizza box on a table in the center of the room, a couple of open newspapers spread next to it. There are a few slices left inside the box, and one half-eaten. Daniel goes round the back. The curtains are open here, too. He can see into the bedroom. The bed is unmade; there are crumpled clothes scattered across the floor. It doesn't look like a break-in. It just looks like Ike Thoreau is a very messy person.

Daniel knocks on the doors of the neighbors, but neither side remembers the last time they saw Ike. Say he keeps long hours, is always out, rarely home, and often forgets to drag his trash cans to the sidewalk.

Daniel goes to the *Cullingworth County Times* offices, asks after him there. The building is next to the town council, where the mayor's office is. There is an electoral poster on the door of the *Cullingworth County Times* as Daniel enters. He's getting tired of seeing Mayor Lyle Smithson's face plastered across every wall and billboard in the county, and he's looking forward to this election being over and done with. Inside the building, he announces himself and gets a meeting with Maria Tisdale, the editor of the newspaper and Ike's boss.

"Is Ike in some kind of trouble?" she says, ushering Daniel into her office and into a seat in front of her desk. She goes to her own, sits down, says, "Can I get you anything? Some water? A coffee maybe?" Maria has black hair, looks like it's been dyed this color. She wears it swept back and over one shoulder, cascading down her pink sweater. Her face is heavily made up, and it seems like she tries to avoid smiling too much so as not to make it crack. Her office is kept neat. There are a few front-page stories framed on her walls, ones he assumes to have been written, or edited, by her. At the front of her desk, ostentatiously placed, is an award, though Daniel doesn't focus too much on what it's for or who it's from.

"No, I'm fine, thank you," Daniel says. "I just want

to ask a few questions, and then I'll get out of your hair."

"Please don't feel like you need to rush," Maria says, spreading her manicured hands out before herself.

"You asked if Ike is in trouble," Daniel says. "Does he often get himself into trouble?"

"Oh, no, nothing like that. It's just with him being gone for so long, and then a deputy from the sheriff's department shows up, I worried that maybe something has happened to him."

"He's gone?"

"I assumed that's what you came here for."

"Have you filed a missing persons report?"

Maria tilts her head, confused. "No," she says. "Has someone else?"

"I don't believe so, no."

"Oh. Then what is it that brought you here? *Is* Ike missing?"

Daniel starts to feel like he's being watched. A feeling he can't shake off. "Let's start over," Daniel says. "It feels like the two of us are wound up in knots as to why I'm here. I'm looking to speak to Ike. I believe he may have been in contact with a friend of mine, a friend I'm having trouble getting in touch with, and I feel Ike perhaps knows how to reach him. At least, I hope he does."

"Okay, then," Maria says. "Well, I'm afraid Ike hasn't been in for almost a week now."

Daniel still feels like he's being watched. He glances to his right, through Maria's windows that look out over her offices, into the bullpen. He catches sight of a pair of female eyes peering over the top of a cubicle, looking back at him. When they meet, the other eyes don't instantly tear away, caught. Instead, they hold his gaze. The woman gets to her feet, then starts reaching into her bag, pulls out a packet of cigarettes, and leaves the newsroom.

"Deputy?"

Daniel turns back to Maria. "Sorry," he says. He makes an excuse. "Thought I saw someone I know. A week, did you say?"

"That's right."

Daniel settles back in his chair, strokes his chin. First Frank, now this Ike, apparently. The two of them connected by a slip of paper in Frank's house, pressed – hidden? – in his laptop. Where've they gone? Are they together? "You have any idea where he might have gone? He say anything?"

"Afraid not. Truth be told, I thought he was working on a story. Ike can get very caught up in his work. A perfectionist, to be honest. I've often felt like he's gunning for my job." She smiles, almost cracks the makeup at the corners of her mouth, quickly returns her face to a pleasantly neutral position.

"Is this the longest he's gone without you hearing from him?"

"I'd say so, yes. He usually checks in every couple of days or so, gives us an update, but this time there hasn't been a peep. If I'm honest with you, Deputy, I'm not too worried. This isn't uncommon, like I said. And Ike can be a little…well, *strange*."

"Strange? How do you mean?"

Maria thinks about her words. "Obsessive," she says. "He can get very caught up in his own…*foibles*, shall we say. He perhaps attributes more importance to some of his stories than they actually deserve. Between the two of us" – she leans across the table, lowers her voice, as if there were anyone near to hear her – "I've sometimes wondered if he maybe has a touch of Asperger's or something like that, y'know."

"There been any differences in his behavior lately? Before he stopped coming to work, I mean."

"Nothing particularly springs to mind," Maria says. "But like I already said, he's always been a little strange."

"All right, then," Daniel says, getting to his feet. "Well, if you hear anything from Ike, be sure to let him know I'd like to talk, will you?"

"Of course." Maria stands with him, walks him to the door of her office. Daniel makes his way through the bullpen, checks the cubicle where he made eye contact with the girl watching him, but she hasn't returned from her smoke break. He glances back at Maria's office. She's watching him, through her window. She waves.

Outside, the woman who caught his eye is waiting for him. She whistles at him as he leaves the building, gets his attention. She's leaning against the wall near the alleyway, and she beckons him over, then slips down the side of the building.

Daniel follows. "Help you with something, ma'am?" he says once they're close enough to talk.

The woman puffs on a cigarette, looks back over her shoulder to the entrance of the alley. "Why're you here?" she says.

Daniel cocks his head. "Excuse me?"

"I heard you tell someone you wanted to talk to Ike. I hear that right?"

"Who are you, ma'am?"

"My name's Lisa," she says. "Lisa Rayner."

"Is Ike a friend of yours?"

"What'd Maria have to say about him disappearing?"

Daniel narrows his eyes. "Are you saying he's gone missing?"

"Isn't that why you're here?"

Lisa looks antsy to Daniel, like she's desperate not to be seen with him, eager to get away and return to her workstation, so he decides not to question her and instead just find out what she has to say about Ike. He tells her what Maria said. During his telling, she finishes her cigarette, pulls out another one, and lights it up.

When he's done, she scoffs. "That's what she said, huh? What a load of shit."

"You have a differing version of events?"

"Hell yeah I do, and so will anyone else in that office, if they have the balls to admit to it. She said Ike's been acting normal? No way. He'd become paranoid. He was secretive. Wouldn't let anyone know what he was working on, but he confided to me – I think because he knew he could trust me – that it was big. Said it was gonna blow this whole county apart."

"The county?"

"That's what he said."

"Why'd he trust you enough to share?"

Lisa brushes a lock of hair behind her ear. "We used to date," she says, almost shyly. "We stayed close."

"Okay. He tell you what his county-shattering story was?"

"No. But I'll tell you this, a major part of the events that I'll bet Maria decided to leave out – the day he disappeared, he went to her with the story."

"And?"

Lisa makes her eyes big. "Whatever he took her, it didn't go down well. They started arguing, the two of them, and I'd never heard Ike raise his voice before. Maria was screaming at him. She kept telling him to kill the story, said whatever it was was ridiculous, a crock of shit. Ike didn't like that."

"You hear what he said back?"

"Well, he was muffled by the glass, but I could hear

him say that the story needed to be told, that they couldn't kill it, he wouldn't let her kill it. That he was going to share the story whether she printed it or not."

"Then?"

"Then he stormed out, and I haven't seen or heard from him since. Listen, I gotta get back –"

"Hold up, just one more question. He ever mention anyone called Frank Aynsley to you? Did he mention a deputy, a cop, anything?"

"No, I've already told you everything he told me about his story."

"It might not be related to the story." Daniel doubts this, though.

"The answer's still no. Never mentioned any Frank to me."

"Where do you think he's gone?"

"You said one more question."

"I was mistaken. This is the last, I promise."

Lisa thinks, blows air out her nose, shakes her head. "I don't know," she says. "But for how spooked he was, how weird he'd been acting – like there were people out to get him – I gotta think he's just *gone*, y'know. Got as far away as he can. But I'll tell you this – the fact he hasn't released the story he swore to Maria he was going to, not online or anywhere, makes me worry." She gives Daniel one last look, with a sense of earnestness about it, like she's counting on him to help Ike out, to find out where he's gone and make sure he's all right. Then she hurries by him, flicking away what's left of her cigarette.

When Daniel gets to the end of the alleyway, he looks toward the front of the office building. Lisa is gone.

11

Tom's few days to cool down are coming to their end. He's alone in his cell now. The night before, while he lay on the bench, trying to sleep, the guards came into the room. The three men he'd beaten had been in the next cell since his return, had glared daggers at him but said nothing. They'd huddled and talked among themselves, kept their backs to him for the most part, occasionally glanced his way to make sure he wasn't listening in. He noticed how the muscular guy rubbed his lower back more now, how he winced with every movement.

Tom was half-asleep when the guards came. He woke fully when the door opened, but kept his eyes closed, peered out through slits, watching. The two guards looked through the bars, watched him for a few minutes. Tom wasn't sure what they wanted. It could be a routine check, though for the most part they'd been blasé about checking on the well-being of their prisoners so far.

They turned away from him finally, satisfied. One of the guards turned to the other. "They asleep, too?"

"Yeah."

"Wake 'em up."

They unlocked the next cell, woke the three guys there, shook them, weren't gentle about it. They cuffed them, dragged them from the cell. The three men were too groggy to speak, mumbled a few things, but nothing Tom could make sense of. "Just keep it moving," one of the guards said. "Let's go."

Tom hasn't seen them since. He's not cut up about it. He prefers the solitude.

Before midday, Daniel and another deputy come to take him out of the cell. Daniel leans on the bars before they unlock the door. "Car ought to be fixed by now, shouldn't it?"

"Damn well should be." Tom will be glad to get back behind the wheel, to get out of this place, follow the sheriff's orders and get out of Cullingworth County. Fuck this place.

Just as soon as he's dealt with Earl. Right after he has the Santa Muerte pendant back.

They take him out of his cell, take him to reclaim his personal effects. He pockets his wallet, and while he's pulling on his jacket, the sheriff appears, drinking from a mug of coffee. "Well," he says, leaning against the door, "remember what I said. Keep your nose outta trouble, and don't let me see you in here again."

Tom nods. His jacket is on. He has his belongings back. He's ready to leave. He turns back to the sheriff, says, "Well, thanks for the hospitality."

Larry takes a drink, raises an eyebrow over the top of the mug, unimpressed. "You're a free man now, Mr. Smith. Be sure to use that freedom wisely." With this, the sheriff leaves.

Tom leaves the station, steps out into the hot midday heat of Kirkwood. He blinks against the glare, his eyes used to the shade of the cell. Looking around, in the daylight, he sees more clearly the differences between Kirkwood and Brenton. They could be a world apart. The sidewalks are as immaculate as he'd thought they were in the dark. The lawn directly opposite the station is lush and grassy. So far as he can see, there isn't a single junkie among all the people on the sidewalks or lounging on the lawn. Everyone here looks happy and healthy and clean. Looks almost like a picture postcard of idealized 1950s Americana. He's almost certain all the homes in this town will have well-maintained lawns and white picket fences.

Tom starts walking, looking for a bus stop or a station. He passes an old couple, and the man tips his hat to Tom. Tom nods, keeps walking. He can't see any bus stop, but he figures there has to be a station in town. If all else fails, he'll get a taxi.

A cruiser pulls up alongside him. Tom keeps walking until he realizes it's keeping pace. He stops, turns. The driver's window rolls down. It's Daniel. "Wanna ride?"

"I'm good," Tom says. He's had enough of riding in police cars for a while.

He's about to start walking again when Daniel says, "Come on, jump in the back. It'll be quicker than a bus, and it won't cost you a dime. I'm heading through that way anyway."

Tom deliberates, then decides there's no harm, it'll save him some time, and he gets in the back. Daniel pulls away, heads out of town. They drive in silence for a while, nothing but the voices on the scanner filling the air, until they make it out into the desert. Tom looks out the window, across the sand, the cacti, the rocks, to the mountainous ranges in the distance.

"So how'd you like your cellmates?" Daniel says, grinning.

"Just a real swell group of guys," Tom says.

"They were pretty swollen by the time you got through with them. What happened?"

"I'm sure there's a report."

"Yeah, but I'm asking you what brought it on."

Tom shrugs, though he doesn't know if Daniel is looking or not. "Just a bunch of assholes, like the guys at the bar."

"You keep beating people up round here, I don't think that excuse is gonna fly much longer."

"You'll notice I've never used it as an excuse."

"I suppose that's true. Well, you can just forget about all that stuff back in the cell now. Ain't like you'll ever see them again."

"Unless I'm real unlucky, and they've gone and booked themselves into Sally's hotel."

Daniel chuckles. "Now that *would* be unlucky. Why would they go and do a thing like that?"

"They said something about being transported to Brenton."

Daniel turns his head a little, eyes narrowed. "They said that? When?"

"In the cell. That first day I was in there with them."

Daniel slows the car, pulls it to a stop at the side of the road. He turns in his seat, looks back at Tom fully. "You sure that's what they said?"

"That's what they said," Tom says. "I wasn't paying all that much attention, but I recognized the name, seeing as that's where I washed up. When they got taken out of the cell, I assumed that's where they were being transported to."

"They didn't come from Brenton. They were picked up in Elliston, for dealing."

"They said something about that, too," Tom says, remembering. "They said they fucked up, got caught, and now they were gonna get sent back to Brenton."

"*Back* to Brenton?"

"That's what they said. I don't know what else to tell you. It don't mean anything to me. They said something about being caught somewhere they weren't supposed to be. Elliston, that place you just mentioned."

Tom sees how Daniel's eyes narrow, how his forehead creases, confused, thinking. "They say why they thought they were gonna be sent back to Brenton?" he says.

"No." Tom shrugs.

"And you're sure that's what they said?"

"They called it a one-way trip."

"They say anything else?"

"Nothin' relevant to what you're asking about."

"Such as?"

"Such as stuff that made me wanna bust their teeth down their throat."

Daniel grunts. "And you came close to doing that."

"It almost felt worth the extra few days locked up."

Daniel laughs. "But they didn't say anything else about Brenton? Anything at all?"

"I already told you, no."

Daniel falls silent, turns back around, and starts driving again. He doesn't talk again the rest of the journey, thinking, evidently confused by what Tom has said. When they get back to Brenton, he asks Tom where he wants to go. "Garage?"

"I gotta go to the hotel first," Tom says. "I need to get my stuff." He thinks of the urn, of his bag, of the picture he has tucked into the mirror.

Daniel drops him out front, has to let him out the back of the cruiser.

"Thanks for the ride," Tom says.

"Don't mention it." Daniel still looks deep in thought, promptly gets back into his car, drives off.

Tom walks up to the hotel. The door is closed, the first time he's seen it so. He reaches out, about to push it open, when he hears something. It stops him in his tracks. He listens.

Gunshots.

12

Tom follows the sound. It's coming from the back of the hotel. He sticks to the side of the building, close to the brickwork. Reaches the corner and peers around.

The back of the hotel is a patch of wasteland. It looks like another building was here, once upon a time. Long since demolished or burned down, or whatever happened to it before its remnants were swept away. Sally stands upon it, a rifle pressed into her shoulder. She has a target pinned to a tree at the other end of the land. Tom watches her shoot. Her aim is close to the bull's-eye, slightly off center. Sally lowers the gun, shields her eyes, and strains to see how she's done. "Damn," she says.

"The target off?" Tom says.

She wheels on him, calms when she sees who it is. "You're back," she says.

"Here I am."

"I heard Earl and his buddies weren't gonna press charges. Thought you'd be back here sooner."

"I got into a different kind of trouble."

"In a jail cell? I'm almost impressed."

Tom crosses the yard, stands next to her, eyeing the distant target. "You got decent aim," he says.

"My dad taught me. He tried to teach Anna, too – she's my sister – but she wasn't as interested, so I got to spend more time practicing."

"Looks like you know what you're doing," Tom says.

"Feel like I'm slipping. I usedta get all bull's-eyes."

"How often you out here?"

"Most days."

"Then you've probably just got your mind on other things. Can't imagine your skills would slip that quickly if you're putting so much practice in."

"Yeah, well, maybe I did have other things on my mind."

"You wanna talk about it?" Tom hopes she does not.

"Not really."

He nods, glad. "You out here practicing daily for a reason?"

"You never know. Better safe than sorry, especially in a town like this. You shoot?"

Tom takes a good look at the rifle. It's an M14. A military rifle. "Been a while since I handled one of those, but yeah. Correct me if I'm wrong, but ain't they illegal for civilians to own?"

"It was my dad's. As well as the hotel, he left me this."

"He was in the army?"

"Yeah."

Tom remembers something the sheriff said. "Did he know the sheriff over in Kirkwood?"

"Larry? Yeah, he knew him." Sally doesn't elaborate, but she doesn't look like her father thought fondly of the sheriff. "You talked to him while you were out there, huh?"

"Yeah, he came in, shook his dick around a little, let me know he was the big man. Mentioned he'd had some buddies in the army."

"Yeah, well, Crispin Blevins was not one of them." She holds the rifle out to him. "Care to refresh your memory?"

"Sure." Tom takes the M14 from her, reacquaints himself with the weight of it. It's been a long time since he last held one. He finds his footing, then raises it to his shoulder. He looks along the sight, spies the bull's-eye, then squeezes the trigger three times. Three bull's-eyes.

Sally whistles through her teeth. "Impressive."

"Thanks." He hands the rifle back. "I came to get my stuff."

"Sure." Sally shoulders the rifle, starts heading back round to the front of the hotel. "You've also lapsed on a few extra payments, I'm afraid. Your recent sojourn courtesy of the Cullingworth County Sheriff's Department has seen to that."

"I'm good for it."

"And I'm glad to hear it, because I rarely do."

They enter the hotel, and Darby is sitting behind the desk, where Sally usually is. "How'd the shooting go, Sally?" he says. He sees Tom follow her in, adds, "Hello, Tom."

"It went well, Darby," Sally says. "Thanks for watching the place."

"Sure." He steps out from behind the counter, looks at Tom both warily and reverently. "I never got to thank you for –" he starts to say.

Tom holds up a hand. "Forget about it." He's not in the mood for gratitude, especially when it's for an act he regrets.

Darby nods, then leaves the lobby, heads out front, to the bench where Tom first saw him. Sally props the rifle against the wall, then reaches down the side of the desk, pulls up a familiar rucksack. "Started to think you weren't coming back. I cleared your room out," she says. "Did it yesterday, so you'll only have to pay up until then. By the way, it was good of you to stand up for Darby the way you did. He told me what happened."

Tom isn't listening anymore. He's grabbed his bag, torn it open, started searching through it on the counter. "Has someone taken the room since?" he says.

"Yes," Sally says.

Tom grows frantic, upends the bag. Sees how Sally's eyes widen at some of the items that fall from it, that he rummages through. The fresh pair of jeans and the spare couple of shirts don't bother her, but the Beretta, the KA-BAR, the half a dozen burner phones cause her to lean forward. "Those are army," she says, pointing to the weapons. He can almost see her remembering his sharpshooting round back, the scene playing over in her mind. "I recognize them. Were you in the army?" Then she sees the urn. Her eyes go wide. She doesn't ask.

Tom ignores her, keeps searching through the clothes, under them, in his pockets. Checks the empty bag again, pushing his hand into its inside pockets. Finds some spare bullets, but not what he's looking for. "I need to go back into the room," he says.

"Just calm down," Sally says. "What's wrong? What's the issue?"

"There was a picture," Tom says. "It's not here."

Sally starts to laugh.

Tom is too tightly wound right now to find anything humorous in the situation. "What's so funny?"

"Is that what's got you so worked up? A picture?

Why didn't you just say so?" She reaches down to her desk, picks something up, hands it to him.

It's the photograph of Alejandra. Tom snatches it out of her hands, checks it for damage, then returns it to his bag, slides it into a safe place, then starts repacking the other items, sure to be careful of the picture as he puts them away.

"I almost missed it," Sally says. "It was up on the mirror – but I suppose you already know that. I thought you'd probably want it kept in a safer place rather than just stuffed into the bag. Who is she? She's very pretty. Girlfriend?"

Tom doesn't answer. Just keeps packing his bag. He notices how Sally checks his hand for a wedding band while he works.

"So, you were army, right?" Sally says, changing the subject when she sees he won't answer about the woman in the picture. "I'm guessing you've left it now. What're you doing with yourself, travelling? When my dad left, he bought this hotel. Left it to me when he died, my only inheritance, along with his rifle, but I've told you that already, haven't I? Keeps me stuck in this shitty little town."

Tom doesn't care about her life story. He's finished packing his bag. "I'm not much longer for your shitty little town, Sally. I got one piece of business to see to, then I'm gone." He slings the bag over his shoulder.

"And what piece of business is that?" Sally says.

"Maybe you can help me," Tom says. "Where's Earl?"

"Earl McQuade?"

"Yes."

She shakes her head. "You don't want to go doing any kind of business with him."

"He took something from me. I'm going to get it back."

Sally looks like she doesn't think this is a good idea. "Whatever it is, just leave it," she says. "It ain't worth the trouble."

"I'll be sure to ask him nicely," Tom says. He has no such intention.

When it's clear that Sally will not tell him what he wants to know, he drops some money on the counter to pay for his room, then leaves the hotel. He does not need her help to find Earl; he has other ways and means. He goes down the road, rounds the corner, heading for the garage, sure his car must be fixed by now, glad to finally be leaving. Through the garage's open roll-up door, he can hear Creedence Clearwater Revival playing, turned up loud. He steps into the opening, sees Lon with his head under a hood, his long hair dangling, his upper body nodding along in time to the bass-heavy rendition of "Heard It Through The Grapevine."

Tom looks the room over, can't see his car. He checks outside, the few cars parked out front, but can't see it there, either. Wonders if there's a back to the garage, if it's there. Probably a good sign, means it's fixed and he can just pay and ride out, find somewhere to lie low for the day before he does what he has to do next.

"Lonnie," he says, stepping into the cool shade.

Lon jerks upright, turns round, a joint hanging from his bottom lip, just like the first time Tom saw him. "Oh – oh, hey, man," Lon says, backing off from the car he's working on. "How you been? Ain't seen you in a while. Thought you were gonna keep checking in?" He chuckles.

Tom thinks he's acting strange. Like he's nervous. His eyes keep darting, around the room and outside, past Tom. Lon keeps backing up, stops when he hits a workbench. His hands start searching behind him, feeling on the bench.

"Where's my car?" Tom says.

"Oh, uh, ha, well, about that –"

Tom walks closer to him and he clamps up, starts, the joint falls from his mouth, hits the floor.

Lon's hands stop searching, settle on something; he swings his arm round. Tom catches him by the wrist. There's not much force in Lon's arm. He's holding a wrench. Tom looks at him, raises an eyebrow, then twists his arm until he drops the wrench and cries out.

"Ah, damn it – I'm sorry, I'm sorry!"

With his other hand, Tom takes a handful of the front of his overalls, lifts him off the ground, and slams him against the nearby tire rack. "Where the fuck is my car?"

"Earl took it – Earl took it!" Lon gulps.

"He *took* it?"

"That's right, he took it!"

"And you let him?"

"You don't say no to Earl McQuade!"

Tom can feel his temper rising. He hoists Lon up again, slams him back down. Lon starts coughing. Tom is having trouble processing what he has been told. "He took my fucking car?" First the pendant, now the car.

Lon nods. "He...he left a message for you..."

"What'd he say?"

Lon is scared to relay it.

Tom leans forward, their noses almost touching. "What did he say?"

Lon swallows. Tom hears something in his throat click. "He...he said, thanks for the necklace, and thanks for the car. He, he told you – these are his words – he said get the fuck out of his town, and enjoy the bus."

13

Tom goes back to the hotel. He's pissed. Sally is surprised to see him again. "You remember you forgot to say goodbye?" she says.

Tom slams his hand down on the counter. "He took my fuckin' car." He doesn't raise his voice. He stays calm despite how he is raging inside.

Sally blinks. "Who did?"

"Earl McQuade."

"He took your car?"

"That's what I said, ain't it?"

"Is that – is that what you meant when you said he'd taken something from you? I'm guessing from the way you're reacting right now that ain't what you were talking about."

"No, that was something different, something more important."

Sally shakes her head. "That son of a bitch," she says, with the weariness of one who has described someone as such many times before. "He's fucking with you. You need to report it. I can call Daniel right now. I'm pretty

sure he'd be more than happy to go out and see Earl and
get your car back."

"You think I should call the cops?" Tom says. "The
same cops who arrested me after a whole bar tried to
beat me down, and believed them when they said *I* was
the one started it?"

"Daniel will –"

"If Daniel has such a problem with Earl, he could've
gone to bat for me, but he didn't, and I've just spent the
last three days locked up. No offense, Sally, but I ain't
gonna rely on your boyfriend's help."

Sally takes a deep breath, looks him in the eye. "I
really think you should call the cops, Tom."

Tom shakes his head. "No. There's something going
on in this town – maybe in Kirkwood, too – and I don't
trust it. I ain't calling the cops." He looks at Sally, holds
her eye. "Where is he?"

"Tom –"

"Where does he live?"

"I'm not going to tell you that."

"You're not the only person I can ask."

"Tom, you've got a gun in your bag. Last time you
saw Earl, you got in a fight with him and his friends,
and right now you look and sound calm and everything,
but I bet you're not, not really. You honestly believe I
think you're just gonna head out there for a polite
conversation, respectfully request your car back from
him and whatever else it was he took? You're going
there looking for a fight, and I'm not gonna encourage
that."

"I don't need your encouragement, and what I do
when I get there ain't none of your concern. Where
is he?"

"My sister's there. I'm not telling you where it is,

Tom, and neither will anyone else in this hotel, or I'll kick them out."

"Your sister?" Tom considers this. "Was she the girl in here the other day with Dean, when I first checked in?"

"That was her."

Tom eyes Sally suspiciously. "And she lives with Earl?"

"She's out at the ranch with him, yes."

"A ranch?"

Sally realizes she has slipped up. "I won't let you put her in danger."

"You happy about her being out there?"

"No, I ain't. Of course I'm not."

"So you ain't gonna do a damn thing. You're content to just let Earl do whatever he wants."

Sally's eyes blaze. She slams her hand down on the counter. "The McQuades are a cancer on this town, on this entire fuckin' county, and I'm mad as hell at Anna for being out there with them, but that's my right to be so. *You* don't have any right to tell me I'm just like everyone else round here who won't stand up to them. My father knew Reggie McQuade his whole life, grew up with him, and he hated that man."

"Who's Reggie?"

"Earl's father. Reginald. Mr. McQuade himself. My father hated him, and that was *before* everything he and his family and friends have done to Brenton. They've destroyed it."

"So what's your sister doing living with them?"

Sally sighs. Her fury drains out of her at this question. "She gave up," she says. "You don't say no to the McQuades, not forever, anyway."

Tom tilts his head, remembering the mechanic saying something similar.

"Just call the cops, Tom," Sally says, sounding tired. "Just report the car and whatever else he took. It ain't worth the trouble. Earl's just trying to piss you off. That's what he's like. He likes to throw his weight around, push people around, show off, show what a big shot he is. Just call the cops and get it over with."

Tom sees that Sally will not assist him. He acts like her words are sinking in. He takes a deep breath. "Look, I'll think about it." He has no intention of doing such a thing.

Sally nods. "Trust me, it's for the best. Don't go getting mixed up with them, especially when you don't have to."

"Okay. Well, in the meantime, I guess I'm stuck here again. I don't suppose you've got another room?"

"I do," Sally says, still sounding tired, but also pleased that he's listened to reason.

"Just keep it rolling again," Tom says.

"Sure." She smiles at him, hands over the room key. "Sleep on it, Tom. You'll be calmer come the morning; you won't feel then how you feel now. Trust me, by then you'll see that the best thing to do is just call the cops."

Tom nods, takes the key, leaves the lobby. Back up the stairs, to his new room. He doesn't plan on being in the hotel much longer. He just needs a place he can store his things and wait for dark.

14

Anna Blevins is half passed out, and she wants to stay this way. Once it ends, she knows, she'll feel terrible. She's coming down. Getting meth isn't hard. She can make herself well again, but Earl rations it, and she's gone through this batch too fast. He'll lecture her, shake his head, express his disappointment, his annoyance, his disgust. He'll give it to her, in the end, but he'll make her jump through hoops first. There's any number of things he might make her do, like she's one of his tweaker customers back in Brenton, and he's bent on humiliating her for his own amusement.

She realizes the reason she's not fully unconscious is because her phone is buzzing. The persistent rattle of a phone call. The phone lies on the bedside table. She's in the room she shares with Earl, but he's not here right now. She can hear him in the sitting room, playing video games with Dean. She picks the phone up. It's Sally.

"Hello?"

"Hey, Anna – you sound terrible. Are you sick?"

Anna clears her throat.

"Or just coming down?" Sally says.

"I'm not coming down," Anna says, looking round the room, sure there is a glass of water somewhere. It's on the windowsill. She drinks it. It's warm, tastes like it's been there a few days, and like she should have checked for a layer of dust resting on the top.

"What can I do for you?" she says, determined to put on a firm voice, to sound how she normally does.

"I just wanted to check if you'd seen something," Sally says.

"Seen something?"

"Yeah."

"Where? Around the ranch? I haven't been anywhere else."

"Right where you are. Has Earl got a new car recently?"

"A new car?"

"Yeah."

"I haven't seen one."

"You sure? It ain't exactly new. A Ford, I think."

"I already told you, I ain't seen one. Why, what's the big deal?"

"One of my customers lost his car recently. He thinks Earl took it. And something else that belongs to him, but he ain't told me what it is. You seen Earl going round with anything else new recently?"

"I'd need a clue about what that 'anything' might be." Something about the Ford sounds familiar to Anna. "Is that the car we saw that guy pushing into town the other day? The one Daniel helped push to the garage."

"Yeah."

"Why would Earl have that? It was an old car, and Earl can afford to buy his own cars. He'd get something newer than that, that hadn't just broke down."

"I don't think he took it to take on a joyride, Anna. I

think he took it to mess with the guy it belongs to. Listen, I'm just asking. If you say you haven't seen it, then you haven't seen it."

"Is this to do with when he came home the other night with a bust nose?"

"I guess so."

"That guy did it to him?"

"That's what I hear. Earl didn't tell you what happened?"

"He never tells me anything."

"So he possibly didn't tell you about the car, either."

"I think I would've noticed if he rolled up with a different car." Anna looks toward the barn at the rear of the property. She doesn't say anything about it to Sally. "Listen, I need to go."

"Anna, before you go, just tell me – you sound sick as fuck, no matter how you try to hide it. Are you high? Are you coming down?"

"For Christ's sake, Sally." This is an argument they've had many times before, and Anna has no interest in rehashing it now, feeling as terrible as she does. "I'm fine, all right? I said as much. I gotta go." She hangs up before her sister can say anything else.

She goes to the mirror, runs her hands down her face, roughly rubs life into her cheeks and the skin under her eyes. She leaves the bedroom. Earl and Dean sit with their backs to her. Neither of them turn, too engrossed in their game, shooting down zombies by the looks of it.

She remembers how Earl was in high school, when he still seemed to be interested in her for more than just the sake of having her. When he still seemed to care, and was cute and funny and kind. Her father had never approved, had chased Earl off on more than one occasion, but that had just made their illicit relationship all the more exciting. The two of them would meet up halfway between the hotel where she lived and the ranch where Earl did, at Dean's house. He'd let them hang out in his bedroom while his parents were at work.

Crispin Blevins and Reginald McQuade had more in common than either of them would care to admit. They were both hardworking, and they were both single parents. Anna's mother had died in a car crash when she and her sister were young, which had resulted in Crispin leaving the army and pouring all his money into the hotel, trying to make a new life for his family while they coped with their grief. Reggie's wife, Sandra, died of leukemia when Earl was five. Both men, perhaps overwhelmed by mourning, never talked of their departed loves.

After Anna's father died five years ago, Earl started pursuing her more aggressively. Anna didn't like this new intensity. Their relationship became off and on, but most of the time it just felt easier to give in to Earl's advances, to just be in a relationship with him and give him what he wanted. It was about a year ago, maybe a little more and maybe a little less, that Anna gave up on any fantasy of having autonomy in her life, and moved onto the ranch with him. Allowed Earl to dictate where she lived and what she did and who she saw. He begrudgingly allows her to visit with her sister still, but he's never happy about it.

Anna saw few other prospects in her life when she moved onto the ranch. Either be with Earl, or run the hotel with her sister. Neither was particularly appealing, but at least with the former she has the drugs, and she finds that the drugs help her to tolerate her shitty situation.

Anna leaves the house, steps out onto the porch. She shields her eyes and looks around the ranch. Looks to the main house, the one the dirt road leading up to the ranch stops directly in front of. There's no sign of Reggie, though he's likely in there right now with Chris Holden, his second-in-command. Chris's house is to the left of the main one. Unlike Chris, Dean doesn't live on the ranch, but he's out here often enough he may as well. Tends to sleep in the spare room in Earl and Anna's place.

Anna steps down off the porch. Her bare feet move through the dirt, kicking up dust. The desertification that has taken over most of Cullingworth County has not yet fully reached McQuade ranch. It's one of the few remaining areas in the county that still has green that isn't a cactus, though there are still a few of those to be found on the perimeter.

As she crosses the yard, the two German Shepherds that reside in the kennels down the side of Reggie's house – Jojo and Georgie, both bitches – sniff at her approach, start circling around each other to get closer to her. Anna scratches their noses through the mesh as she goes by, makes her way over to the barn. Her feet brush through grass now. It's long and untended.

"Anna!" It's Earl's voice.

She's a few paces from the derelict barn at the base of the hills that rise behind the ranch, wondering if the car Sally mentioned is inside, but she stops and turns.

Earl and Dean have left the house. They're carrying a bucket. Earl waves her over. "I didn't know you were up," he says.

"I walked right by you," she says, looking into the bucket and seeing raw meat for the dogs. "Two of you were busy killing monsters."

"C'mon," Earl says, heading to the kennels. "We're gonna feed the girls."

Anna joins them. They go to the mesh, slip bits of

meat through the gaps in the fence for the dogs to take from their fingertips. Anna hears the door to the main house open. She glances back, sees Reggie and Chris emerge. Reggie sees them feeding the dogs, turns his head to the side, spits off the porch, then strides over to join them, Chris by his side.

Anna has always gotten the impression Reggie doesn't particularly care for her being there. Merely tolerates her presence, knowing that his son wants her around. Reggie and Chris are old friends, but they look like they could be brothers. They both have the same broad shoulders, square jaws, combed dark hair. Earl has not inherited his father's almost-handsome looks. He looks more like his mother, who, in pictures Anna has seen, had a narrow face and buckteeth. Earl's front teeth don't protrude like hers did, but they do have the same shape, like they're growing almost to a point.

Reggie's midsection is a little softer than Chris's, and, unlike Chris, he is not clean-shaven. He wears a mustache and regularly has stubble on his cheeks. He looks over what his son and Dean and Anna are doing. "Stop messing around with the dogs and just feed them already," he says. "We ain't got the time for this."

Earl glances at his watch. "We got a few hours yet."

Reggie side-eyes Anna while he talks to his son. "We got somewhere important to be. Don't be fuckin' late 'cause you couldn't help yourself from messing around."

Wherever they are going, Anna will not be joining them. She's kept in the dark on everything. Most likely, this is at Reggie's command.

Reggie looks at his son, narrows his eyes. "That ain't healed yet?"

Earl presses the scab on the bridge of his nose. "No," he says. "Not yet. Better'n it was, though."

Reggie turns to Dean, sees the bruising still on his face, but doesn't comment on it. "We're going over there now," he says. "Make sure everything's set. We'll see you there."

"Sure," Earl says. "And we'll be right on time."

Reggie stares at his son, looking like he wants to admonish him further, but decides against it and heads off to his truck with Chris, his silent companion, in tow.

Earl pulls another piece of meat from the bucket, pokes it through the gap in the mesh for Georgie to take from his fingers, scratches her nose as she does so.

A couple of hours later, Earl and Dean head out to meet up with his father, wherever it is they go. Anna sits on her hands in their home, still coming down, and tries not to think about how terrible she feels. She'd wanted to ask Earl for help, for him to make it better, but she knew his annoyance at her would just make her feel worse. She tells herself if she can wait until tomorrow, tough it out until then, he won't be so pissy about it. She thinks setting herself the goal will make things easier, but tomorrow feels like it is forever away.

She's alone on the ranch save for a couple of men who patrol the perimeter, armed with automatic rifles. They puff on cigarettes and don't pay her any mind. If she's going to make it through until tomorrow, when she'll brave asking Earl for a top-up, she needs to keep her mind occupied. Keep the depression and the aches at bay. She sits with the dogs for a while, plays with them through the cage, then looks over at the barn. A bygone relic of a time the ranch was operational. She goes over to it, as she earlier intended, tries the door, but it's locked. She goes down the side, to one of the gaps in its dilapidated walls where a plank of wood has come loose, and peers inside.

The barn is usually empty. She sees a car. She's never

seen it at the ranch before, but she recognizes it. The day she saw the man pushing it into Brenton. It fits Sally's description.

Anna steps away from the barn, shakes her head, returns to the house. She won't call Sally, won't tell her what she has found, that she was right, that he's stolen the car. Anna is used to Earl's behavior, resigned to it, by now. It would just be easier for everyone else if they did the same.

15

Tom leaves his room before it gets dark, looks for a back way out of the hotel so he doesn't have to pass Sally in the lobby. The fire escape will probably be his best bet, though he knows sometimes these doors can be alarmed.

His new room is on the fourth floor. He goes down to the third, where his old one was. He finds Darby leaning on the railing. Tom waves him over as he reaches the foot of the stairs. "Hey, man," Darby says. "What's up?"

Tom points a thumb toward the door for the fire escape. "You know if that's alarmed?"

"I don't think so," Darby says. "I see people smoking on it from time to time, and I sure don't think they know the code. How come you're asking?"

"'Cause I'm going to use it, and I don't wanna set any alarm off." He adds, "Don't mention it to Sally."

"Um, sure. All right. You trying to avoid her or something?"

"Yeah."

"Oh." Darby seems surprised by this. "Why?"

Tom shakes his head, steps to the door. "Don't matter. Just don't tell her. You owe me one, keep that in mind."

"I don't know why you might think you've gotta hide something from her, but Sally's good people. A lot of folk have given up on this town, but she ain't."

At the door, Tom turns back. "You sure about that?"

"It might've beat her down some, but deep down, in her heart, she's still holding out for it to get better. That's what keeps her going. That's why she looks after all of us here, in this hotel."

"Looks after you?"

"Some of us here, we've gotten in deep, y'know? You really think, when you've got a habit that bad, that you can pay the rates? Sure, we contribute what we can, when we can, and I help her out with the hotel, but a lot of the time Sally is cutting us some slack on account of she knows we got nowhere else to go. There's a lot of people would just let us die out on the streets, cold and coming down, but she lets us stay here, where we at least don't have to worry about where we're gonna spend the night."

"Why's she do that?"

"I dunno. She's a good person, I guess. I think it has somethin' to do with her daddy, too. He was a good man, from everything I've heard. He cared about this town, looked out for it, kept Reggie McQuade in check."

"Is Reggie McQuade as big an asshole as his son?"

Darby smirks. "Different kind of asshole."

"Figures." Tom opens the door. No alarm sounds. He looks back at Darby. "Not a word," he says.

"Sure," Darby says. "Like you said, I owe you one. Hell, reckon I owe you more than one."

"Keep your mouth shut and we'll call it even."

"Seems unfair to you, but if that's how you want it, we got a deal."

Tom steps out, descends the fire escape, rounds the corner, and goes back to the garage. Lon is closing up for the night. It's the first time Tom has seen him without overalls, but his regular clothes – jeans and a Metallica T-shirt – look just as unwashed and crumpled. He's pulling down the shutters. With a joint, as ever, dangling from the corner of his mouth, he fumbles for his keys to lock up. Tom steps up behind him, takes a handful of his greasy hair, and slams his face into the shutters. The joint falls from his lips.

"Ah, man, what the fuck!" When he turns to see his assailant, still holding his hair, his eyes go wide at the sight of Tom. Lon's nose is bloodied. "Look, man, I don't know what you want, I already told you what happened. Ain't anything I can do about it now. I already told you that!"

"You *can* do somethin' for me, Lon," Tom says. "You can loan me a car."

Lonnie doesn't take much persuasion. He gives Tom the keys to a green Chevy, then finishes locking up his garage and hurries off into the night. Tom takes the car, drives it past the hotel, past another couple of buildings, then parks it down a side alley. The bar is a few more buildings down on the opposite side of the road. Tom parks with the front facing forward so he can see. He gets out of the car and goes over to the bar.

Tonight must be a quiet night. Only one of the dealers from the night before – the one who was pushing Darby around, who sized Tom up – is present. He's busy selling to a meth head, is preoccupied, doesn't see Tom as he enters. Doesn't notice the hush that falls over the room, either.

Everyone else sees Tom. Tom recognizes a few faces.

Some of them are still sporting the bruises he gave them, whereas his have mostly healed. They're quick to look away, but they continue to watch out of the corner of their eyes.

Tom starts moving. Strides over to the drug dealer sitting in his regular booth. The room goes tense at Tom's approach. The meth head the dealer is selling to senses it. Senses the shift in the air as he prepares for impending trouble. The tweaker steps back, gets out of the way. The dealer looks confused. Their transaction is not finished. He opens his mouth, about to say something; then the next thing he knows, Tom places a hand on the back of his head, slams his face down into the table.

Tom has dazed him. Before he can recover, he drags him out of the booth, drives his knee up hard into the center of his face. The dealer goes limp. Tom drops him, lets him fall. He rolls onto his back, lies spread-eagled on the floor.

The room watches Tom, wide-eyed. There's no Earl present to tell them to jump in, so none of them move.

Tom pats the dealer down and finds the stash: about two dozen baggies, maybe more, in a brown paper bag in the inside pocket of his jacket. Tom takes the bag, leaves the bar with the stash. He takes the long way around back to the car, so no one sees where he goes. He throws the drugs onto the passenger seat, gets back behind the wheel, watches the front of the bar, and he waits.

16

E arl remembers, the day after they'd been in the fight with that guy in the bar, Dean told him how he first saw him come into town. Pushing his car along the road. Earl's mind started to work at the thought of the car and of the man who had given him and his boys, and their customers, such a beating.

Earl got in touch with Lonnie, asked him if the car was fixed yet. Lonnie said the part would arrive the next day. "You get hold of it, you call me," Earl said.

"Uh…why?"

"Because I fuckin' told you to, Lonnie, that's why. You want me to have to come along and check for myself, see if you've got it?"

"No, Earl, it's cool. I'll call you."

Earl wasn't impressed by the vehicle when they reached the garage. Whistled low, laughed. "Piece of shit, ain't it? No wonder it broke down on the uptight motherfucker." He stepped around the car, giving it a good looking-over, seeing the spots of rust low down on its sill. He patted the roof. "Well, I think he just gifted us his car, as an apology for the ruckus he caused in the bar the other night."

Now as they drive to meet Earl's father, Dean asks, "You worried your dad will be pissed when he finds out you took that guy's car?"

"Naw, I know *for sure* he'll be pissed." Earl doesn't fear anyone, but he sure as hell doesn't want to get on the wrong side of his father. "Remember how mad he was when he found out about the bar fight?"

Dean nods, solemn. He's remembering.

Earl remembers, too. The yelling, the cussing. It wasn't anything he hadn't heard before, many times. *The fuck were you thinking? I've told you a thousand times now, keep your fuckin' noses clean, don't go causing trouble, and don't make any goddamn noise! Especially not* now, *for Christ's sake. Do you know how important this all is? Last thing we need right now is any kind of noise.*

"If he knew I'd taken the car, who knows what the crazy old fucker would do about it," Earl says.

"So what *are* you gonna do? Just keep it hidden in the barn? He's bound to notice it eventually."

"He never goes in there. When was the last time he went out to the barn? Ain't nothin' in there; he don't care about it. I reckon I'll give it at least two weeks. By then, he'll have calmed down, and everything happening right now will be over and done with, and he won't be so damn uptight."

"He's kinda always uptight, though," Dean says.

"That's true, but who knows? Maybe this thing comes through after the election and we'll see a new side to old daddy dearest. Could be he'll actually crack a smile – you imagine? I ain't even sure his face still remembers how to do that."

Dean laughs.

"Plus, that motherfucker – what was his name, you find it out?"

"It was Tom," Dean says. "Tom Smith."

"*Tom Smith* will be *long* gone by then, so wouldn't be like he could make me give it back. Tom will be gone, and we'll take that car out into the desert and do donuts 'til it flips."

"There's that necklace, too," Dean says.

"So?" Earl says.

"He was real mad when you took that off him. Took those cops to hold him back."

Earl laughs. "It's just some fuckin' trinket." Earl has it now; he's wearing it. It's under his shirt. He can feel it press against his chest. He pulls it out so Dean can see it. Dean grins.

"Looks familiar," Dean says.

"It's one've those things you see the spics paint, and that they have statues to, that kinda shit."

Dean nods. "You reckon he'd make you give it back? Your daddy, I mean. The car."

Earl shrugs. "Can never tell what he's gonna do exactly. Sometimes he likes to try and 'make an example'. You'd think he woulda given up on that kinda shit by now."

Dean's phone starts ringing. "It's Carl," he says.

He answers. Earl can only hear Dean's end of the conversation. "The same guy? You sure? He did *what*? Shit… All right, yeah, I'll tell Earl. Just hang tight." Dean lowers the phone, turns to Earl. "Speak of the fuckin' Devil…" he says.

"What is it?"

"Tom Smith's just gone back to the bar, knocked Carl out, took his stash."

Earl is surprised. "Sure it was him?"

"Carl says he didn't get a look at him, guy hit him

from behind, but everyone else saw him, and that's who they say it was. They didn't know his name, but they recognized him."

"And he took the stash?"

"Yeah."

Earl starts laughing. "That dumb son of a bitch ain't left town yet?"

"What we gonna do? We gotta sort this out. Your dad can't hear about this, 'specially not if you don't want him to know about your new set of wheels."

Earl thinks. He eases off on the accelerator, starts to slow. Reggie is expecting them, wants them there early; he'll be pissed if they turn up late. At the same time, they've gotta do something about this Tom Smith. They can't just let it slide, can't just let him beat up one of their own and take their stash. And Dean is right – they can't let his father know about this.

Earl thinks about the stolen car. *"Shit…"* His father hears about the stash being stolen from the bar, about Tom causing trouble because Earl took his car, he's gonna drop a world of shit and pain on top of him.

"What we gonna do?" Dean says.

"You still got Carl on the line?"

"Yeah."

Earl swerves the car across the road in a wild U-turn, points it back toward Brenton. "Tell him we're on our way." He slams his foot to the accelerator, floors it. They're going to have to be fast.

17

I t doesn't take long before Earl and Dean arrive. Tom sits low in the Chevy, watches over the top of the steering wheel as they screech to a halt in front of the bar in a car that is not his. They jump out of their vehicle, rush inside. They look like they're in a hurry. Tom watches and waits.

A couple of minutes pass by, presumably while they get the story of what has happened. They leave the bar, cross the road. Tom has to lean forward, peer out past the corner of the building to see where they go. To the hotel. They go inside. The dealer he beat up isn't with them. Still in the bar, licking his wounds.

Earl and Dean want to know where Tom is. They want their stash back. Tom doesn't care if Sally takes them straight up to his room; they're not going to find it there.

They step back out a moment later. Too soon to have been up to his room, to have searched it. They're walking backwards, shouting, waving their arms. Sally follows them to the door. She's shouting, too. Chasing them off. Tom is intrigued. He's impressed. He winds the window down a little to see if he can pick up on anything they're saying.

"– the fuck away from my hotel," Sally says. "I don't give a shit what you think he's done. You ain't going up to his room!"

Earl jabs his finger at her, though he's on the road and still walking back, back toward his car. "When I got more time, Sally, we'll be back, you fuckin' hear? We'll come back!" He glares at her, then spins on his heel, and he and Dean go back to the bar. The beaten dealer is standing in the doorway now. They talk to him briefly. Tom puts his window back up.

Earl and Dean get into the car. The dealer doesn't get in with them. Instead, he stumbles off down the sidewalk, dabbing at his face. Tom looks back toward the hotel. Sally has disappeared inside. Earl and Dean spin the car round, drive back the way they came.

Tom counts to five, then starts the engine and pulls out after them, follows at a safe distance. He'll follow them back to McQuade ranch, he'll find out where they've got his car and the Santa Muerte pendant, and then he'll take them both back. And if any of them try to stop him…

Well.

That's just too bad for them.

18

Tom follows the car, keeps his distance. They leave town. It gets dark. Where they're going, there doesn't seem to be anyone else on the road. Tom can't see anyone up ahead, can't see anyone behind. There are no lights, nothing belonging to either a car or a streetlight. Tom turns his headlights off, doesn't want them to know he's behind them. Just keeps following their taillights through the night.

They drive for a long time. Tom starts to wonder how far away from Brenton the McQuade ranch is. Wonders if they're still in Cullingworth County. He looks round, and it doesn't seem like there's anything here. No towns, no gas stations, no signs of life.

Suddenly, Tom finds himself closing in on the red lights. They're slowing. He slows in turn, holds back. The taillights have stopped. He stops. Watches. Sees one of the two, too far away to tell if it's either Earl or Dean, get out of the car, a dark shadow running around the front of the car and to the fence. The car passes slowly through the fence, then it stops on the other side. Tom waits until the person on foot gets back in the car and it starts moving again, then he rolls forward, reaches the point where they stopped. There's a gate. It's marked 'Prohibited.' Tom can't see the taillights anymore. They've disappeared into the darkness, gone over a hill and down the other side.

Tom gets out, checks the gate. It's held in place by a latch. There is a chain, with a padlock, but it is unlocked. He has the feeling that, in their rush, Earl and Dean have forgotten to lock it after themselves. He pushes the gate wide, gets back in the Chevy, pulls it through. Just in case anyone else comes and an open gate will raise an alarm, he closes it after himself.

This road is old and in disrepair; has not been tended for years by the looks and feel of it. It leads through the desert, to the hill Earl and Dean have disappeared over. Once he crests the hill, he can see where they are going. Catches sight of their taillights again, farther away now, off in the distance.

They drive toward a building. It looks like it used to be a factory, once upon a time. The moonlight shines down into the open space it occupies. Tom doesn't go any farther, idles on the hill. He gets a good look at the building. It is derelict. A lot of the windows are smashed. It does not look occupied. He doesn't need to be told that this is not the ranch. Wonders if it is beyond this opening, past this building, but then he sees the brake lights begin to flash. They're at the far corner of the building. Tom can see a circle of light there, as if the rear of the building is lit up. The car has slowed almost to a complete stop. They ease around the side of the building. They're stopping. They're not going any farther.

Tom has a feeling the ranch is nowhere near here. Seeing that they're not going any farther, that they're unlikely to lead him to his car and his pendant, he pulls the Chevy to one side. He can either turn round and leave, or he can wait until they're finished with whatever they're doing here, and continue to follow them.

He considers his options. Chances are, Earl will have the pendant on him. The car is not such a big deal, he can leave that behind and continue on with the Chevy Lon has loaned him. Furthermore, he's already beat up one of their dealers tonight. They're going to be more cautious going forward. Sticking with Earl now might be better than trying to catch back up with him later.

Then, before he has to make up his mind, he notices a man appear at the corner of the factory, opposite to the one Earl and Dean pulled around. He looks left and right, peers out into the darkness. He's carrying a gun. In the darkness, and at this distance, it looks like an automatic rifle.

The man is a sentry. He's on guard duty. He's on lookout. He turns around, walks away, back the way he came.

Tom sucks his teeth. He can't help himself. He's intrigued. He parks the Chevy off to the side, behind a patch of cacti, out of view. Before he goes any farther, he checks the factory, the area around it. Watches the windows, the ground and upper floors. Checks for more sentries. Doesn't see any. He goes to the building, keeping low, eyes alert and scanning. It's hard to tell if he's heading for the front or the back of the former factory. He thinks it's the back. Whatever side it is, he presses up close to it. Through a smashed window, he can see inside, but there's nothing *to* see. An opening, the factory floor, where whatever this building used to make was manufactured.

He goes up to the corner, where Earl and Dean's car disappeared. Can't see anything down the side, but he can see the lights at the rear of the building, can hear more activity. The sound of running engines, a few calls and shouts.

A guard appears. Tom steps back into the shadows, sidesteps along the wall until he reaches one of the smashed windows. He leaps inside. He ducks low, waits. Through the window, he can hear the guard approaching. The guard is walking slow, taking his time; there's no concern about him. He's just doing his job. Not expecting to come across anything of note.

He reaches the window. Tom stands, moves fast, reaches out the window, and wraps his arms around the sentry's throat and head, drags him into the factory through the opening. Inside, he squeezes, cutting off the man's windpipe to prevent him crying out. His right arm is across the guard's neck. He shifts it around, puts pressure on the carotid. He moves the left from the guard's face and mouth and puts it behind his head. Holds him tight, keeps the hold until the man stops struggling, passes out.

Tom checks him when he's down. The only gun he's carrying is the M16. Tom dismantles it, scatters the parts. Doesn't want him to have a gun within easy reach when he comes back around.

He looks outside, then climbs back out the broken window. He goes around the corner, creeps along. Peers out when he reaches the edge where the car disappeared.

There is a lot of activity. People are coming out from the factory, carrying boxes. He spots Earl and Dean standing to one side, leaning on the back of their car, arms folded. In the middle of it all, there is another man, heavyset, mustached, directing traffic. Two more men stand near him. One of them has a similar build, and the other is thinner, younger, wears a suit. He looks out of place. Watches everything going on with a cool detachment.

The man with the mustache looks up, seems to realize that Earl and Dean have just arrived. He signals the similar-looking man near him to take over, keep an eye on things, then goes over to them. He doesn't look happy. Starts pointing at his watch. "Fuckin' time you call this?"

"We had somethin' to deal with," Earl says.

"I don't give a shit – I told you to get here early. You fuckin' promised me you'd be here early –"

"Dad, listen, we had somethin' to deal with. It was important –"

Earl's father, the man in charge, slaps him around the side of the head. He jabs a finger into Earl's chest, then down at the ground. "I told you to be *here*."

"Reggie, Reginald, uh, Mr. McQuade, sir," Dean says, "it wasn't our fault –"

Reggie spins on Dean. His eyes flash, and Dean falls silent. Reggie turns back to Earl, pokes his finger into his chest again, holds it there, drills it in so Earl is leaning back over the car. "I'm getting real tired of your shit. This is serious. What, you think it's a fuckin' joke? *Answer me.*"

"No, Dad –"

"No, *sir*," Reggie says.

"No, sir," Earl corrects himself. "No, it's not a joke."

Reggie takes his finger back, allows Earl to straighten up, but he's still pissed. "So what was so important?"

Tom is curious how Earl will answer.

"It's nothin'," he says. "Nothin' that can't wait. We'll tell you later."

Reggie glares at his son a moment longer, then turns and walks back over to the bulk of activity, calls out to the man he has left in charge. Calls him Chris. Tom watches Earl and Dean. They exchange glances.

Tom turns back to the workers carrying out boxes. The boxes are unmarked. No one mentions what is inside. He peers around, leans out from the corner as far as he dares risk, tries to see the inside of the factory, where the men are coming from. There is a door. It does not lead directly into the rear of the building. Seems to lead into the side. It's double wide, and both doors are hooked open. Tom can see men coming up and going down a flight of steps. Wherever they're going is not inside the factory, it is underneath it.

Tom remains aware of the man he has choked out. He won't stay unconscious for much longer. Probably still a few more minutes before he comes back around, before the oxygen fully returns to his brain.

The men finish bringing out the boxes. They're piled up. No one is doing anything. They stand around. Reggie and Chris talk to the suited man. Earl and Dean remain to one side. The workers wait. Everyone is waiting.

They start to perk up when they hear the approach of engines. They come from the opposite direction to which Earl and Dean, and Tom, have arrived. Tom's ears perk up. It is a mix of engines, but some of them are louder than others, like motorcycles.

There is a hill at the back of the factory, much like the one at the front. The approaching vehicles come over the top and, sure enough, there are two motorcycles. Then there is a van following close behind.

Tom watches. They look like a biker gang. Bandanas wrapped around their heads, with tattoos up and down their arms – and, more tellingly, they wear kuttes. The bikers pull up and park to one side, near to Reggie and the others. The van turns around, backs up to the boxes.

The two bikers go over to Reggie, Chris, and the third man. They're all smiling at each other; they shake hands, embrace. The back doors of the van and the driver and passenger door open. There are three men inside. They're bikers too, wearing kuttes. One of them turns. Tom gets a good look at their name. The Forever Road Dogs. Texas chapter. Their patch is a snarling dog, crowned, fire for eyes. The tattoos on their arms are varied: flames, guns, snakes, dragons, dollar signs, the acronym FRD. Tom also spots a weeping Christ.

One of the men from the bikes looks like he is in charge. He talks with Reggie, then steps to the boxes. He opens one up, checks the contents. Reggie raises an eyebrow. "What's this, Brad? No trust, huh?"

"When you known me not to check?" Brad says.

Tom strains his eyes. Can see a Sergeant At Arms tag on the front of his kutte. The other four bikers don't appear to have any kind of leadership patches. Brad pulls out the contents of one of the boxes, looks it over, holds it out to his brother bikers. It's in a bag. Tom can't see what it is, but he has a good idea.

"What you reckon?" Brad says. "It look good to y'all?"

One of the bikers steps forward, the heaviest looking of the five. He takes the bag, opens it up, pulls out a crystal. Meth. Tom figured as much. The McQuades are cooking meth. Wouldn't surprise him if under the derelict factory there is a lab, likely a super-lab, judging by the quantities they are producing. They're cooking it and selling it, and it looks like they're selling it to the Forever Road Dogs for wider distribution and profit.

The fat biker – his tag reads 'Heavy,' and Tom doubts this is his birth name – turns one of the broken crystals left and right, holds it up to his eye. "I dunno, man," he says to Brad. "I hate to say it, but looks like standards might be slipping."

Brad turns back to Reggie. "See? This is why we check the quality."

"Bullshit," Reggie says. "Good as it ever is." He stands up straighter, puffs his chest out, affronted. By his side, Chris bristles.

"See, just 'good' might be the problem," Brad says.

"Fine, then," Reggie says, "it's outstanding, the best in the county – hell, the best in the *country* – same as it ever is."

Brad and Heavy start laughing. "Just busting your balls, man," Brad says. Heavy returns the crystal to the bag. "You know we gotta check. What you think Wyatt would do, we took it back unseen?"

"Same thing I'd do to one of my boys, they pulled that shit with me," Reggie says, shooting a look toward his son.

"All right," Brad says. He circles a finger in the air. "Pack it up!"

Brad and Reggie step to one side, talk. The bikers and the McQuade workers start packing the boxes into the back of the van.

Tom has seen enough. He doesn't need to know any more, and enough time has passed since he choked out the guard. He makes to turn. The barrel of a gun is pressed into the back of his head, just below his left ear. "Who the fuck are you?" the man at the other end of the gun says.

Tom raises his hands slowly, feeling foolish. He should have been listening. Should have heard this guard's approach. The loud arrival of the motorcycles, the sight of their patches, has distracted him. He looks back over at the meth exchange. No one is looking their way; no one has sensed his seeming capture. The sentry has not raised the alarm. Tom knows it is only a matter of time, seconds, before he calls out, draws attention over here.

Tom spins to his right. The sentry is not expecting this, looks alarmed as Tom rises to his feet, slams the palm of his hand up into his nose. The sentry's nose folds in on itself, the bone driven up into his brain. Tom hit him harder than he intended to, meant only to incapacitate him, but the gun pressed to his head has made his blood hot.

The sentry falls, blood spilling from his nose, dead before he hits the ground.

The gun goes off. A brief burst of fire that draws everyone's attention.

Tom doesn't bother to look back. He starts running, back to the Chevy.

Behind him, he hears shouts, calls of alarm. He hears these shouts begin to follow, pursuing him back to the car. Hears a gunshot. It flies wide. He starts to zigzag. He isn't going to make it easy for them.

He reaches the car and dives across its hood, glances back as he does so. Sees the combined force of the McQuades and their men and the Forever Road Dogs giving chase. They fire at the car he hides behind, where he is pressing himself into a ball up against the wheel.

Bullets rattle the car, shake it on its suspension, rock it back and forth. He hears windows smash, tires burst. The window above his head shatters; the glass rains down around and upon him.

The shooting stops. A voice calls out to him. Reggie's. "If you're still breathing back there, you'd better come out with your hands empty and up in the air."

Tom brushes broken glass from the back of his head, tangled in his hair. Considers his options. He's unarmed. Hadn't planned on coming out here, and hadn't expected to take part in a noisy operation. He could make a break for it, try to get back to the road, but they've all got their guns pointed in his direction, could likely mow him down before he makes it five paces. And if he does get to the road, then what? There's nothing out here. It's too far back to Brenton, and they'll all be searching, would run him down before dawn. Decides his best course of action is to do as Reggie says, take his chances.

"I gotta start counting?" Reggie says.

"I'm comin' out," Tom says, then raises his empty hands over the hood of the car. He steps out, goes to the side of the car, stands in front of them. The McQuades and the Road Dogs head up the crowd. There's about a dozen men at their backs.

Earl steps forward, realizing who they're looking at. "Well, look who it is," he says. He strides up to Tom, punches him across the face. Tom doesn't fall, doesn't lose ground. Stands exactly where he is. Earl is surprised by this. His eyes blaze. Expected him to go down. He raises his arm, is going to hit him again, determined not to be embarrassed like this in front of all these men, but before he can do anything, Reggie stops him.

"Step back, Earl," he says, "you fuckin' idiot."

Even in the dark, Tom can see how Earl's cheeks redden. He steps back, looking mad as hell, his balled fists shaking down by his sides.

Reggie motions to two of his men. One of them is Chris. "Take him down there," he says, "around the back."

The two men come forward, grab Tom by an arm each, drag him away from the shot-out car. Before they're too far, he can hear Reggie address Earl. "Who is that?" he says. "Sounds like you know him." His tone is not happy. It demands an explanation. "He the guy from the bar?"

Then Tom is dragged too far to hear anything said next.

fter Sally sees off Earl and Dean, she stays by the window inside the lobby and watches until they drive away. Once they're out of sight, she goes up to Tom's room, knocks on his door.

"Tom, it's me. Open up." She knocks again. He doesn't answer. She presses her ear to the wood, can't hear anything inside. No movement, nor is the television on, and the shower isn't running. "You there?" No response.

Sally goes back down to the lobby, gets her master key, heads back up to his room. She passes a small group heading outside. Darby is among them. "You seen Tom?" she says.

"Huh?"

"You seen Tom? I ain't see him leave, but doesn't seem like he's in his room, either."

"Uh, no, no, I haven't," Darby says, but he hurries on, buries himself into the group and rushes out with them.

Sally stands on the stairs, watches them go. Thinks about calling Darby back, but doesn't. Figures he's probably hurting, in a rush to get a fix. She continues on to Tom's room, knocks again, though she's not expecting an answer. "If you're in there, call out, 'cause I'm about to come in." She slides the key into the lock, waits a beat, hears nothing, and steps in.

The room is empty. She's not surprised. She looks round. The bed is made, looks like it hasn't been so much as sat on. She steps deeper into the room, spots his rucksack on the chair at the desk. Remembers how worked up he got when he thought his stuff was missing, how pissed off he is about his car being taken, remembers the *urn*, and she doubts he has skipped town. He's going to come back here, if only for his bag and the urn and the picture of the woman safely stashed away inside. Sally notices it isn't pinned up to the mirror this time.

She returns to her desk, takes a seat, pulls out her phone, and calls Daniel.

"Hey," he says, answering on the fourth ring. "How you doing?" He sounds hopeful, almost like he thinks she's going to invite him around, they'll finally have their long-awaited next date, and maybe this time they won't get interrupted by a bar fight.

"Listen, I just wanted to let you know about something," Sally says.

"Sure." He sounds less hopeful now, almost wary.

"Earl and Dean were just 'round here. They were looking for Tom."

"They say why?"

"No. But they were pissed, like they were wanting to hurt him."

Daniel sighs down the line. "This son of a bitch," he says. "He ain't left yet? The sheriff told him the first thing he'd better do is get outta town."

Sally thinks about his stolen car.

"Sally? You still there?"

"I know why he ain't left."

"Oh?"

"He was gonna. But Earl took his car."

"What? When?"

"While he was locked up. Took something else from him too, though he wouldn't say what it was. Think he was more worked up about that than the car."

Daniel is silent for a moment, then he says, "The necklace? Earl grabbed a necklace off him the other night when he was getting taken away."

"A necklace?" Sally frowns. It sounds excessive to get worked up over something so trivial as a necklace. "What kind was it?"

"I dunno. I didn't get a good look."

"Maybe it's something else, then. He might not care about the necklace. It might be something else altogether."

"*That* motherfucker," Daniel says, sighing again, referring to Earl. "Jesus Christ, but he just can't help himself, can he?"

"Earl's always been an asshole, you know that. We shouldn't be shocked."

"Guess I'm not. Guess I'm just annoyed. Has Tom reported it?"

"I doubt it. He seemed reluctant to do so, which is why I'm calling you. I told him he should, but he was pretty adamant he didn't wanna do that. Said he'd sleep on it though; then next thing I know a couple of hours later, I got Earl and Dean charging into the lobby, demanding to know if he's in the hotel, which room he's in."

"What'd you do?"

"I told them to fuck off."

"Jesus, Sally…"

"They ain't gonna do nothin' to me."

"You don't know that for sure."

"Yeah, well, I don't give a shit if I hurt Earl's little feelings, either. Listen, we're getting off track. I've just been up to Tom's room, give him a heads-up, but he ain't there."

"Shit."

"Yeah, that's what I thought. So I'm calling you to let you know what's going on, that maybe Earl has a reason to be pissed at Tom, maybe he's actually done something, or else maybe Earl's just heard he's out and wants to fuck with him some more – either way, it feels like trouble."

"I hear you. I'll keep an eye and an ear out, but the chances I'm gonna find anything are slim. Tom comes back to the hotel, you call me, all right? I'll come and talk to him, see if I can't talk some sense into him, get him to report his car as stolen. Then I might actually be able to do something about it."

"Just be careful. Like I said, I got a feeling."

"Yeah. Talk later."

They hang up, and Sally sits back in her seat. She gets up and goes to the door, steps out onto the sidewalk, and looks down toward the bar. She can see Darby, the group he was with, hanging outside the door, talking among themselves, looking concerned. Darby sees her watching, motions to the others, and they head inside, out of sight.

Sally sits back down. She thinks about Earl and about Tom. "Jesus Christ," she says, running her hands back through her hair. "All these men, looking for trouble. I'm surrounded by macho assholes."

20

Tom sits on the ground at the back of the factory, arms bound behind his back, a gun trained on him from behind. It's taken a little time for them all to reorganize after the chaos he has caused. They've found the guard he killed, carried his body into the clearing, and laid him down next to Earl's car, and they've found the one he choked out, too. He stands to one side, rubbing his neck and every so often staring daggers Tom's way. Tom winks at him, and he quickly looks elsewhere.

Tom has had time to look around. He's close to the side door that the boxes are coming up from, that leads down to underneath the factory. He can smell chemicals wafting out of it. Can hear the churning of machinery. He turns his head a little, to his guard. "What you got down there?"

The guard ignores him.

"Cooking meth? That a lab?"

The guard scoffs.

"Oh, I see. A *super*lab, huh?"

"Shut up," the guard says, but Tom has his answer.

The boxes are nearly all packed into the back of the van now. The main players stand to one side, looking back at Tom, deciding what to do with him. One of them, the out-of-place-looking thin man in the suit, is bouncing where he stands, his face visibly red even in the half-light, jabbing a finger in Tom's direction.

"He's seen my fucking face!" he keeps saying over and over. "Do you know how bad that is? For Christ's sake, he's seen my fucking *face!*"

"Shut the fuck up, Brian," Reggie says, finally snapping. The thin man, Brian, clamps his mouth shut, lowers his pointing arm, but continues to bounce. "It ain't gonna matter before long anyway."

Tom has been watching and listening. Picking up on names. The names of the Forever Road Dogs in particular. Sometimes they call each other by their first names, sometimes by their last, sometimes by monikers. He's pieced them all together. Brad Smithson is the Sergeant At Arms. There's something in Brad's face that's familiar to him, though he can't place it. He's never met this man before, but feels like he recognizes him. Feels like the beard and the long hair are preventing him from putting his finger on it fully, but knows it's there, in the back of his head, just waiting to be remembered.

Heavy he was already aware of, from their arrival. His real name is Henry Harding; the 'Heavy' nickname is obviously in reference to his weight. Also present is Heavy's brother, Matt. The other two are Willie Pence and Kelvin Maynard (though Tom isn't sure he's got this last name the right way around).

The huddle consists of Reggie, Brian, Chris, Brad, Earl, and Dean. Tom knows what the end result of their discussion will be, and isn't sure why it's taking them so long to come to this conclusion. Whatever it is, Tom will have to think of something quick, to keep them from putting a bullet in the back of his head and dumping him out in the desert.

Tom notices Brad has been quiet in the management huddle. For the most part, he's stroked his beard and watched Tom. Right now, however, the topic of discussion has moved from Tom to Earl.

Reggie is still pissed at him. He slaps him around the head again. "The fuck were you *thinking*?" he says. "You take a man's car, what you think he was gonna do?"

"I thought he was gonna do the smart thing and just get the fuck outta town," Earl says.

Reggie slaps him silent. "Then you're a fucking moron. That what you would do? Honest to Christ, Earl, I don't know what the fuck I'm gonna do with you. I feel like we should tie you up over there with him. You try and pull this shit *now*? Now, of all fuckin' times. You know how important this all is?"

It looks like Earl knows better than to answer. He just lowers his eyes, nods.

"You know it, but you still do it." Reggie hits him again. Tom thinks he can see tears in Earl's eyes. He blinks hard, desperate to chase them away, to not cry in front of all these men who either work for him and his father, or intimidate him. "Don't think I don't know why you didn't tell me about the car," Reggie says. "'Cause I woulda made you send it back, that's right. You think that kind of embarrassment would've been worse than this, huh?"

Earl shakes his head. "I've said I'm sorry," he says.

Reggie slaps him. The sound echoes. "And I wanna hear it a million more times, you stupid fuck!" He wheels on Dean now, who starts and visibly gulps. "You know about this?"

"Yuh-yes, yes, sir," Dean says, not attempting to deny it, knowing better than that.

"You didn't try and talk him out of it? You didn't explain to him the stupidity of such an act, at this moment in time in particular? Or is it that you're just as dumb as he is?"

Dean bites his lips, seals them closed, and this is all the answer that Reggie needs.

"The fuckin' two of you," he says, "you're both as bad as each other. Once this is done, we're all gonna sit down and have a long talk. We're gonna do somethin' about that junkie whore you're keeping at the ranch, too."

"Can we get back on track?" Brian says, still shaking, having kept his mouth closed for as long as he's been able, but now looking like he's about to burst. "What about *him*?" He points at Tom.

They all look his way. Tom stares back, defiant. When he talks, he talks to Earl, looks right at him. "Give me back the car and the pendant, and I'll leave, and maybe you'll never hear from me again."

Brad laughs. "Maybe, huh?"

Reggie turns to Earl. "Pendant? What fuckin' pendant?"

Dean looks sideways at Earl.

Earl shrugs, looks at his father. "So I took his fuckin' necklace, so fuckin' what?"

Reggie turns to Tom now, brow furrowed. "A necklace?"

"And I want it back," Tom says.

"You've killed one of my men," Reggie says, "and you've caused all this hassle tonight, for a fuckin' *necklace*?"

"And I'll do more, and I'll do worse, if I'm not given it back now."

Brad laughs. "This guy," he says. "I like this guy. I

like the balls on him. Tell you what, we'll deal with him."

The rest of the men turn to Brad.

"He ain't your problem," Reggie says. "He ain't your mess, and you shouldn't have to clean him up. We don't have no issue dealing with him."

Brad smiles. "It ain't no problem," he says. "Me and the boys might just have some fun with him first. What'd you say his name was?" He looks at Earl.

"Tom," Earl says, realizing he's being questioned. "Tom, uh, Smith."

"Looks like you'll get to keep that car after all," Brad says, winking at Earl; then he separates himself from the group. He approaches Tom, crouches down in front of him. Behind him, the group decide the discussion is at its end; they're all nearly done here with the exchange. They slowly disperse. Brian, in particular, seems eager to get away, stands by his car, but doesn't want to leave before the rest do. Everyone else seems to be hanging around, seeing this through, and he won't be the first to go. Instead, he continues to bounce by his car.

"So you like to run your mouth, huh?" Brad says.

"I never say anythin' I don't mean," Tom says.

"So you're a tough guy, too."

Tom shrugs one shoulder. "Cut me loose and let's find out together."

Brad grins, shows his teeth through his beard. "Careful what you wish for, man. I might just do that."

Brad gets to his feet. "All right," he says. He glances round. "Looks like we're done here." He motions to Matt and Heavy, and they come forward, hoist Tom to his feet, and carry him to the van. They put him in the side door, push him in to where there's a space behind the two front seats. Kelvin Maynard (or Maynard

Kelvin) gets in with him, pulls a handgun out from his waist, points it into Tom's face. He grins from behind it.

Outside, through the still-open door, Tom can see Brad shaking hands with Reggie. They say their good-byes. Brad and Willie are riding on the bikes. The Harding brothers get into the front of the van. Heavy is driving. The door slides shut behind Kelvin, locking Tom in with him, staring down the barrel of his gun.

21

The van doesn't go far.

They go back over the hill from where they came, drive a couple of miles into the desert, then stop. The gun is still pointed at Tom. He looks beyond it, at Kelvin. Kelvin grins. The door behind him opens. Willie stands there. "All right, get him out," he says.

Kelvin keeps the gun on Tom. With his other hand, he grabs him by the back of the shirt, drags him out of the van. Doesn't give Tom a chance to get to his feet. Pulls him down onto his back, drags him across the ground, dumps him down onto the sand.

"Stand him up," someone says.

All five of the Road Dogs are on foot now. Kelvin and Willie pull Tom up to his feet. Brad and the Harding brothers stand to one side. Brad pops his knuckles. He grins. "You're gonna get your wish," he says. "We're gonna cut you loose."

It's cold in the desert. It's quiet, too. The sky is clear. The moon is low, and Tom figures it must be between midnight and early morning.

"Soften this motherfucker up first," Brad says. "We don't want him bolting for it soon as we get those bindings off."

Next thing Tom knows, someone hits him hard in the lower back, a kidney shot. The direction it came from, he thinks it must have been Kelvin. Tom cries out, goes down to his knees. It was a hard shot. It's likely he's gonna piss blood for a couple of days.

From the other side, Willie's side, a clubbing blow lands across the top of his shoulders, drives his face down into the sand. He feels a boot on the back of his head, grinding his face down into the desert. He can't breathe. Sand gets into his mouth and up his nose. When it finally releases him, he spits and gasps. Grit grinds in his teeth.

They hoist him up to his feet and start pushing him around. Brad takes a step back, folds his arms, conserves his energy, while the other four pass him in their square, each of them taking a turn landing a blow. Heavy puts all his weight behind a shot to the gut. It lands hard. Tom feels bile rise in his throat, burn the back of it. He spits it out, aims for the nearest pair of boots.

Matt starts laughing. "He just don't quit, do he?"

Then someone, probably Matt, kicks him in the ribs. Tom rolls onto his back. His wrists and arms are still bound behind his back. His shoulders twist and strain, feeling like they're about to pop from their sockets.

Brad strides forward. "All right," he says. "Reckon that's soft enough. You ain't gonna try and run out on us now, are you, Tommy boy?" He takes a knee next to Tom, brushes sand from his face, away from his mouth, then looks around at the other bikers. "Who reckons they can take this guy?"

They all laugh. They all say they can. One-on-one, no problem. They're all ready to step up.

Brad turns back to Tom. "Who do you like your chances with? Don't be afraid, take a good look."

Tom doesn't look around. Looks up at Brad. "How about you?"

Brad pats his cheek. "You ain't worth my time, Tommy. I ain't got nothin' to prove by wiping the floor with you."

Again, even in Tom's beaten state, there is something familiar about Brad's face, something Tom can't put his finger on. The eyes, the nose, the mouth – they're all there – they just look wrong, somehow.

Brad stands, turns to the others. "Y'all wanna draw straws, or what? You civilized enough to work it out between yourselves?"

"You see when the McQuade boy hit him?" Heavy says. He's laughing at the memory. "Threw everything he had into that punch, barely moved him. You see the look on the kid's face?" He laughs harder, shakes his head. "Fuck it, let me do it. I wanna see how well he holds up with a real fuckin' punch."

Brad looks round. "Any objections?"

No one does. Matt pats his brother on the back, nods.

"We gonna take bets?" Willie says.

"Ain't a bad idea," Brad says.

"Bets on what?" Matt says.

"How long he'll last," Willie says.

"I'd lay a ten he goes down on the first punch," Matt says.

"A ten?" Kelvin says. "That it?"

"All I got on me right now," Matt says.

"And we've got faith that you're good for it when we get back to the clubhouse," Willie says.

"Bro, c'mon," Heavy says, nudging Matt and winking at him.

"All right, all right," Matt says, throwing up his hands. "Fuck it, fifty. Fifty that this guy goes down on the first fuckin' punch." He turns to his brother, points at him. "Don't you let me down on this."

Heavy rubs his hands together. "Don't intend to."

Kelvin, Maynard, whatever his name is, licks his lips. He takes Brad to one side while the others place their bets on how fast Tom will go down, says something that Tom isn't supposed to hear. "Who gets to waste him?"

"You askin'?" Brad says.

"You know my birthday's comin' up," Kelvin says.

"Ain't plannin' on waiting that long to get rid of him."

"Sure, I know that. Make it an early gift."

"And here I was plannin' on buying you a beer. Sure." He slaps Kelvin on the back. Kelvin turns back around, satisfied.

The bikers are still talking among themselves, still placing bets, arguing over amounts. Tom pushes himself to a sitting position, manages to get up to his knees. "We gonna do this thing, or what?"

Heavy looks at him, raises his eyebrows.

Brad laughs. "I knew we were gonna have some fun with this one," he says. "Look at him, so eager to go."

"Then he's a dumb bastard," Willie says, shaking his head and laughing along with Brad. "But are you a tough one? That's the real question, man. You might regret hurrying this along, real soon."

"I ain't got all night," Tom says.

"Oh no?" Brad says. "Where else you think you're gonna go?"

"I already told you, back there," Tom says. "I'm gonna get my car back, and my pendant."

They laugh at him.

"The necklace, right?" Brad says. "That's a hell of a thing to go and get yourself killed over."

"I don't intend on getting myself killed."

"Then you've gone about it the wrong way, buddy."

"Just cut me loose and let's get to it."

Brad nods at his boys. Kelvin and Willie step forward, pull Tom from the ground, throw him up against the side of the van, chest first. They press him up against it; then one of them cuts him loose. They give him another shove, then step back. Tom turns, spits blood and sand out the corner of his mouth. Heavy comes forward, running his hands over each other, over his knuckles. Tom plants his feet, sets his stance. He needs a way out of this. Right now, he doesn't see any other option than to fight. If he runs, they'll chase him down – or else they'll just shoot him. Each one of them is armed. Fighting at least gives him a chance to search for an opening, might buy him some time for an unexpected opportunity to present itself.

"All right, then," Brad says. He motions for Heavy to get started. "Have at it. Let's see what this guy's got."

"He's nothin' but talk," Heavy says. He comes forward, as slow as Tom expected such a big guy to be. Heavy is relying on his power, on landing that one punch that will end the whole thing. Tom ducks his first attack, skips out of reach. The bikers jeer it.

"That didn't land!" Matt says. "So that don't count."

Heavy follows, but Tom doesn't go too far. He keeps his fists raised, waits for Heavy to try again. He doesn't have to wait long. Heavy gets close, takes a swing. Tom dodges it. Heavy throws another, but Tom was watching, ready for this follow-up, and again he dodges it easily. Heavy gets frustrated, grabs at Tom with both arms, but Tom is too fast for him. Stays out of his reach. Heavy is already breathing hard.

"Thought you wanted this fight, Tommy," Brad says. "Stop dancing around and throw some fuckin' fists."

Tom ignores him. Tom fights to win; he doesn't have anything to prove to these men.

Heavy sucks air, keeps his fists raised. "You gonna stand still?"

"I'm right here, big man," Tom says.

Heavy swings for him again. Tom ducks it, but doesn't move out of range this time. He comes up, nails an uppercut. Heavy's teeth clamp together; he steps back, rocked. He shakes his head.

Tom follows through, nails him with a left jab, then a right hook. Heavy doesn't go down, but he looks like it won't take much more. His face is red from exertion. He tries to punch Tom, one last desperate throw, but Tom catches his arm, hooks it under his armpit and holds it to his ribs, then throws rights hard into Heavy's face until he goes down.

The bikers are silent, shocked at what they have seen. Matt goes to his fallen brother, cradles his head, wipes the blood from his face.

Brad looks pissed. He speaks to Willie and Kelvin, to Matt. "Put this son of a bitch down."

22

D aniel doesn't see or hear anything of Earl or Tom through the night. He decides to go out to the ranch, despite the late hour, check things for himself. Just a friendly little visit, nothing official about it. Just making sure everything's all right, no one's having any trouble, nothing bad's happening. And, while he's there, he'll keep an eye out for the stolen car, too.

It's well after midnight when Daniel reaches the ranch, and unlikely that anyone will still be awake. Daniel doesn't mind getting them out of bed. Two dogs go wild in their kennels as he gets out of his car and starts walking up to the main door. They howl aggressively, gnash their teeth. Almost like they're trying to help him wake the ranch up. He knows really that they're trying to get at him, to maul the stranger. He wonders if the uniform has anything to do with their bloodlust, if they've been taught to hate it, and he's glad of the meshing that separates him from them.

Daniel bangs the side of his fist hard against the

door, rattles it in its frame. While he waits for an answer, he steps to the edge of the porch, ignores the wild dogs, and looks around. Doesn't see any sign of the car. Notices the curtains twitch in the house to the side, where he knows Earl lives.

The door opens. He turns and sees Chris. Chris is scowling.

"Evening, Chris," Daniel says, tipping the brim of his hat. "You find your tongue today?"

Chris grunts.

"Well, I just don't know whether I should take that as a yes or a no." Daniel smiles at him. Chris does not return it. Daniel can see Chris isn't going to ask him what he wants, isn't going to engage, seems content to scowl in the doorway like an angry Lurch. "Reggie home?"

Chris has to clear his throat to speak. "I'll get him," he says. "Wait here."

Daniel takes a step back, leans against one of the frames, folds his arms.

Reggie takes his time coming to the door. Keeps the deputy waiting. When he finally arrives, he's yawning, rubbing his eyes like he's just woke up, though he's still dressed. Daniel feels like it's all a bit acted out.

"Evening, Reggie," he says. "Or, hell, what time's it? Should I be saying good morning instead?" He tilts his chin. "I wake you?" Looking past him, he can see that Chris remains close by, standing a few paces back from his friend, within earshot. His eyes are on Daniel, burning through him.

"You sure have, Deputy," Reggie says. "But I don't think that's a surprise to you, considering the fuckin' time."

"Justice don't sleep, Mr. McQuade."

Reggie stops making a show of rubbing his eyes, lets his arms drop. "There a reason you're here, Deputy Murphy?"

"I was close by, figured I'd call in, make sure everything's all right for y'all, all the way out here."

"Any reason why it wouldn't be?"

"I heard a little rumor your one and only son has been pissing people off. Just wanted to check none of that hassle has been landing at your door."

"You'd have to ask him about that, but he ain't gonna thank you for waking him up, either."

"So you ain't heard nothin' about it?"

"Are you askin' me if someone's come out here, to my home, looking to cause trouble?"

"Well? Have they?"

"No. But I'll tell you this, too – if they did, we wouldn't need any fuckin' cops to come and take care of it for us. We can more than deal with it our own selves."

"I don't doubt that, Reggie. I'm out here checking on the other guy."

"You're gonna have to check elsewhere, 'cause I ain't seen him."

Daniel nods. "But if you do, now, you'll be sure to ring the sheriff's department right away, right?"

"Yeah, sure, I'll do just that. There anything else, Murphy?"

"Naw, I guess not." Daniel starts to turn away, then stops himself, turns back. Snaps his fingers, like he's just remembered something. "Say, y'all come into a new car recently?"

"What're you talkin' about?"

"A Ford," Daniel says. "Blue one. Nothin' flashy, pretty basic. I heard Earl was seen driving one round. I figured he musta just got that, right? 'Cause that ain't what he usually drives."

"Whoever you been talkin' to, they musta seen someone else. They didn't see Earl. He ain't got no new car – you can see his regular one for yourself; it's right there parked in front of his place."

"So it is. Seems strange, though. They were adamant it was him."

"You see it here?"

"No, I don't. That's why I'm asking."

"I ain't seen no blue Ford. Think I would've noticed somethin' like that."

"I'm sure you would've," Daniel says. He isn't sure how much he believes any of what Reggie is saying. The exaggerated rubbing of his eyes when he first came to the door hasn't done him any favors, has only served to make Daniel suspicious. He's been too defensive in his answers about Tom, too, and the same again when Daniel asked about the car.

"Guess that's all I wanted to know," Daniel says. He's not going to get anything more out of the tight-lipped Reginald McQuade. "I'll get myself out your hair. Sure hope you're able to get back to sleep, Reggie."

"I'm sure I'll manage, Murphy," Reggie says, then steps back inside the house and closes the door.

The dogs start barking again as Daniel walks by. As he reaches the cruiser, the door to Earl's house opens. Daniel looks back, but it's not Earl coming out. It's Anna. She's wearing a long T-shirt a couple of sizes too big for her, presumably what she sleeps in.

"Daniel," she says, coming closer. Despite the chill in the night air and how little she is wearing, she doesn't seem to be feeling it. "What're you doing out here this time of night?"

"Just checking on a few things," Daniel says, unsure how much information Anna can be trusted with. "Nothin' important."

"Yeah, well, for nothin' important, you've really riled up Jojo and Georgie."

"They the dogs?" Daniel glances back at their kennel. The dogs have quieted now, but they're both still standing side by side, watching him.

Anna points them out. "That one's Jojo. That one's Georgie."

They both look the same to Daniel.

"So," Anna says, "you manage to get my sister to leave that fuckin' hotel for a night?"

"Not yet, but I'm working on it."

Anna rolls her eyes. "That woman," she says, exasperated. "What's she so scared about? The place'll fall down when she's not around?"

"Might not fall down, but it could get pulled down," Daniel says. "I've seen the people staying there."

Anna waves this off. "Naw, they love Sally. She's their Florence Nightingale. They'd never do anythin' to hurt her."

"From what I've heard, once the need gets to be too much, ain't nothin' a tweaker won't do to get a fix. Sell their own grandmother, like as not."

Anna falls silent at this, avoids his gaze, and at this moment Daniel notices the lines in her face, even in the dark, and the red in the whites of her eyes. Sees how she looks older now than Sally, her older sister.

Daniel clears his throat, feeling awkward. "How you been, anyway?"

"I'm good," she says. "I'm fine."

"What you get up to this evening?"

"Nothin' much. Watched some TV. I was all alone, all I had for company was the fuckin' TV."

"You were alone?"

"Yeah."

"Where was Earl?"

She shrugs. "I dunno. Wherever it is he goes with his dad and all their buddies. They only got back a little while ago."

Daniel mulls this over. It ties in to his belief that Reggie was playacting being tired. "Hey, Anna, has Earl gotten a new car recently?"

Anna's eyebrows rise, something about the question. Before she can answer, however, Earl appears on the porch. "Anna," he says, "what're you doin', girl? Get on back over here. You look like you're gonna freeze."

Anna dutifully does as he says, returns to the house while Earl comes down the porch steps, approaches Daniel with his eyes narrowed. "What're you doin' out here, Dan?" he says.

"You can ask your dad about it," he says. "But for now, I was just saying hello to Anna."

"Well, now you've said it, so now you can fuck off."

Daniel notices that Earl appears to have bruising on the side of his head, between the corner of his eye and his ear. The bruises compliment the scab across the bridge of his nose. "Now that ain't very friendly of you, Earl."

"I don't gotta be friendly. This is my home."

"Why so tense, Earl? Somethin' to do with all those bruises?"

Dean appears on the porch, ushers Anna into the house. Daniel thinks of the McQuades and their henchmen – Chris with Reggie, and Dean with Earl, not to mention all their other buddies in town, the ones who, if asked, would describe their employment as 'ranch hands.' The McQuades always make sure they have backup.

"They ain't none of your damn business," Earl says.

"No," Daniel says, "I suppose you're right. Well, Earl, I'll get myself off of your property now. Enjoy the rest of your night, y'hear?" Daniel tips his brim, then gets into his cruiser. Earl doesn't respond, just stands and seethes, his fists opening and closing like he wants to take a swing. Daniel turns the car round, winks at Earl as he passes, then leaves the ranch. He's been on duty all night, doesn't have much longer left, and he's starting to get tired.

He reaches the road, points himself back toward Kirkwood, to the station. Thinks he might call in on Sally on his way back, as he passes through Brenton. It'll be getting close to dawn by the time he gets there, and she usually has late nights and early starts. He'll let her know face-to-face that he didn't hear anything during the night.

In the distance, approaching, it looks like a convoy is coming his way. Daniel slows the car for a better look. They're still a distance off, but he starts to make sense of the vehicles. Two motorcyclists leading the way, a van following close behind. Almost like it's being escorted.

Something about the scene feels off to Daniel. The feeling only intensifies as the convoy draws nearer. The motorcyclists do not wear kuttes, but they still have the appearance of a gang. He can see two men in the front of the van, similar menacing builds to the two men riding the bikes. Something is wrong with the driver's face. It looks swollen.

The convoy passes him by. Daniel turns his head. He sees gang tattoos on their arms. FRD. He knows the name – Forever Road Dogs. He's heard of them. He looks into the rearview as they go.

It doesn't feel right. A couple of bikers, a van following close behind – what's inside the van? What's in the back?

Daniel wants a closer look. He turns the cruiser around, accelerates. It might be nothing, it might be something – either way, he wants to know for sure. He flashes his lights, turns on the siren. The bikes out front continue on their way, but the van begins to slow. It pulls to the side of the road.

23

T he Road Dogs weren't happy about Tom's victory over Heavy. None of them had bet on him.

They were quick to follow Brad's orders to put him down. Tom saw that perhaps this was the opportunity he was waiting for. Four bikers didn't worry him. He'd already put down their biggest member with relative ease. They were armed, sure, but that played to his advantage. All he needed was for one of them to get close enough he could grab the handgun at their side, shoot his way out of the situation, and take their van to get out of the desert.

It didn't go down like that. They attacked him as one, but they kept to his left, Brad on his right. Brad pulled out his gun, kept it trained on Tom. "You're gonna take this beating," Brad said.

Matt reached him first, spurred on by the sight of his fallen brother. His anger made him sloppy. Tom grabbed him, raised his knee into his stomach, moved his body to use him as a shield against Brad. Willie was quick to charge from the left, too, following Matt through. Tom lashed out, kicked his leg, knocked it out from under him and put him down flat on his face.

With all the distractions, he didn't notice as Kelvin came up behind him. Struck him across the back of the head with something hard – his gun. Tom's grip on Matt weakened. Matt shoved him off, punched him across the face. Tom went down.

"Now," Brad said, "hit him *now*, fer Christ's sake!"

The three did, laying in with their boots. Tom barely felt it. The blow to the back of the head had done its damage. His vision was blurring at the edges. The night was getting darker.

Tom isn't sure how long he's been out for. It's still night. He's lying front-down in the sand. He opens one eye. Can feel blood crusting his brow. Everything hurts. They've done a number on him while he's been out. They're standing to the side, smoking, talking among themselves. Tom can't raise his head to see them all, sees four pairs of legs. Someone is missing.

That someone soon presents themselves to him. It's Kelvin. He crouches down in front of Tom, blocks his one-eyed view, turns his head to better see him. "You waking up?" he says. The tip of his tongue pokes out, runs over his lips. He reaches out, pokes a finger into the back of Tom's head. Tom feels a sharp pain ripple through his body. He grits his teeth. Kelvin sees. "That hurt, does it? I'll bet. It's a deep gash I put in ya. Looks almost like a pussy."

"He woke up?" The voice comes from behind Kelvin. It's Brad.

"Looks it," Kelvin says, stepping back.

Brad comes forward, presses the flat of his boot to Tom's side, rolls him over onto his back. Tom realizes now his other eye, the left, has swollen shut. At some point while he was out, one of the bikers either punched or kicked him there. Brad looks down on him. "You get a reprieve, Tommy," he says. "I'll admit, I was pissed off at first, when you put Heavy down so fast."

Heavy glares at him, nursing his jaw.

"But while you've been having your nap here, I got to thinking. Ain't that exactly what I wanted from you? A fighter. Some fun. You're coming back with us, Tommy. Plenty boys back at the clubhouse would like to go a round with you. Wyatt particularly – I just know he'll be itching to try his hand, 'specially once he hears what you did to Heavy."

This isn't the worst thing. The journey gives Tom time. He has no intention of allowing them to reach their clubhouse.

"We hang around here any longer and it's gonna be dawn before we know it," Willie says.

"You ain't wrong," Brad says. "Let's saddle up, boys. Get back on the road."

Before they set off, they remove their kuttes, throw them into the back of the van. Tom figures it makes sense, not to ride around while transporting a large amount of meth wearing gang colors. They bind Tom's wrists back together, then drag him into the van after the kuttes. Kelvin climbs in after him, grinning, gun pulled again and stuck in his face.

They're on the road now. The cut throbs at the back of Tom's head. It's been a long night, a painful night, but he's had longer. He wants to rest, but he won't let himself. Needs to remain alert. He's been trained for such situations, for captivity, for torture. He puts his mind elsewhere, ignores the pain in his head, ignores the taste of blood in the back of his throat. If he sees an opportunity to get out of this situation, he will be ready to take it.

Kelvin keeps the grin on his face while he watches

him. Lets the gun wave around a little. "You're a tough son of a bitch, I'll give you that," he says.

Tom shifts his weight where he sits, tries to get a little more comfortable, but it's a losing battle.

"You musta done some fighting, right? You trained in something? A martial art, maybe?"

In the front, Heavy is driving the van. Matt rides passenger, twists around at the sound of Kelvin's voice. "He got lucky, that's all." Defending his brother's honor.

Tom stares at them both with his one eye.

"Really ain't talking much anymore, is he?" Matt says. "Couldn't shut him up a few hours ago."

"Ain't the most conversational, not now," Kelvin says. "It's gonna be a *long* fuckin' ride, you don't feel like talkin', man."

"How long 'til we get where we're going?" Tom says.

"Well, lookit that," Kelvin says. "His voice has come back."

"Might regret that before long," Matt says. "He was a sassy son of a bitch last time he let his mouth run."

"Yeah, well, last time it got him into some real trouble, and I don't think he's gonna make that mistake again. You ain't that stupid, are you?"

"I've been accused of being worse," Tom says. "How long we got?"

"You ain't gotta worry about that," Kelvin says. "This ride will be over before you know it."

"Can't wait. Give me an ETA."

Kelvin looks at Matt.

"Estimated time of arrival," Matt says.

Kelvin turns back to Tom. "What's your rush, man? You ain't gonna like it when we get there."

"It's for your benefit, really," Tom says. "The reason I ask, I mean."

"Oh yeah?" Kelvin says. "And why's that?"

"I'm just wondering how much longer y'all have got to live."

At first, they don't look impressed by this. Then Kelvin starts to laugh. "Awful confident, ain't ya? For a guy tied up in the back of a van with a hole in the back of his head."

Tom's legs are free. He can kick Kelvin into submission. Get him down, stomp on his face. The two in the front won't be able to do anything fast enough. They'll have to pull over, stop the van, and that will take too long. By then, Kelvin will be dead, Tom will be free, and he'll have his gun.

Tom smiles at Kelvin. Something in it makes Kelvin's grin falter. He understands the intent behind it, the menace.

Tom gets ready. He's about to make his move.

Before he can do anything, Heavy speaks up. "Shit," he says. "Everyone shut up and sit down. Fuckin' cop's pulling us over."

"The fuck?" Matt says, twisting back round.

"Lie down," Kelvin says to Tom. "Get down, low as you can."

Tom stops himself from lashing out, delivering the first kick to the center of Kelvin's face. This unexpected occurrence could play in his favor. He plays at being weak, shuffles a little, makes like he's in too much pain to move ably, until Kelvin gets annoyed and grabs him, pushes him down flat.

"What's he doin' out here?" Matt says. "This fuckin' road's supposed to be clear."

"Just shut up," Heavy says. "I'll do the talking. Everyone else just be quiet. Kelvin, make sure that motherfucker doesn't make a *peep*."

"Got it." Kelvin lies down next to Tom, sticks the gun in his face.

The van slows. Sand and gravel crunch beneath them as they pull to the side of the road. Tom can hear the siren. It stops as the van stops. Kelvin's eyes are locked on his. "We don't wanna have to kill a cop," Kelvin says, whispering, "but we'll do it, so you'd better believe I won't think twice about pulling this fuckin' trigger right in your fuckin' face."

Tom keeps his eyes on Kelvin's, watching. Waiting. Tom grits his teeth. Braces himself.

"Here he comes," Heavy says, presumably watching the mirror. He winds down his window.

"Just be cool, man," Matt says.

"I *am* cool," Heavy says. "You stay quiet."

Tom listens. Can hear the policeman's approach. He reaches the window. "Evening, sir," he says. His voice is familiar, but Tom doesn't have time to think about that. "How y'all doing?"

Tom's eyes are on Kelvin's. Kelvin's face is pinched, the tendons in his cheeks twitch. His eyes flicker toward the front of the van, the cop. Tom makes his move.

He drops his head, ducks it under the gun, drives his forehead into the center of Kelvin's face with everything he has at such close quarters. It's enough. Kelvin's nose crunches, bursts, sprays blood. Kelvin cries out, and the gun goes off. It's next to Tom's ear. The sound rattles through his skull.

Tom keeps moving. Rolls back, uses the momentum to get up to his feet, hurries back to Kelvin, and starts kicking. Stomps him in the ribs, in the face. Subdues him.

There are more gunshots. They come from outside the van, from inside the van. Tom ignores them for now.

Concentrates on what he's doing. Kelvin has a knife on his belt. Tom lowers himself down to it, feels for it, pulls it free. Flips it round in his hands, working blind. Uses the knife to cut himself free. It's hard to do, unable to see, but the knife is sharp. It cuts through the rope. It slices into his hands, too, but he ignores it. His blood makes his grip slippery, but he works through it, tightens his hold on the handle, until the rope is frayed enough that he's able to pull his hands apart, split the rope.

Kelvin is coming round. He's dazed, but he still has the gun. Before he can raise it, Tom dives to him, the knife held two-handed, drives it through his chest, into his heart. Tom looks into Kelvin's shocked eyes as he dies, then picks up the gun and gets to his feet.

In the front, Heavy is slumped over the steering wheel, dead. Matt is screaming, using his body for cover, leaning over and firing out the window. Matt is unaware of what has transpired in the back of the van, has assumed that a bound man has been no further trouble for Kelvin. Tom raises the gun, shoots Matt in the back of the head. His blood sprays across the inside of the windshield, then he falls across the body of his brother.

24

D aniel ducks at the sound of the gunshot from the back of the van, pulls his piece. At the same time, the two men in the front of the van pull theirs. The fat man behind the wheel starts to turn on Daniel, the gun raised. It happens in slow motion. Daniel feels his eyes go wide. The fat man's arm comes out the window. The gun is almost in his face.

Daniel fires. His first shot hits the door as he raises the gun. The fat man fires. It goes wide, but Daniel can feel the air split at the side of his head. He flinches, raises his own gun higher, squeezes it twice. Both bullets hit the fat man, the first in the throat, the second in the chest. Blood squirts, the fat man drops his gun. Panicked, Daniel shoots again, hits him in the chest, to the left this time. The driver's body twists, falls over the wheel.

Daniel can't move. He's never shot anyone before. Never killed anyone. He feels like he's going to be sick.

Then the passenger starts hollering, and he's raising his own gun, about to fire, and Daniel is able to move.

He ducks. The gunshots cut through the space he

was occupying. Daniel runs for the nearest cover, a boulder on the opposite side of the road to where the van has stopped. He dives behind it, hears bullets tear into the rock.

He hears something else. The motorcycles, the two that continued on when he pulled over the van – they're coming back. He peers over the top. Both bikers have guns pulled, and they're firing at him now, too.

Daniel ducks down. He peers around the side of the boulder, judging the distance back to his cruiser, if he can make it, call in support. Even if he were somehow able to make it without catching a bullet, what then? He'll still have to wait for backup. Still have to defend himself until they get here, and he's outnumbered. His chances don't look good.

Something happens in the van. He sees it out the corner of his eye. The passenger stops shooting. His brains splash across the dashboard. The side door is pulled open. A man emerges. He carries a gun, but he doesn't look like the others.

He looks familiar.

25

T om probes at the swelling round his left eye. It's tender, filled with blood. He can't see enough out of it. He reaches into the front of the van, pulls on Matt's body, rolls him back so he can see his belt, if there's a knife there, one cleaner than the one sticking out of Kelvin's chest.

There is. He pulls it loose, checks the sharpness of the blade, then sticks the point into the skin below his eye, slices it open. The blood bursts from it like a blister. He drops the knife. Uses the tips of his fingers to squeeze out as much of the blood as he can, blinks hard as bleary vision slowly returns to the eye.

Outside, there are gunshots still. He pulls open the side door. It's dark still, but lighter than it was in the van. It hurts his already aching eyes. Blinking, he looks round, takes in what is happening. Sees the cop pinned behind the boulder on the other side of the road. Sees Brad and Willie bearing down on him, shooting. They haven't seen Tom yet, haven't seen what's happened in the van.

Tom gets out of the vehicle, raises the gun two-handed. Willie is closest to him. Tom takes aim, takes his time. He squeezes the trigger. The bullet tears off the lower half of Willie's face. Willie loses control of his bike, swerves, crashes into Brad. Brad flips, goes over the top of the bike, hits the road face-first and skids along it.

Tom keeps the gun high, goes closer. Checks Willie first. He's dead. Goes to Brad. There is a streak of red along the road, leading up to where Brad has stopped. Using the toe of his boot, Tom rolls Brad over.

Most of Brad's face is on the road now. Half of his nose is gone, his chin and the beard there have been scraped off. Tom can see his teeth through his cheek. He's still alive, though. Barely. He coughs blood, looks up at Tom. He's trying to speak. Tom gives him a moment to get the words out.

"Who the fuck *are* you?" he says.

Tom doesn't answer. Shoots him through what's left of his face.

"Tom?" It's the cop. Tom turns, sees that he's approaching cautiously, his gun still raised. "That you?"

Tom wipes blood from his face. The cop is Daniel. "Yeah."

Daniel doesn't come any closer. "I'm gonna pretend for a second that I didn't just watch you shoot that man through the face in cold blood," he says, "if you tell me what the hell is going on here."

26

D aniel has called in what happened. The sheriff intercepted the call, alarmed at the report of a shoot-out, said he'd be out soon.

In the meantime, Daniel and Tom wait. "You look like hell, Tom," Daniel says. "What they done to you?"

Tom is leaning against the cruiser, sipping from a bottle of water Daniel has given him. He swishes it around his mouth, cleans it out, spits it onto the road. There's sand and blood in it. It's dawn now. The sun is beginning to rise. Soon, his bloodied spit will be baking on the asphalt. "Guess they must've worn out their old punching bag," he says. "They wanted to see if I could fight."

"And could you?"

"Yes. More than they expected. They weren't happy about that."

Daniel nods, but he doesn't know what to say. Still stunned by all that has happened, and by his discovery of what is in the back of the van. He turns away, goes back to the van. He's cordoned off the road, but there's not much more he can do until support arrives.

He opened up one of the boxes earlier. Now he peers into it again. Looks at the meth. Shakes his head. His earlier reaction was not so subdued. Tom doesn't think Daniel believed him about the meth until he saw it for himself. He'd shook his head until it looked like it might fall from his shoulders. He ran his hand down his face, covered his mouth, stared at the crystals. He'd gone pale. He looked sick to his stomach. "Y'know," he says, turning back to Tom. "I shouldn't be surprised, but, I mean...*fuck*. Look at this. This is a lot of fuckin' meth. This is a major operation."

Tom nods, drinks the water. Runs some into his hand and splashes it back into his face, runs it over the top of his head, through his hair. He probes tentatively at the gash at the back of his skull, where Kelvin hit him with the gun. It doesn't feel as bad as he feared. It might not need stitches, though he won't know for sure until he's able to clean it out and get a good look at it.

Daniel steps into the middle of the road, looks up and down. There's no one coming. This is an old and unused road, the long way to get anywhere when the interstate is so much quicker. He can understand why the bikers were using it to transport their drugs. Drugs cooked up by the McQuades.

Again, Daniel knows he shouldn't be surprised, but he is alarmed at the extent of their operation. At most, he thought they had a small lab hidden away some-where, in a trailer perhaps, cooking up enough small batches to sell in Brenton and turn a neat profit. But this is a much broader scale than he ever anticipated. And, from what Tom has told him he's seen, it sounds like they have a superlab beneath the factory where Daniel's own father used to work.

"Taking their time, ain't they?" Tom says.

Daniel grunts.

"You look distracted, Deputy."

"I am. I'm just trying to wrap my head around all this, around just how...*big* this all is. Where were they taking it all?" He points at the meth in the back of the van. "Are they selling it all through Texas? Has it gone further? The McQuades are fuckin' meth kingpins. This is way bigger than I ever expected it to be. Makes me wonder what they're doing living in that rickety old ranch all these years."

"They suddenly build themselves a McMansion, that's gonna raise more than a few eyebrows," Tom says. "Likely just saving it all until they've got enough to retire on, then they'll get the fuck outta here, start over somewhere the cops don't know them by name."

Daniel starts to laugh. "Maybe that was the plan, but that ain't gonna happen now." Finally, *finally*, after so many years of wanting to do *something*, *anything* to bring the McQuades to account, they have all the evidence they need. All the evidence they could ever need. The cooking, sale, and distribution of meth, the kidnapping of Tom, not to mention their biker buddies attempting to murder him, a lawman. And if it transpires the Forever Road Dogs were transporting the meth across state lines, well, then it becomes a matter for the feds, and the McQuades are never gonna see the outside of a prison cell again in their lives.

Daniel hears cars approach. He looks up, sees three cruisers coming their way. He raises an arm in salute, waves them down. The cars all slow, pull to a stop at the edge of Daniel's cordon. The sheriff leads the way. He takes in the carnage before him with his hands on his hips, whistles through his teeth. "Well," he says, "looks like you've had a busy night." Larry steps into the scene, still looking around. His eyes settle on Tom leaning on the hood of the cruiser, drinking water.

Tom nods at him. "Sheriff," he says.

"What the hell is he doing here?" Larry says, wheeling on Daniel.

"He was the hostage I mentioned," Daniel says.

Larry spits out the corner of his mouth, steps closer to Tom. "Didn't I tell you – *twice* now – to keep yourself out of trouble?"

Tom shrugs one shoulder. "Guess it has a way of finding me."

"Tom saved my life, sir," Daniel says.

Larry considers this. "How exactly did a hostage, and one looking as beat up as he does, manage to save your life?"

"I got free," Tom says.

"Yeah, well, you can tell us all about your Houdini escapades back at the station. We're gonna need a statement about what's gone on here."

Tom finishes the water. "Sure," he says. "Just make it quick."

"Oh?" Larry raises an eyebrow. "You got somewhere you need to be?"

"Sure," Tom says. "I need to leave the county, just like you said."

Larry gives him a look, unimpressed.

Daniel exchanges brief greetings with the other deputies who have accompanied the sheriff. It's a who's who of some of Larry's favorite boys – Jake King, Shaun Keenan, Lloyd Taylor, and David Johnson. Jake pats Daniel on the back as he passes by, on his way to the van to check out the contents. "Looks like some fancy shooting here, Daniel," he says. "Didn't know you had it in you."

"I don't," Daniel says, but Jake is already gone, looking into the open box, feeling around inside it.

"You've had a hell of a week, ain't ya?" Larry says to Daniel. "Trying to track down Frank, now this."

"You heard anything from him yet?"

"I do, you and Mark will be the first I tell about it, get the two of you off my back."

"Well, I'll be glad of that. What're we gonna do here?"

"We'd best get this place more fully secured, call in the forensics boys. For now, this one needs to be taken to the station." He tilts his head in Tom's direction. "Lloyd, David, you two escort Mr. Rollins here back to the station, take his statement."

"Yes, sir," Lloyd says. They walk Tom to their cruiser.

"Just like old times, huh?" Tom says, recognising them as the two deputies who took him into custody after the bar fight. "Y'all got more water?"

Daniel watches them go. When he turns back, Larry has gone to the back of the van, is standing with Jake. Daniel joins them. "Hey, Jake, can I get a minute with the sheriff?"

"Sure," Jake says, sliding away, going to join Shaun, who is looking at the fallen bikers. They're probably all going to stare for a while before they do anything to mark up evidence. Nothing like this has happened around here before.

"What's up?" Larry says.

Daniel did not mention the McQuade involvement on the radio, on the off chance they have a scanner out at McQuade ranch. He's eager to share that knowledge now, though.

"All this," Daniel says, patting a box, "all this was cooked by the McQuades."

Larry raises an eyebrow.

"Tom saw them do it. He was there for the exchange, saw it all go down. They're cooking it in a superlab, selling it on to the Forever Road Dogs, and then they're taking it elsewhere – this could be statewide, sir. It could be *bigger*."

Daniel feels himself getting giddy. Once he's done, they'll go to McQuade ranch; they'll start making arrests. This is it. This is the moment he's hoped for but didn't believe would ever come.

"Hold on. Slow down," Larry says. "Let me get this straight. The McQuades are cooking *all* this meth, then selling it on to this biker gang, and they're distributing it…well, we don't know how far exactly, but we reckon *far*. Is that right?"

"That's right."

"And the McQuades are definitely, one hundred percent, behind all this?"

Daniel is nodding. "Tom saw them. Knew them by name. Said there was only one guy in the group he didn't recognise, seemed to be running things. A guy in a suit, he said, who looked out of place and was real pissed off that Tom saw his face."

"And your boy Tom will attest to all this?"

"I reckon so," Daniel says, "soon as he gets to the station."

"What was he doing out there?"

"They stole his car."

Larry grins. "They stole his car?"

"That's what he says."

"And he was trying to get it back, I suppose."

"Sounds like it."

"Goddamn, that boy don't have much sense."

Daniel chuckles, but he's eager to keep things moving. "We need to go to the ranch now, right now," he says, "before they get a chance to hear what's happened. We gotta catch them by surprise before they can run."

Larry nods. "Yeah, you're right about that."

Then, out of nowhere, Larry punches Daniel across the jaw.

It's a hard blow, unexpected. Daniel has no time to guard against it, and he goes down, hits the back of his head on the road. His first thought is that someone has sucker-punched him. Maybe one of the bikers wasn't as dead as they thought; he's sneaked up out of nowhere and dealt Daniel one hell of a haymaker in retaliation for his fallen brothers. Daniel's mind will not comprehend that it is the sheriff who has struck him. It happened so fast. He never saw it coming.

He blinks, feeling dizzy and sick. Through his blurry eyes, he sees Larry looking down at him. He spits out the corner of his mouth. He shakes his head, looks almost disappointed. "I always knew you were gonna be a problem, kid," he says. "You shoulda just left this all alone. You shoulda left Frank alone." He takes a deep breath, raises a boot, then kicks Daniel in the face. Daniel's head rocks back and bounces off the road again. Still struggling to believe what has happened to him, he fades into darkness.

27

The two deputies take Tom to the station. It is not a place he wanted to return to. They sit him down in the interrogation room, bring him a bottle of water, then leave him alone.

Halfway back to the station, the deputy riding shotgun – David – had pulled out his phone, checked it like he'd gotten a message. He frowned at the screen as he read it, then got the driver's – Lloyd's – attention, showed him whatever the message said. The two of them looked at each other, nodded, then turned their collective attention back to the road.

They didn't say anything about the message, and Tom didn't ask. He sits in the interrogation room and sips his water. Probably wouldn't have given the message a second thought if they hadn't left him alone for so long.

A couple of hours pass; then the sheriff comes to visit. "Sorry to keep you waiting so long, Tom," he says, standing at the opposite side of the table, not sitting down. "But the things that have happened, you understand we're kinda busy 'round here at the minute."

"Sure. Except no one's asked me any questions. No one's taken my statement."

"Like I say, we'll be with you soon as we can."

"Or how about this – you leave me a pen and some paper, I'll fill in my statement, and you can call me with any questions you might have. How about that?"

Larry smiles. "We ain't gonna be able to do that, I'm afraid."

Tom takes a deep breath, sits back in his chair. "This is beginning to feel like some kind of joke," he says.

"I'm sorry you feel that way," Larry says, but he doesn't sound like he means it. "But as you may have noticed, we're a small-town sheriff's department, and things like roadside shoot-outs with biker gangs don't happen all that often 'round here. Just bear with us. We're doing the best we can."

"Where's Daniel?" Tom says.

"He's still out at the scene."

"Taking a while for y'all to get it sorted out, ain't it?"

"Well, like I already explained. You were listening, weren't you?"

"Of course. What else can I do? This conversation is the most riveting thing that's happened to me in the past few hours."

"Well, after the busy night you've had, that sure is saying something, ain't it?"

"Guess that's why I can't keep away from this place. The entertainment value."

"Well," Larry says, backing off toward the door, "that ain't our first priority, but I'm pleased to find that's a service we didn't even realize we offered. Sit tight, Mr. Smith. We'll be with you as soon as we can."

The sheriff leaves, and Tom goes back to waiting. He finishes the bottle of water he has, and soon after that finds he needs to use the bathroom. He knocks on the door and the two-way mirror, calls out, but no one responds. He takes the bottle to the corner, pisses into it, puts the cap back on, and lets it stand in the middle of the interrogation table for whoever will have to clear it up.

He folds his arms and waits. Time ticks by. Another hour passes. Another two. He feels himself starting to doze off in the chair, the events of the night and day catching up to him.

When the door is finally opened again, Tom is resting facedown on the table, asleep. He jolts awake, unsure how long he's been out.

The two deputies who enter are the same two that brought him here. David and Lloyd. David squints at the piss bottle in the middle of the table. "That what I think it is?" he says.

"It sure ain't lemonade," Tom says.

"That's disgusting," David says.

"You'd rather I did it in the corner, let it stink the room up?"

"People have done worse," Lloyd says, with a smirk.

David shakes his head, like he's maybe remembering something he'd rather remained forgotten. "We're wasting time here – come on, we gotta move." He signals for Tom to get to his feet.

"Where we going?" Tom says.

"We've heard some alarming things," Lloyd says. "We've gotta move you to a more secure facility."

"What alarming things? What secure facility?" Tom does not stand, sits and wonders what is more secure than the sheriff's department.

Lloyd and David take him by an elbow each, but they're cautious as they pull him up to his feet. No doubt they've heard what he's capable of. "Listen, let's not waste time, okay?" Lloyd says. "Let's just get out of here. We can explain on the way."

Tom shakes their hands off. "I can walk," he says, "and I ain't under arrest, so I don't need either of you touching me."

Lloyd holds up both hands as a sign of peace. "Sure," he says. "Have it your way. Let's just move, okay? We gotta get you out of here."

Tom doesn't move. "I ain't going nowhere 'til I hear what this issue is."

Lloyd and David exchange glances. David answers, "You really think you can waste five bikers at the side of the road and there ain't gonna be repercussions? Their buddies have found out, and they're on their way here now, and I reckon it's gonna be more than just the one chapter. Sheriff wants us to move you, keep you safe."

"I don't need protecting."

"Yeah, but the county might, and we can't preoccupy ourselves with you when a whole load of bikers are headed our way. We get you to a safe house, deal with them; then we can take your statement."

Something feels off to Tom. "Where's Daniel?" he says.

"Don't worry about Daniel," Lloyd says. "This is his job; he can take care of himself." They lead Tom out of the room. He lets them, eager for a change of scenery.

Almost immediately, Tom stops walking. The hallway is empty save for the three of them. He thinks they're taking him out a back way, as he hasn't seen this part of the station before. "I'm starting to think this is all just a waste of my time," he says.

Lloyd and David look at each other, the same way they did when they received the message earlier in the cruiser. "Mr. Smith, please," Lloyd says. "Just come with us. It's far safer for you and the people of this county this way. Just let us do our job, please."

Tom doesn't move.

"If it'll make it easier, we can place you under arrest," David says.

"For what?" Tom says.

David shrugs. "Obstruction. I'm sure we can think of something."

Tom would like to leave the station. He's tired of sitting around, waiting to give a report no one seems interested in taking. "Fine," he says, and starts walking again. "Just get me the fuck out of here."

The two deputies stand on either side of him. They escort him to the back door. Lloyd holds it open. Before he exits, Tom turns back to David. "You forgot the piss bottle," he says.

"Oh, I didn't forget it," David says. "I chose not to touch it. Let the next asshole in there deal with it."

28

A gain, Tom finds himself in the back of a cruiser. It's dusk as they leave Kirkwood. "So where we going?" Tom says.

"Not right now," Lloyd says, holding up a hand. David is driving. "We're concentrating."

"On what?"

"Your safety."

Tom looks out the windows. There's nothing to see. Just desert. "From what? A cactus?"

Lloyd turns round a little. "You might not take this very seriously, Mr. Smith, but we do. This is our job, and right now, you're our responsibility." With the mesh separating them, Lloyd is sure to make his voice firmer, a real big man once there's a barrier between them.

This feels wrong. "Sheriff ain't joining us?" Tom says.

"Sheriff's a busy man," Lloyd says.

Tom grunts. "Uh-huh. Coming this far out, it's gonna take you a real long time to get back to town and keep it safe from the big bad bikers."

"We'd really appreciate some silence now, Mr.

Smith," David says, the first words he's spoken since they got in the car. "Like Deputy Taylor here said, we need to concentrate. Gotta keep our eyes peeled."

Tom sits forward, puts his face close to the mesh. "I don't believe a word you're telling me," he says. "The bikers don't know shit. They ain't coming here. They don't know a damn thing about me or what happened to their boys. So how about we all act like adults, and the two of you tell me what it is you're doing."

"Just sit back and shut up, will ya?" David says.

Lloyd holds up a hand, calms his partner. "Just ignore him," he says. "It ain't gonna matter much longer."

Tom feels like he's in the back of the biker's van again. Trapped, looking for a way out. The deputies have been lying to him. "How many of y'all are dirty?" Tom says.

Lloyd looks back at him, eyebrows raised, grin plastered across his face. "Too late to smarten up, man. Shoulda realized that *before* you got in the backseat."

Tom hates to admit it, but the deputy isn't wrong. He's not too concerned. He leans close to the mesh, close to Lloyd's face. There are only inches between them. "You really think this can keep me from you?"

A flicker of doubt passes Lloyd's expression.

"Forget him," David says. "We're here."

Tom looks. It's gotten dark outside. There's nothing to see. They're in the middle of nowhere.

David slows the car, pulls it to the side of the road. He looks around. "Say, ain't this where we stopped the other night?"

"Think so," Lloyd says. "Looks about right. In fact, yeah, that cactus there –" He points through the windscreen. "Looks like a dick, don't it? This is the place. How's that for a coincidence?" The two of them chuckle.

David turns round. "Hey, remember your buddies from the cell? Those three dumb-fuck dealers you beat up? You're gonna get reacquainted with them real soon."

"Can't wait," Tom says. "We're due a catch-up."

Lloyd pulls out his gun, pokes the tip of the barrel through the mesh. "Sit very still," he says. "David, get him out."

David has pulled his own gun. He taps it against the mesh, makes sure Tom gets a good look at it. "With pleasure," he says.

Tom understands. The deputies have brought him out to the desert for the same reason the bikers did – to execute him. He doubts he'll be able to impress them with his fighting prowess to earn a reprieve.

For now, he does as Lloyd says and sits very still in the back of the car as David gets out, opens the back door. Tom is compliant. He needs to play this carefully. David takes him by an arm, pulls him outside.

Tom plays dumb. "What's the problem?" he says, acting like he doesn't understand, like he can't possibly comprehend what they're planning on doing. "What's happening? What are you doing?"

"Shut the fuck up, will ya?" David hits him in the back of the head with the handle of his gun. Not hard enough to knock him out, but with enough force to make him dizzy, give him a lump next to the gash he's already sporting.

Lloyd gets out of the car, keeps his gun raised. "Step back from the vehicle."

Tom raises his hands in defeat, in surrender, steps back from the cruiser.

"Now start walking into the desert," Lloyd says.

"We'll be right behind you," David says. Tom can hear the snicker in his voice.

Tom needs to keep the distance between them close. If he goes off into the desert, starts walking and puts space between them, there's nothing he can do. He's unarmed; he needs this to remain close quarters.

"All right," he says. Takes a showy gulp, like he's not about to try something. "All right, I'm going." He starts to turn slowly. About to go round the back of the car and out into the desert, just like they've said.

David is standing too close to him. David's mistake is thinking that just because he has a gun, he is safe.

Tom twists, a quick movement they're not expecting. David fires, startled, but Tom is too quick. He slips behind David, puts an arm across his throat, and grabs at his gun arm with his other hand, keeps it away from himself. Alarmed, David pulls the trigger again. This bullet bounces off the top of the car.

Lloyd flinches, almost jumps out of his skin, thinks that Tom is aiming David's gun arm his way, trying to take him out. Lloyd starts shooting. Tom falls back behind the car, dragging David along with him, using him as a shield, keeping him under control with the choking grip across his neck.

They duck low and move down the side of the car to the front, David's feet dragging. Lloyd is panicking; he keeps shooting at the car. Bullets tear into the hood, trying to reach them. Tom reaches for David's hand clutching the gun. He squeezes his fingers into the grip until David lets go. He takes the gun, stands, still using the deputy as his shield. Tom snaps off a quick couple of rounds, then ducks back down. One shot goes wide, disappears off into the night, but the other finds its mark. Lloyd cries out, and Tom hears him go down. David is dead weight in Tom's arms. He drops him, sees he has served his job as a shield and taken two bullets in the chest. He's not breathing.

Tom rushes around the front of the car. Lloyd attempts to drag himself along the road, clutching his shoulder where the bullet hit him. He sees Tom and fires, but the shot is wild. Tom kicks the gun from his hand. It skitters across the road.

Tom kneels down, grabs Lloyd, hoists him into a seated position, and slams him against the side of the police cruiser. "Talk to me," Tom says.

Lloyd spits at him. "Fuck you."

Tom strikes him across the face with the gun, tears open his cheek.

"Fuck you!" Lloyd says.

Tom grabs his shoulder, the left one where the bullet has struck, and squeezes. Lloyd screams. Blood begins to cover Tom's hand. His thumb slips into the bullet hole, and Lloyd screams harder. He turns so pale he's almost glowing in the dark.

"Okay, okay," Lloyd begs, breathing hard. "Let go, please, let go."

Tom eases his grip, but doesn't let go completely. A reminder he can hurt him again at any moment.

Lloyd sucks air, winces, tries to pull his wounded shoulder away from Tom, but Tom won't let go.

"You were gonna execute me?" Tom says.

Lloyd nods.

"Why?"

"'Cause we were told to."

"By who?"

"The sheriff."

Tom absorbs this information, but his demeanor does not change. "And why'd he give that order? I don't believe you just ignorantly do as he says when it comes to things like this. You know more than you want me to believe, ain't that right, Deputy Taylor?"

Lloyd is gasping still. Looks like he's about to throw

up. "Because you know too much – because you've seen it all. And because you're a troublemaking son of a bitch, and he's had enough of your shit."

"The McQuades tell him to do it?"

Lloyd nods.

"What they got on him? Tell me everything, Lloyd. I don't want this information in dribs and drabs. I want you to spit it all out." He squeezes the injured shoulder, not enough to hurt, but enough to remind Lloyd of where exactly his hand is and what it can do.

Lloyd freezes at the pressure, bracing himself. He relaxes when he realizes nothing more is coming, but he understands. "The McQuades don't have nothing on the sheriff other than the fact they're in business together. Larry and Reggie have known each other since they were young. They're old friends. Reggie cooks the meth. Larry makes sure no one hassles him for it, keeps everything on the down low, and he takes his share."

"They're partners?"

"Yeah."

"And how many of y'all are on the payroll?"

"In the department?" Lloyd looks to the side, starts doing some math. "About a third."

"And the rest? They're all in the dark?"

"Yeah."

"What about Daniel? He know?"

"Daniel don't know shit, that dumb motherfucker," Lloyd says, and Tom picks up on his genuine disdain. He imagines the deputies on the meth payroll feel the same for all the others, the ones who are clean, the ones just trying to do their jobs. "He thinks Reggie's behind it all, that he and his boy and their buddies are cooking up meth and selling it in Brenton. Daniel doesn't have a damn clue what's going on, how big this all is, how tiny a cog he really is."

"I don't need theatricals, Lloyd," Tom says. "You ain't some super villain explaining his grand scheme, so you just answer my questions and keep the histrionics to yourself."

Lloyd looks like he doesn't know how to react to this.

"What's the deal with Brenton? Why are the drugs sold there? Why's it look like hell when Kirkwood looks so clean?"

"People wanna get high in Cullingworth County, they stay in Brenton. While back, we scooped up and deposited all the junkies and the dealers there, let them rot in their own filth. We keep the rest of the county clean, and that's the ticket the sheriff rides back into office on each term. Course, the people of Brenton are encouraged to vote that way, too. Most of 'em don't mind. It's their own little drugstore paradise, and they don't wanna lose that."

"So the dealers I was in the cell with, they tried to sell elsewhere?"

Lloyd nods. He winces, pained. "They'd already been warned. You sell in Brenton, or else you don't sell. They tried to call our bluffs on that, and, well... We brought them out here."

"Executed them."

Lloyd begins to laugh, but it's cut short when he starts to cough. "Man, you wouldn't believe the bodies buried out in this here desert."

Tom frowns. "Is Daniel one of them?"

"Not yet. But he's gonna be, once things calm down. Course, he could always take Larry up on his offer, way the rest of us did, but we all know what Danny boy's like. Far too upstanding for that. He's gonna go the same way as his pal Frank."

"Who's Frank?"

Lloyd starts coughing again, can't speak. He gasps for air.

Tom has more questions. He needs to know if there's anyone else involved – he thinks of the suited man he saw at the exchange.

Lloyd's cough begins to calm, but his eyes are flickering, he's fading out. His eyes close; he slumps over. Passed out from shock and loss of blood. Tom slaps his cheeks, says his name, but he doesn't come around. He squeezes his shoulder again. Lloyd roars awake, looks around, blinking, but promptly passes back out.

Tom leaves him where he is for now, opens the driver's door of the cruiser. The keys aren't in the ignition. He goes to David's body, finds them in his pocket, returns to the car, and tries the ignition. The car is dead, damaged by Lloyd's wild shooting.

Tom gets back out of the car, and as he does so, Lloyd has gotten back to his feet. He lunges for him. He wasn't unconscious, he was just playing possum. Tom shoots him. Lloyd goes down. This time, he's not faking. He's not breathing.

Tom looks round. He needs to keep moving. From what Lloyd has said, not all of the department is on the meth payroll, but Tom has no way of knowing who is and who isn't, other than Daniel. And he doesn't know where Daniel is.

He pockets the gun, then searches on the road until he finds the other gun, the one he kicked from Lloyd's hand. Removes the clip, pockets it, then strides out into the desert. Once he gets his bearings, he'll head back for Brenton. Beyond that, he isn't sure yet, but he'll think of something on the way.

29

T he first time Daniel comes around, his throat is dry and his jaw is throbbing. When he runs his tongue around the inside of his mouth, he can feel the jagged edges of a couple of broken back teeth. The feeling makes him wince.

He blinks, takes a look around. Doesn't know where he is. His arms are bound behind his back, around a wooden strut. The ground is dirt. He looks up, sees the arched roof. He's in a barn. There's a car in front of him. It's familiar. It's Tom's car.

"Sounds like someone's awake." The sheriff stands up, hidden at the front of the car. Jake King stands with him. Looks like the two of them have been waiting for him to regain consciousness.

Daniel remembers the punch in the face, then the kick.

Larry reaches the back of the car, where Daniel is, leans against it, folds his arms. Jake remains to one side, thumbs hooked through his belt loops.

"This is the McQuade barn, ain't it?" Daniel says.

"That's right."

"And that's Tom Smith's car, ain't it?"

Larry looks down at the vehicle he's leaning against. "Think you can see that for yourself. It ain't all that dark in here."

Daniel blows air. "So you're working for the McQuades."

"*With,*" Larry says. "Reggie and me, we work together."

Daniel lets his head hang, shakes it, feeling like a fool. How had he never seen it? "And that's why, ain't it?"

"Why what?" Larry says.

"Why they've been getting away with it for so long. Why we've never made a single arrest against them. Why Brenton is allowed to rot."

"But the upside is," Larry says, "that we've all gotten very rich in the process."

"Not all of us," Daniel says.

"That's true, not everyone. Just a selected, trusted few. It can be that way for you, Daniel."

Daniel snorts. "So, what? Y'all are a bunch of bikers or somethin'?"

"Bikers? What're you talkin' about?"

"The Forever Road Dogs."

Larry waves his hands. "Them? Those boys are just a means to an end. It's gotta get moved somehow. Besides, we all had a mutual friend, put us in touch with one another."

"And who was that?"

"Ah, c'mon now, son, I ain't gonna tell you that. What do you think I am, some kinda idiot?"

Daniel probes at the jagged edges of his broken teeth with the tip of his tongue. "What're you gonna do to me?"

Larry pushes himself off the car, steps forward,

hitches up his belt. He crouches down in front of Daniel. "Well, y'see, that hinges on you. How we play this going forward depends on the choices you make."

"And what are my choices?"

Larry smiles. "Well, you can either join us – me and Jake here and a half a dozen others – or… C'mon now, Daniel, I'm sure you can guess what the alternative is."

Daniel feels himself run cold all over. He tries not to let it show. Leans past the sheriff, calls to Jake. "That how he got you, Jake? You see some stuff you weren't supposed to, you have to make the choice between either doing what you know is wrong or eating a bullet?"

"No good trying to appeal to his moral center," Larry says. "Jake's been in on this with us from damn near the start."

Jake chuckles.

Daniel's mind races, struggling to comprehend what he has been told. These men he works with, these men who, until a brief few moments ago, he trusted with his life, how many of them work for – or with, whatever – the McQuades, flooding the town of Brenton, the county, the state, with drugs? And all while aligned with a biker group who thought nothing of pulling a gun on Daniel, attempting to shoot him in the face. If any of his fellow deputies had been present, would they have fired back? Would they have tried to save him? Would they have even sent the help he called for, had Tom not been there?

"Where's Tom?" he says.

"Never you mind about him," Larry says.

"You killed him?"

Larry looks at Jake, turns back to Daniel, shrugs, decides there's no harm in telling him the truth. "Not yet. He's in a similar situation as you. We gotta be careful. Things weren't how they are, we'd have dealt with him at the scene of the shoot-out."

"What about me? You'd have dealt with me there, too?"

"No, Daniel. I don't wanna have to kill my boys. You should know me better'n that. I wanna give each of them the opportunity to have what I do – I want y'all to get rich. I want y'all to make your money too, to get yourselves safe, to never have to worry about another dollar bill the rest of your lives, but it don't work like I can just do the rounds and offer y'all an invite. We gotta know who's smart enough to take it, who's smart enough to see the way the land lies, who's gonna actually do somethin' with their lives instead of just flushing them down the toilet."

"How are things now?"

Larry blinks. "What?"

"You said you couldn't deal with Tom the way you'd like because of how things are. What things are you referring to? The election? That's the only thing I can think of going on right now."

"You don't have to worry about none of that."

"Sounds like I do. 'Cause if there wasn't all this extra activity coming to the county, I'm thinking I would've been wasted at the shoot-out, too."

"He's no good, Chief," Jake says. "He's like you said. Can't be trusted to keep his mouth shut. Just wasting your breath at this point."

"Yeah, well," Larry says, "had to give him the offer at least, didn't I? We've known this kid how long now? Eight years? Had to dangle that carrot, see if it didn't interest him just a little."

Larry straightens up. His knees crack. "Unfortunately, I'm starting to think that Jake is right. You ain't gonna see sense, kid."

"I think y'all are the ones who've lost sight of sense," Daniel says. "I can't believe what I'm fuckin' hearing here." Daniel's stomach is clenched tight, like a fist. The horrified understanding of what has been happening right under his nose. Who can he even trust?

He thinks Mark Colt, maybe. Possibly. Mark is an old friend. Daniel's known him since they were both kids. Surely if Mark had gotten involved with the sheriff, surely…

"Where's Frank?" Daniel says.

"Penny's dropped," Jake says.

Larry rolls his head round on his shoulders, pops the tendons in his neck. He sighs. "Frank found himself in a similar predicament to the one you're currently in," he says. "Frank found out somethin' he wasn't supposed to know. He started talking to some journalist –"

"Ike Thoreau?"

Larry looks down at him. "How'd you know that?"

"Jesus…" Daniel shakes his head. "You killed them? Both of them? How many fuckin' people have you killed just to cover up what you're doing?"

"Well, see, I'm gonna have to stop you there." Larry holds up a finger. "What Frank found out, that didn't have nothing to do with *us* per se. He and his buddy hadn't linked it back to us, not yet, but I suppose it was only a matter of time. We just had to tidy it up, do a favor for that same mutual friend who put us in touch with the Forever Road Dogs. Really, it was all about them, it was their mess to clean up, but they ain't exactly readily available, so it fell to us."

"The night he was picked up from his home, they were cops in that car, weren't they?" Daniel says, remembering what Frank's neighbor told him she had seen. "Who did it – was it you? Was it the two of you? Motherfuckers, who killed him?"

Larry looks down at him, prone against the support pole, the way he shuffles in the dirt. "Wouldn't you like to know? All you really need to know, Daniel, is that Frank found himself with the same options before you, and he chose wrong."

"What did he find out?"

"I already told you, Daniel. We ain't fuckin' idiots."

Larry and Jake stand together, start walking like they're going to leave the barn. "So what the fuck are you going to do with me? Just leave me here?"

"That's right," Larry says, stopping and looking back. "You can think on all I've said. You've got until after the election is done, and that's only because I've always had a soft spot for ya, kid. After that, it's on you."

"Even if I agreed to work with you on this, what makes you think you could trust me?"

The sheriff raises his eyebrows as he puts on his hat. "Oh, we'd make sure, Daniel. You wouldn't have to worry about that."

They leave him alone then. Daniel sits back against the pole, thinks over everything he has been told, everything he has learned.

After a while, he stops feeling sorry for himself, tries to work his hands free in the ropes that bind him. His arms begin to ache.

The ropes are too tight; he can't get them loose. They just burn at his wrists, tear the skin from him. He tilts his head back against the pole, catches his breath. It's cold in the barn. Through gaps in the planks, he can see faint sunlight, but the warmth out there doesn't make its way inside.

It's always dark in the barn. There are gaps in the planks it's made from, but not enough light gets through. Daniel thinks it's late evening. It feels cold enough. He doesn't see anyone for a few more hours, then Earl comes to pay him a visit, and Daniel wishes he were still alone.

"Thought I'd come say hello," Earl says, picking up one of the small stools the sheriff and Jake were earlier sitting on at the front of the car, moves it in front of Daniel and perches himself on it. "How you doin', pal?" Earl smiles, looking very pleased with the situation he finds Daniel in.

"Been better," Daniel says.

"I'm sure."

"You just come out here to taunt me?"

"Naw. Figured you'd be getting lonely. Thought you might enjoy some company."

"You ain't the kind of company I was hoping for."

"I'll bet. You were probably hoping for Sally to come walking through that door, right?"

Daniel doesn't respond to this.

Earl smiles with the corner of his mouth. "She sure is a piece of work. She'd be a fine piece of ass if she smiled every once in a while, and if she wasn't such a bitch."

"She ain't a bitch to everyone. Just the people she don't like."

"Oh, I don't doubt that. I bet she smiles at you, too. Come on, tell me, Daniel, what's she like?"

"What d'you mean?" Daniel thinks he knows what he means, but he's not playing into his hands.

"In the sack." Earl raises his eyebrows. "I mean, Anna can be pretty wild – usedta be, anyway – but Sally's always been more button-down, so I'm just curious how the two sisters match up, you understand? If they got any similar kind of moves, anything like that."

"You're a vile little man," Daniel says.

Earl laughs. "You even fucked her yet? The two of

you been seeing each other for how long now? And you still struggle to get her to agree to a date. So I gotta wonder, she ever find the time to jump your bones?"

Daniel grits his teeth, but has to stop as the nerves in his broken teeth begin to scream.

"I reckon she ain't. 'Cause if she *had* emptied your balls on occasion, you wouldn't be walking round with such a stick up your ass."

"You can think what you want," Daniel says. "Ain't no skin off my nose."

"Sounds like someone wants to admit something, but wants to be a gentleman at the same time. A gentleman don't kiss and tell, that right? Come on, man, it's just the two of us in here. You can tell your old pal Earl."

"We ain't pals," Daniel says. "And we never have been, so you certainly ain't an *old* friend. And you wanna know where the stick up my ass came from? It's from the likes of you and all your pals strutting round like you own the place, without any consequences for your actions – and now I know, I fucking *know*, why y'all ain't ever suffered any fuckin' consequences."

"Calm down, Danny boy. Don't get yourself so worked up." Earl stands, takes a walk around the pole. He crouches down at the ropes, checks them over. He clicks his tongue. "Naughty, naughty," he says. "Looks like someone's been trying to break loose." He tightens the ropes. Daniel bites his lip to stop from crying out. Earl leans round the pole from the side, his face close to Daniel's. "You're not enjoying your stay at Chez McQuade?"

"The accommodation leaves a lot to be desired."

"I'll be sure to pass your criticism on to the management." Earl stands to one side, looking down on Daniel in much the same way Larry had. Earl looks like he's enjoying himself.

"Anna know I'm here?" Daniel says.

"Anna knows what she needs to know," Earl says. He reaches into his pocket, pulls out a rag. "Don't think you're gonna be able to call out for her, man. You ain't goin' nowhere." He forces the rag into Daniel's mouth, then ties it round the back of his head. A gag. "There we go," Earl says, patting Daniel's cheek. "That's better, ain't it? Don't want you making too much noise, do we? Well, then."

The job done, Earl gets back to his feet and makes to leave. "I'll see you 'round, Daniel. Ain't like you're going anywhere."

30

L arry sits behind his desk, absently reads a report to look busy. His mind is elsewhere. He's waiting to hear back from David and Lloyd. He checks his phone under the desk, but there's nothing. No missed calls, no messages. Time is ticking. They've been gone a few hours. He adds it up in his head, works out what they've done step by step, how long it should have taken, where they should be at by now. Does this a few times while pretending to read the report. Each time, he comes up with the same answer – even if they've driven farther than usual, then executed Tom and buried the body, he should have heard something by now.

It's getting late. Too late. It's after midnight now. He'd expected them to be back when he returned from the McQuade's ranch, after his talk with Daniel.

He calls Jake, gets him to come to his office. "What's up?" Jake says, striding in and taking a seat.

Larry puts down the report. "You heard anything back from David and Lloyd yet?"

Jake shakes his head, pulls a roll of nicotine gum

from his pocket, shakes out two pieces, and pops them in his mouth. "Uh-uh," he says. "But it's too soon for them to be back."

"I know that," Larry says, annoyed that he's having to spell it out, "but we should've *heard* somethin' by now."

This gets Jake's attention. "They ain't been in touch?"

"Not with me, that's why I've called you in here. Figured that woulda been pretty fuckin' obvious by now, buddy."

"I ain't heard from them."

"*Thank you*, hallelujah, Jesus fucking Christ, that's all I wanted to know, Jake."

"Then why didn't you just say that?"

Larry rolls his eyes.

"You getting nervous?"

"Starting to."

"Tried calling them?"

"I was holding off. I'll do it now. You try 'em on the radio, use the private channel."

Jake salutes him with two fingers, then leaves the office to use his radio. Larry brings up David's number on his phone, dials it. It rings a long time, then goes to voicemail. He tries Lloyd next, but gets the same result. Jake hasn't returned yet, so he tries again, both numbers. Again, nothing.

Jake comes back shaking his head. "No answer," he says.

"Now I'm nervous," Larry says.

Jake agrees. "Same. Think we should head out there?"

"I don't think we've got any fuckin' choice."

They leave the station, take a cruiser. Jake drives. He

goes fast. "They say they were going to the usual place?"

"The latest place," Larry says. "Where they took those asshole dealers the other night."

"That's where I meant."

"Then say what you fuckin' mean," Larry says, turning Jake's earlier statement around on him.

Larry's stomach does flips as they get closer. He keeps checking his phone, keeps trying to get them on the radio, on the private line, but nothing.

"I got a bad feeling," Jake says.

"Me too," Larry says. "This ain't good. They woulda been in touch by now. Something's happened."

Jake sucks on his teeth. "This guy, this fuckin' Tom guy, he was beaten half to death, he's been in a gunfight – what could he have done? David and Lloyd ain't small guys. They were bigger than him, anyway. He didn't look like he was breaking six foot."

Larry broods, watches the road. They're getting close.

"You think he has friends?"

"I hope not."

The road is quiet. Most of these roads are, the ones that lead mostly to and from Brenton, that don't go anywhere near Kirkwood or the other towns in Culling-worth County. Then, up ahead, Larry spots something. He sees it before Jake says anything.

"Oh, *fuck*…" Jake says. He slows the car.

Their cruiser is there, pulled to the side of the road. It's riddled with bullets. On the road they can see bodies. "Get a little closer, then stop," Larry says.

They get close enough that he can see the nearest body splayed in the middle of the road. It's Lloyd. The pair of legs poking out from the side of the car must belong to David. Neither of them are moving.

Jake covers his mouth with a hand. He swallows his nicotine gum. "Holy fuck…"

Larry pulls his gun, gets out of the cruiser, keeps the door open, and remains covered behind it. Jake follows his lead. "Smith!" Larry shouts, looking into the dark. "Smith, you there? If you're here, you better show your ass!"

Jake looks into the dark too, but he's jumpy. Doesn't keep his cool like the sheriff. "I don't think he's still here," Jake says.

"Then why didn't he take the car?"

"'Cause it looks shot to shit. It's probably crippled."

Larry leaves his cover, creeps forward, takes his time. Keeps one eye on the dark desert, watching for movement, straining his eyes as they struggle to adjust. He checks on Lloyd, then David, then the car. All dead. Larry straightens up, holsters his gun. "He ain't here."

Jake steps up next to him. "Where's he gone?"

Larry shoots him a look, doesn't bother to respond. He surveys the scene, decides their next steps. "All right, here's what we're gonna do. Get on the radio, get in touch with all our boys, everyone on the payroll. I don't care if they've got time off, call 'em all in. We're gonna clean this up and keep it quiet for now, until we have Smith. We can't spook him by spreading the word of what he's done here – we do that, he might try and spill his guts about what he knows, what David and Lloyd were gonna do to him. By now he knows too much, and he can use that against us. So we gotta find him, and we ain't gonna take him alive."

Jake nods along. He puts some more nicotine gum into his mouth, chews furiously. "Soon as we lay eyes on this piece of shit, we blast him."

"That's right," Larry says. "Make sure they all know that. We ain't taking any chances. I want him dead.

Then, once we've dealt with him, we let people know what he's done here."

"And what exactly has he done here?"

"Tom Smith, a dangerous and psychotic loner and drifter, mercilessly executed two brave young deputies while they performed a routine traffic stop, then fled into the night."

"What about their dash cams? They'll have had them turned off, but we gotta make sure they're destroyed."

Larry nods. Every so often, Jake raises a good point. "I'll go deal with that now. You get on the radio. Tell them he's probably on foot, get them to search the roads from this point onwards, though he's likely gone north, as we've come from the south, and we didn't see a damn thing."

"The desert?"

"He'd have to be pretty dumb to go too deep into the desert. Tell them to keep their flashlights on the sides of the roads. He hears a car coming, he might try and hide."

"Okay," Jake says.

"You got all that?"

"Yeah."

"Then get to it, damn it! We ain't got all night, and I want this son of a bitch *found*!"

31

T he sun is up, and Tom is deep in the desert.

Last night – or this morning, whatever time it was – when it was still dark and Tom left the scene where David and Lloyd were going to execute him, he noticed footprints in the sand a little way down from where the cruiser was stopped. Five sets, heading out into the desert.

Tom followed them. He had to duck down low in the dark to make them out. They went a ways out. Then they stopped, and the five became two. Two sets, walking away. They were probably counting on wind to blow their tracks away. Lazy.

The sand was slightly higher there, a mound that would easily have been missed had the tracks not led him to it. Tom started digging. Didn't have to go deep. Less than two feet, a shallow grave, and then he found bodies. Brushed sand from their faces. His cellmates. All three of them. He cleared them, checked their pockets. The fat guy had a lighter. Tom took it. From the muscular guy, he took his T-shirt, thinking of the hot sun coming up in the next few hours. He didn't bother filling the shallow grave back in before he continued on his way.

As the sun began to rise, Tom took the muscular guy's T-shirt from where he'd tucked it down the back of his jeans, wrapped it around his head to protect himself from the sun. He's been walking a while now, heading back in the direction they came. He's far from the road, can't see it, can't even hear the passing of vehicles. Just keeps putting one foot in front of the other, tries not to think about how hot it is, or how his body burns as the rays of the sun beat down upon it, even through his clothes. Tries not to think about the grumbling in his stomach, either, or the dryness in his throat.

He doesn't know how long it will take him to get back to Brenton. He starts checking the cacti, searching for a fishhook barrel cactus. Remembers his father's lessons, from when he was young. Every day after school and all weekend long. Remembers how the liquid inside the other cacti will make him sick, can potentially kill him, but the water inside the fishhook barrel can be drunk – so long as he's eaten something first. Otherwise it could make him shit himself, give him diarrhea, and that's the last thing he needs out in the desert, already severely dehydrated and no sign of water.

So far, the only animals he's seen have been small rodents and snakes. Most of them scatter as he makes his way through. He decides to go for a snake. It's been a long time since he ate snake. Been a long time since he had to catch one, too. He finds a handful of dried and broken sticks with which to make a fire, keeps hold of the biggest one. He keeps the rest of the sticks safely to one side, then finds a small rock with a jagged edge. He scrapes it against the nearest boulder, sharpens it as best he can. Done, he puts it with the firewood. He stands one of the sticks up to mark the position of the rest, then he goes in search.

He looks under rocks, checks round the back of boulders. He taps the ground lightly, trying to draw attention. His eyes scan the area. The sun continues to burn him, to cook him. Sweat gets in his eyes.

His ears prick at a familiar sound. A rattlesnake. Its tail. Tom follows the sound. It comes from behind a boulder. Tom climbs on top, moving slow, careful, doesn't want to make too much sound, doesn't want to disturb the snake. He gets on top, looks down the other side. The snake is there, curled up. Its head rests upon its long body.

Tom lowers the tip of the stick to the ground in front of the snake. A foot in front of it. He taps the ground again, just lightly, like the feet of a rodent. The snake feels the vibrations. It raises its head. It rattles. Tom waits. He taps some more. The snake raises its head higher. Tom reaches down behind it, careful, keeping it distracted.

He drops the stick, grabs the snake from behind just below the head, pinches it, controls its movement. The rest of its body starts to thrash, it tries to wrap itself around his arm. He puts it against the rock, then plucks the gun from his waistband and crushes its skull with the handle.

He carries the body back to his bundle of sticks. It takes a while for the dead snake to stop moving, to stop curling and writhing. While it does, Tom stacks the sticks, takes the fat guy's lighter from his pocket. They're dry, kindling. They catch with ease. While it gets hot, he skins the snake. Uses his makeshift tool, the rock he has sharpened on the boulder. Cuts the head off first. Has to saw through the tough skin. He skins it next, starting at the tail. It's hard and bloody work. Tom perseveres. He's done this in the past, but he had a knife then, and that made things easier. He wishes he brought his KA-BAR when he left the hotel. Of course, with everything that has happened, it would have been taken from him at some point, and he would still be without it.

The skin finally gone, he tears the guts out. They slide out in a long tube. He throws them to one side, then wipes out the insides as best he's able on his jeans, using the point of his knee to get in deep. Then he wraps it around the long stick he used to distract it, and starts to cook.

It's still hot when he eats it, and it burns the roof of his mouth, but he's too hungry to care. When he's done, he starts moving again. Can't hang around.

Finally, after what feels like another mile, out the corner of his eye he spots the red flowers that grow from the top of the fishhook barrel cactus. The only splash of color amidst all the desolation. He stumbles to it, pulling his sharpened rock from his pocket. He uses it to cut flesh from the cactus. Its hooks poke at his skin, catch him. He ignores them. Again, if he had his knife, if he weren't hot, thirsty, and tired, this would all be a lot easier. Cutting through the cactus with the sharp rock is as difficult as skinning the snake.

He cuts out chunks of the flesh, removes the T-shirt from his head, wraps the flesh in it, squeezes it, wrings out the water into his mouth. Sucks it from the fibers of the shirt. He repeats the process on the other pieces he has cut free, sucks them dry. It's not as much as he needs, but it might be just enough to keep him going.

Tom gets to his feet, wraps the wet T-shirt back round his head. It's sticky but it's cool, and he's grateful for this. He starts walking again.

32

The sheriff hasn't heard anything about Tom yet, and he's getting nervous. There is a constant fluttering in his stomach, like it doesn't know whether it wants to shit or throw up.

Goddamn son of a bitch. Tom has been nothing but trouble since he arrived. A damn nuisance he should have escorted out of Cullingworth County himself, made sure he was good and gone.

He calls Reggie, lets him know what's happened.

Reggie is silent while he explains. When he's done, all he has to say is, "He's killed two of your boys?"

Larry is in his cruiser, pulled to the side of the road, away from the station. He's told Jake to call him on the private channel if there are any new developments. He presses his phone hard to the side of his face. "Yes, he has. Two good boys."

"He's killed one of mine. Hurt a couple of others. Guess you're probably leading in the damages department."

"And he's killed five Forever Road Dogs – how do you think they're gonna react?"

"I already got our boy to talk to them, told them to keep their cool and hold off for the time being. Told them we'd deal with it. They agreed, on account he's got more reason to be pissed off than they do, on account of it being his cousin and all."

Larry grunts. "How was he when you spoke to him?"

"How do you think? He's pissed."

"We're all pissed."

"I know that. He's gonna be mad as all hell, though, when he finds out your boys have fucked up a task as simple as shooting a man in the back of the head in the desert."

Larry grits his teeth, doesn't bite at the reminder of his failure. "We'll get him. We don't need to tell our boy anything just yet; he don't need to know. It ain't a risk to him yet."

"You sure you can clear things up before he needs to know?"

"Yes."

"It's on you, then."

"Well, that's what I'm calling for. Warn you he might be on his way to you, so keep your fuckin' eyes open. He shows up, take him out on sight, then get in touch with me straight away."

"Why would he come here? For your errant deputy?"

"Could be, or maybe he'll be after his car – the car your boy took. Your boy hadn't taken his fucking car, none of this would be an issue right now, you understand that, right?"

Reggie is silent a moment. Larry knows Earl's behavior, his immaturity, is a point of contention for his father. "I've spoken to him about that," he says.

"Spoken to him?" Larry says. "That all?"

"How I discipline my son ain't no concern of yours."

"Sounds like it's *all* of our concern. Look at the fuckin' mess he's caused us. Every morning he wakes up, you ought to give him a smack in the mouth, up until the day he finally starts behaving himself."

Larry can hear Reggie bristling at the other end of the line.

"You can criticize my mistakes all you want, Reggie, but you'd better make sure your house is in order first. Get that fuckin' son of yours on a damn leash."

"Just deal with it," Reggie says, sounding like the words are uttered through his teeth. "Get this son of a bitch dead, and then we can discuss these things properly."

"I'll look forward to it." Larry hangs up, knowing he's pissed his old friend off. It's not hard to do. Reggie has always had a short fuse. Has always been quick to dole out criticism, but never been able to take it.

Larry starts his car up, continues on to Brenton. He goes to the hotel, on the off chance Tom has made it back to town, has checked back in and is hiding out. Sally sits behind her desk. She looks tired. Larry leans on the counter. "Looks like you're working yourself too hard, Miss Blevins," he says, smiling.

"Could be," Sally says, remaining seated. "What can I do for you, Sheriff?"

Larry clears his throat. "Tom Smith was staying in your hotel, ain't that right?"

Sally raises her eyebrows. "Feels like every other day I've got people coming in here asking after that man."

"That so? Who else?"

"Earl and Dean were here not that long ago."

"Oh really? And what did they want?"

Sally shrugs. "Same thing you do, I imagine."

"And what's that?"

"To know where he is."

"And you don't know?"

"Why should I? He's nothing to me. People seem to think I'm keeping track of his movements, when all he did was check into my hotel for a short stay."

"So he ain't come back?"

"He ain't been back since y'all arrested him for the fight at the bar. Came back to collect his stuff and pay his bill, and I ain't seen him since."

Larry wonders how much he should believe. Is Sally telling the truth – Tom is nothing to her, and she doesn't know where he is – or is there more to their relationship and she's covering for him, for whatever reason? As long as he looks at her, though, she doesn't give anything away. Sally Blevins has always been a cool customer. Her demeanor never changes. Just like her father. "Reckon I could take a look at his room?"

"You *could*," Sally says, with an emphasis that lets him know a *but* is coming, "but I doubt you'd find anything. It's been occupied since he left, and you'd have to disrupt the two new guests sharing it. I mean, feel free. It's your call."

Larry doesn't want to have to deal with a couple of stinking tweakers on the off chance he might find something that could lead him to Tom, especially when it's such a slim chance. "No, that's fine. But listen, if Mr. Smith returns to this hotel, you give me a call, huh? I'd like to talk with him."

"Sure. What about?"

"Now, that's a private matter, Miss Blevins, and I can't very well go sharing Mr. Smith's business with everyone who asks."

He's about to leave when Sally says, "You know where Daniel is? I ain't heard from him since early yesterday."

Larry doesn't hesitate. "Daniel called in sick," he says, just as cool as Sally looks. "Said he had a bug, that he felt contagious, so he was locking himself away in his room, gonna try and sleep it off."

Sally doesn't say anything, doesn't nod, doesn't react. But Larry wonders, is that a hint of doubt he sees in her eyes?

"Well," she says, "if you hear from him before I do, let him know I hope he's feeling better."

"Will do," Larry says, tapping the brim of his hat. "And if Tom Smith comes back, you remember to give me a call. He don't need to know about it, just give me a little call, and he and I can have a private chat."

"Sure."

Larry leaves the hotel, heads back to the station. On the way, he calls his boys, checks in. None of them have anything. No sign of Tom. Larry doesn't express his frustration to them, but inside he is burning. Back in his office, he goes back to Tom's files. He gave them a cursory glance the last time he looked, wasn't expecting to find anything of importance. Starting to feel like he's maybe missed something.

He reads through the file again, but nothing catches his eye. There's nothing special about Tom Smith. Hell, even his name sounds bland as all get-out. Larry looks at the picture of him. He taps the file with one finger, staring at the picture, seeing something familiar there. Something he can't quite –

Larry sits up, eyes narrowed. He's thinking about Dallas. It's been years since he last went to Dallas. He can't imagine why he would think of Dallas now, nor why looking at Tom Smith's picture brings it to mind.

He remembers reading about the bomb scare they had a couple of months ago, seeing it on the news. It was all over the media – on the TV, in the papers. Larry likes to keep himself abreast of everything going on in the rest of Texas. Keeps his eyes peeled primarily for anything to do with the Forever Road Dogs, any trouble they might get themselves into, especially if they're carrying or transporting meth. He watches for anything that could be traced back to Cullingworth County.

For a long time, all the news could talk about was Dallas. What happened. The van full of explosives that almost went off right outside the synagogue where some senator was praying with his family.

And there was the man who stopped it all. The man who appeared from out of nowhere and disappeared just as quickly. The man whose face was everywhere, but no one knew how to find.

Larry raises the picture to his face. Tom Smith. He studies him hard. He covers his beard and his hair with his thumbs. He drops the file and gets on his computer, searches the news. Finds the story. Finds the picture.

Tom Rollins.

Tom Smith.

It's him.

Tom Rollins was the man in Dallas that day. Tom Rollins is the man the sheriff is looking for.

He sits back, covering his mouth with his hand. This changes things. This changes everything.

Larry skims the article on his computer. Rollins was in the army. It says that he went AWOL, and that he's wanted for that reason. Larry closes the online article, goes back into the database. Searches for him under his real name.

Rollins wasn't just in the army. He was in the CIA, though it's not clear in what capacity. Larry can read between the lines – black ops shit, stuff no one would want him talking about. Larry thinks how the news article said he was wanted for going AWOL from the army, but the timeline doesn't work out for what he's now reading. Rollins couldn't have gone AWOL from the army. He left the CIA.

"Well, shit," Larry says, exhaling the words with his breath.

He reads the file, goes deep into Rollins's past. Reads about his family. Gets hits on his brother first – Anthony Rollins, four years younger, and a criminal record the length of Larry's arm, all for petty misdemeanors. Nothing that brought anything serious, no jail time, just a lot of trouble and, in some cases, a lot of fines.

Mary Rollins, mother, deceased. Died when Tom was nine years old from cervical cancer. Nothing to see there.

Then Larry reaches the father. A man with a record of his own, though seems to have mellowed out in his later years, after he had children. Jeffrey Rollins. Left to raise two young boys after his wife died. Larry's attention is piqued when he gets to the bottom of Jeffrey Rollins's file, when it explains his recent activities.

Jeffrey is a survivalist. More than that, he's living off-grid now, and his last known location was as part of a doomsday-prepping community in New Mexico.

Was this how Tom was raised? Larry feels antsy. His knee bounces under his desk, the thrill of knowing he suspected something, of following it through and finding the answer. Now he feels something else, knows that the answer to catching Rollins is somewhere in these files. He scratches his chin, reads it back over. There's no mention of Tom growing up in such a community, but it was likely his father has been living that lifestyle for a long time.

While he was raising his two boys.

In New Mexico, a state that probably has just as much desert as Texas.

Larry stops. He thinks.

Desert.

Larry gets on the radio. "Get off-road," he tells them. "Look *in* the desert. He's had survivalist training. He could be *in* it."

"We sure as shit ain't having any luck finding him at the side of the road," Shaun Keenan says. "We'll get out there now."

"Everyone head back to where he killed David and Lloyd," Larry says. "Meet up there, then split up. I want each car heading in a different direction out through the desert. Go get this motherfucker."

Larry sits back in his chair, knowing it's too early to breathe a sigh of relief, but breathing one anyway. He feels lighter. There's a sensation of hope replacing the horrible sinking feeling that has been draining him. He knows who 'Tom Smith' really is, now. He knows every-thing about him. And now, he's pretty sure, he knows where they're going to find him.

The phone on his desk begins to ring.

Larry looks at it, peers out of his office to where his secretary sits. She's not on the line. She's standing by her filing cabinet, putting documents away. The phone call has come through direct to the sheriff.

Larry picks it up. "Cullingworth County Sheriff's Department," he says, "Sheriff Larry Collins speaking."

"Hello there, Sheriff," says the voice on the other end. It's firm, commanding, has a Texas accent but enunciates every word. It says something that makes Larry's stomach sink deeper than it was before. "This is Senior Special Agent Eric Thompson. I'm calling you from the FBI field office here in Houston. How are you doing out there in Cullingworth County?"

"We're good, thanks for asking." Larry swallows. There's a dry click at the back of his throat that he hopes does not carry through the phone. "What can I do for you, Agent Thompson?" He's pleased to hear that his voice does not waver.

"Couldn't help but notice you accessed some files recently on a Mr. Tom Rollins."

"Uh, yes, that's right."

"I was just curious as to why, Sheriff." Agent Thompson's voice gives nothing away. Larry is on edge.

He thinks fast. "Turns out I had the wrong Tom Rollins," he says. "I accessed the wrong files by mistake."

"Oh, I see. For an accident, you certainly took a deep dive into Mr. Rollins's background. You looked into his brother, his father?"

"Well, I gotta admit to you, Agent Thompson, we're kinda quiet round here, and I was just passing the time, found them to be an interesting read."

"Is that so?"

Larry doesn't say anything to this. The agent is waiting for him to slip up, to say something wrong. He's already said too much.

"Well, Sheriff, since you're aware of Tom Rollins now – the one you've been reading the files on, I mean – how about you do me a favor, and if on the off chance you ever *do* come into contact with him, you give me a call. Just call this branch and ask for Eric Thompson. Did you get that?"

"Y-yeah, I got it."

"Excellent. Keep it written down. People think it's an easy name to remember, but they often forget. Well, it has certainly been a pleasure talking with you, Sheriff. I'll let you get back to your quiet little town."

"Uh, yeah, yeah."

"Oh, before I go. The Tom Rollins you *did* pick up – you know, the wrong one, not the one from the files you were looking at – what was it he did? What was he arrested for?"

Larry clenches his jaw.

"Sheriff? Are you there?"

"Sorry, yes, I'm here. He got himself a little too drunk in one of our towns, got himself into a fight. Nothing major. No one pressed any charges, he paid for the damages, and he's on his way now. Long gone by now, I reckon."

"That story certainly has a cheery resolution, doesn't it? Okay, Sheriff, I won't keep you any longer. You have a good day. I understand your mayor is looking like a frontrunner for the governorship."

Larry wishes the agent would just get off the line. "That's right."

"He came out of nowhere, didn't he? Same thing when he became mayor, from what I've been reading – out of nowhere, next thing you know he's in charge." Eric chuckles lightly. "That's impressive. Is he a good man?"

"He's very popular, yes."

"That isn't what I asked, Sheriff – is he doing a good job? I want to know what kind of governor we're about to get ourselves."

"He's done a great job around here," Larry says. "I've enjoyed working with him very much."

"I'm very much glad to hear that. Okay, Sheriff, this time I mean it, you have a good day." The line goes dead.

Larry stares at the phone. He feels cold all over.

And now he's asking himself, not for the first time, *Who the fuck is this guy? Who the fuck is Tom Rollins?*

33

Tom hears a car.

He stops walking, listens. Looks around. It's midday. The sun is at its highest point. He sees heat rising from the sand. Tom isn't near any road. The car must be travelling over the desert. It sounds like it's coming from behind him. He turns. Sees the sand it's kicking up in its wake. He can't see the car, but guesses it must be the sheriff's department, looking for him.

There is a grouping of cacti and boulders to his left. He goes behind it, ducks, peers over the top until the vehicle comes into view. It's a cruiser. He was right. They're going slow, looking for him. He can see them inside, their heads on a swivel. He ducks down again, out of sight, but he knows they're going to check behind this rock. They're going to check behind everything a person could use as a hiding place.

Tom pulls the gun he took from Lloyd and David, holds it in front of himself, weighs up his options as the cruiser draws nearer. He can't guarantee they're on the meth payroll. Can't guarantee they aren't just good cops, like Daniel, trying to do their jobs, looking for the man who has killed two of their friends.

Tom knows how this goes. They're looking for a cop killer. They're going to shoot on sight. They're not going to ask him any questions. He won't get a chance to talk.

Tom stays low, listens. Tries to formulate a plan, but he's hot and thirsty and tired, and he can't think straight. He bites the inside of his cheek, hoping the pain will sharpen his focus. It helps, a little. He spits blood into the sand. Uses the T-shirt wrapped round his head to wipe the sweat from his face.

The car gets closer. He can hear its tires skidding in the sand. They're nearly on top of him.

Tom stands, aims the gun, hits the windshield in the middle, between the two of them. It cracks, spider-webs, blinds them. He sees them both panic. The cruiser skids. He aims again, takes out the tire on the driver's side. It lurches to the left, comes to a hard stop.

Tom approaches, gun raised. "Don't move," he says, keeping a safe distance from the driver's open window. "Throw out your guns."

The driver is dazed, has a cut across his forehead, blood running down into his eyes and face. Must have hit it on the steering wheel as they were brought to a stop.

The passenger door opens, the other deputy gets out. He falls to the ground, dazed. Tom reaches into the car, grabs the driver by his shirt. Undoes his safety belt, pulls him out.

Still no way to tell if these men are with the sheriff. If they're on the meth payroll. If they're not, he won't kill them. He'll subdue them. Incapacitate them both, then either leave them in the shade, or tie them up and put them in the trunk of the cruiser, which he's planning on taking so long as it has a spare tire and he's able to change it for the shot-out one on the driver's side.

The passenger is on his feet at the other side of the car, gun raised, resting on the roof. Tom hoists the driver to his feet, uses him as a shield, same as he did to David. The other deputy has more sense than Lloyd did. He sees what Tom has done, does not shoot, though he keeps his gun up.

"Drop it," Tom says.

"Fuck you," he says. "You first."

Tom presses his gun to the temple of the deputy he's holding. "Drop it *now*," he says. "I don't need him breathing for him to be a shield."

The other deputy scrapes his teeth along his bottom lip, deciding what to do. Tom realizes he recognizes him. He was one of the deputies who turned up with the sheriff after the shoot-out with the Forever Road Dogs. Tom still can't guarantee this means he's on the payroll.

"Drop the gun," Tom says. "I don't wanna have to keep repeating myself."

The deputy's arms shake. He roars in frustration, throws down his gun. Holds up his arms in surrender.

"I know you," Tom says.

"You don't fuckin' know me, asshole."

"I know your face. I've seen you before."

The deputy nods. "After you wasted the bikers."

"What's your name?"

The deputy hesitates, then says, "Shaun."

"Uh-huh. What's the sheriff told you about me, Shaun?"

"That you're a cop-killing piece of shit."

"That all he had to say?"

Shaun's eyes flicker to the deputy Tom holds. "Like what?" he says.

"Shaun, I ain't gonna keep dancing round here. You work for the sheriff, or do you work for the sheriff and the McQuades?"

Shaun's face doesn't change, but he doesn't respond, either.

"Sounds like I got my answer," Tom says. "The sheriff tell you to kill me on sight, that what he said? Or does he want you to bring me in?"

Shaun's eyes flicker to the other deputy held up by Tom's arm, again. His eyes narrow as they turn back to Tom. "He said to waste you, you dumb piece of shit." Shaun dives for his gun then. Before Tom can do anything, the deputy he's holding drives an elbow back into his chest, catches him by surprise. Tom thinks back to when Lloyd tried to get the drop on him, wonders if the Cullingworth County Sheriff's Department takes acting lessons to get so good at playing possum, or if it just comes naturally. He blasts the escaping deputy twice in the back before he can get more than three paces, then rolls sideways, comes up on his knees, aiming. Shaun has reached his gun, is on his side, is pointing it back at the space Tom previously occupied. Before he can turn, Tom shoots him in the gut.

Shaun cries out, drops his gun. Tom goes to him, picks the gun up, throws it to one side. Shaun writhes on the ground, both hands pressed to his stomach. Blood spills out between his fingers, soaks into his uniform.

Tom goes to the other deputy, checks him. He's dead. He returns to Shaun. Shaun is screaming. *"Fuck!"* Tears stream from his eyes, snot runs from his nose. Spit hangs from his bottom lip.

"Looks painful," Tom says.

"Course it's fuckin' painful!"

"One of the worst places to get shot," Tom says.

"You know why? First off, as you can well tell, it's damn painful. Secondly, all that shit you got swimming round in your intestines, it's gonna get into your blood and start swimming round in *there*. It's gonna poison you slowly, and you're gonna die slowly, right here, under this hot sun."

Shaun looks up at him, slack-jawed, horrified.

"It's a nasty way to die. That's what I'd do to my worst enemy. I'd gut shoot him, leave him somewhere nice and secluded, and watch him die slow, screaming, begging for mercy, crying for his mama. You, though, you ain't my worst enemy."

Tom crouches down, gets to eye level with Shaun. "So all this blood poisoning I'm talking about, that's what happens if I don't take you to a hospital."

"Please," Shaun says, "*please –*"

"You one of the sheriff's special boys?"

Shaun nods.

Tom jerks his head back toward the dead deputy. "Was he?"

Shaun nods again, too pained to speak.

"Then I suppose that's one body off my conscience. Where's Daniel?"

Shaun shakes his head, eyes closed tight, in agony. He gulps air like a fish out of water. "*Please…*" He manages to say again, his voice barely above a whisper.

"Where is Daniel?"

"I don't know," Shaun says. "Sheriff…took him… somewhere… I don't…know…"

"You sure you don't know?"

"I p-promise…"

Tom watches him until he opens his eyes, looks back. Tom sees the pain and the fear in them. "I believe you," Tom says, then puts a bullet through his face.

He goes to the back of the cruiser then, searches for

the spare tire. Finds it. He swaps it for the one at the front, then gets inside. The keys are still in the ignition, but the car has stalled. He turns the key, hoping the engine starts, knowing he should have checked this first before he went through the hassle of changing the wheel. He was too hopeful, too desperate to have a car to travel in, to get out of the desert.

The car starts. Tom cranks the AC. It blows cool on his hot, sweating skin. He closes the driver's door and notices a bottle of water in its pocket. He pours it all down his throat without stopping for air. It's warm, but he doesn't care. Checks the rest of the car, finds another bottle in the passenger door. Drinks it down, takes his time with this one. Feels a little better when it's gone, though his thirst is not entirely slaked.

He takes the T-shirt from his head, drops it into the passenger footwell, then turns the car around, peering between the cracks in the windshield so he can see where he's going. He sticks to the desert, stays away from the road. There'll be more cruisers out there looking for him. One with a shattered windshield is going to draw a lot of unwanted attention.

34

A nna is in the kitchen, eating cereal, when Reggie comes inside. He doesn't bother to knock, just throws the door open and strides in. "Uh, good morning," Anna says. She's wearing only the oversized shirt she sleeps in, pulls it down to cover her bare legs.

Reggie ignores her, continues on straight to the front room, where Earl and Dean are smoking weed and playing video games. "The fuck are the two of you doin'?" he says, looking around, unimpressed.

"What's it look like?" Earl says.

"Two of you just woke up?"

"Naw, we've been up a while."

Anna is on the side of the kitchen table facing the door through into the sitting room. She can see what's happening without having to turn her head. She starts watching as Reggie turns to Dean. "You ever go home?"

"Uh –" Before Dean has to formulate a coherent response, Earl answers for him.

"Dean lives here, with me and Anna," he says. "I told you that already, long time ago."

"Uh-huh." Reggie turns back to Earl. "He pay rent?"

"*Yes*," Earl says.

Anna knows this is a lie. Dean doesn't pay any rent, same way she doesn't.

Reggie looks at them both a moment longer, Earl sitting defiant with the joint hanging from the corner of his mouth, Dean avoiding his gaze, looking at the floor, feeling awkward. "Both of you, up," he says. "Outside. We need to have a word."

"So say it here," Earl says.

Reggie turns, looks back at Anna, at her watching them all while she lifts another spoonful of cereal and milk to her mouth. "Outside," he repeats, then leaves the house. He glances down at Anna as he goes, curls his lip, but says nothing further. Anna doesn't mind. She can deal with his dirty looks, though they sometimes make her run cold, shrivel up inside. It's when he decides he has something to say to her she doesn't like. Reggie is terrifying. She can understand why her father never liked him.

Earl and Dean follow him out, though they drag their feet and take their time. "Stay there," Earl says, as if she were planning on joining them.

"Okay," Anna says.

Earl closes the door after himself. Another meeting Anna is to be left out of. She leans back in her chair, peers out the window through the slats in the blinds. None of them are looking her way. Reggie already looks worked up, red in the face. His voice is muffled through the glass, but she manages to pick up on a few things he says.

" – *your fault! You just left it alone – have happened!*"

He slaps Earl in the back of the head, and Anna winces. It's not the first time she's seen him do this, doubts it will be the last, but it makes her flinch every time. She doesn't know how Earl is able to stand there and take it, how those blows don't make his ears ring, knock him to the ground. He's received them all his life, though. Always done something, whether little or small, to piss his father off. Probably numb to these blows by now.

Reggie continues to shout. It sounds like he's telling Earl off for something, and admonishing Dean for not stopping Earl from doing that something, but his volume is just a little lower now, and she can't make out any of the words he says.

She glances up at the main house, something there catching her attention out of the corner of her eye, and she sees Chris on the porch. He's looking right back at her.

Anna gets a shock, falls away from the window; her chair falls back on four legs. She returns to her cereal, acting casual.

A moment later, Earl and Dean return indoors. Reggie is not with them. She's glad. Earl slams the door shut after himself.

"What's wrong?" Anna says.

"Nothing," Earl says, his face red.

Dean continues back through to the front room, doesn't say a word.

"You sure?" Anna says.

"I said nothing!" Earl says. "Jesus Christ, mind your fuckin' business, will ya?"

Anna clams up.

"Just finish your cereal and go smoke another bowl, why don't ya? *Fuck...*" Earl storms away, shaking his head, following Dean back through to their video game.

There isn't much left of her cereal, but Anna isn't hungry anymore. She leaves the kitchen, goes to the bedroom. She slams the door shut before she can stop herself, then freezes in place and braces herself, worried Earl will come through after her, demanding to know what she thinks she's doing. He doesn't, though. More worked up about whatever it is his father has said to him.

She takes a seat on the edge of the bed, thinks about maybe just doing what he told her to and getting high. That's all they think of her, everyone on this fucking ranch – just a dirty fucking junkie. Not good for anything, apart from the times Earl feels like throwing a fuck into her, except these days when he's home, he seems more interested in playing video games with Dean and doing nothing else.

Once upon a time he made her feel special. Now he makes her feel like dirt.

She doesn't understand. He has her, but now it's like he doesn't want her. Acts like he doesn't care if she stays or goes, except he won't let her leave.

It's the classic case, she figures, of wanting what you don't and can't have, until you get it. Then you don't want it anymore.

Of course, Anna knows she hasn't exactly done anything to make him still want her. She gets high to tolerate being near him, living with him. She gets high in the hope he'll finally have enough and just let her go, but now she doesn't want to go, because this is where she gets her meth free of charge. Well, not *totally* free, but close enough. He's trapped her in a Catch-22.

Now she's tired. Tired of always being left out of the loop, of being looked down on, as being viewed as nothing more than Earl's junkie girlfriend. His property. Like some kind of trophy – the daughter of Crispin Blevins, great enemy of the McQuades.

Anna doesn't get high. She gets dressed instead. She goes through to the bathroom and washes her face.

Rubs life back into her cheeks. Ignores the cravings that threaten to possess her completely, because she has a point to prove.

"I'm gonna go see Sally," she says, in the sitting room.

"No you ain't," Earl says.

Anna blinks. "I – I am."

Earl pauses his game with a sigh. "No, you *ain't*. Dean can't take you."

"I don't need Dean to take me. I can go myself. I just need a car to borrow."

"There ain't no spare cars."

"Well, I can get a ride from one of the guys. They'll probably be heading that way. They usually are."

"Not today. No one's going that way today." Earl stares at her levelly.

Anna flounders. "Well, I –"

"You're not going anywhere, so you may as well just make yourself comfortable."

"Why the hell not?"

"Because we're too busy. There's too much going on at the minute."

"Y'all don't look very busy."

Earl jumps to his feet. "Damn it, Anna, don't fucking question me!"

Anna takes a step back, feels her heart rate quicken.

"If I say we're too busy, then we're too fuckin' busy! If I say you can't go and visit your bitch sister, then you can't go and visit your fuckin' bitch sister! Is that clear? Is that getting through to that fuckin' junkie brain of yours?"

Anna's eyes burn. She blinks, over and over, won't cry.

Earl sneers. She sees how pathetic she is in his eyes. "Just go back to the fuckin' room already," he says. Then he turns around, sits back down, and resumes his game with Dean.

Dean doesn't turn around. Just keeps his eyes on the screen, makes like everything going on right here in the room with him isn't.

Anna returns to the bedroom, flees from Earl's fury and Dean's cowardice. She closes the door, slams it again, doesn't care this time. She presses her back against the wood and holds her breath and closes her eyes.

She won't cry.

Fuck him.

She won't cry.

35

S ally tries to get in touch with Daniel, leaves him a voice message. "Give me a call when you get this. I'm starting to get worried about you."

She sits at her desk and tries not to keep glancing at her phone, but she can't help herself. Finds she keeps picking it up, staring at the blank screen, willing it to start ringing, or to receive some kind of message in response. How sick can he really be that he can't even look at his phone and respond to her, let her know how he's doing?

She has a bad feeling. Butterflies. A sense that things aren't quite as they seem.

And then Tom appears in the lobby, seemingly out of nowhere. Sally jumps in her seat. He hasn't come through the front door. He's come from the stairwell. "Jesus Christ!" she says, one hand on her chest. "Where'd you come from?"

"Back door," Tom says, his voice a croak.

Sally's eyes widen as she gets a good look at him. He looks like hell. His skin is dried out and burnt red from the sun. His lips are chapped, cracking. There are some cuts and bruises on his face, almost disguised by the sunburn. "What the hell's happened to you?" she says. "You look like shit."

"That's how I feel. You got water?"

"Sure, sure, just wait here." Sally walks past him into the stairwell, to her room. Fills him a glass of water from the sink. As she returns it to him, she finds he has stepped into her home, closed the door after himself. "Uh, I don't mean to be rude, Tom, but I'd rather you had this outside."

Tom holds his hand out for the glass until she hands it over. He gulps it all down. Some of it spills out of his mouth, down his chin, cuts streaks through the dirt on his face. He finishes, gasps, hands the glass back. "Need to keep out of view of the road," he says. "Can't be seen."

"By who?"

"The McQuade boys or the sheriff's department, maybe a few others I'm unaware of right now."

Sally cocks her head. "What do you mean? What's happened?"

Tom looks at her. He tells her everything, holding her gaze all the while. Sally listens, feels her eyes get wider, her jaw hang loose. When he finally finishes, she has to take a moment to comprehend everything he has told her.

All she's able to say is, "My father never liked the McQuades. He always hated Reggie, knew him since they were both young. Said he was a bully until my dad stepped up to him and punched him in the mouth, put him down on his ass in front of all his friends. Said Reggie despised him ever since that incident, but the feeling was mutual."

"Well, your father sounds like he was a good judge of character."

"And Daniel," she says, managing to finally get her wits back about her. "He's not involved in this?"

"Oh, he's definitely involved, but not in the way you mean. He's got himself wrapped up in it all, he's probably in danger right now – unless they've already killed him – but no, he's not one of the sheriff's chosen boys."

Sally swallows. She clears her throat to speak. "If they haven't killed him, do you know where they might be keeping him?"

"Guy I asked didn't know," Tom says. "But it's gotta be a slim chance that they're keeping him alive."

The thought that Daniel might be dead already gives Sally a stabbing pain in her chest, makes her breath catch. Makes her regret all the times she chose the hotel over spending time with him. She grits her teeth. Feeling sorry for herself, for how she treated him, won't fix anything. "The sheriff came by looking for you," she says.

"Don't surprise me," Tom says.

"I told him you hadn't been back since they'd arrested you for the bar fight."

Tom raises an eyebrow. "Why'd you lie?"

"Because they shouldn't have arrested you in the first place. And because Earl McQuade is an asshole, and he shouldn't have taken your car, and I was just hopeful you'd beat his sorry ass down and taken your car back and that's what the sheriff was coming round to see you about."

"So you didn't take him up to my room?"

"No, that's still yours."

Tom nods. "I need you to do me a favor. Firstly, I need to use your shower. They might have eyes on my room. I can't go back to it. Secondly, I need you to go up and get my bag, bring it back down here. It's got clothes in it, and…"

He trails off, and Sally assumes he's referring to his weapons. "I know what's in the bag," she says. "I've seen it. The shower's through there." She points. "I'll be right back."

Tom gives her a grateful look, then turns and heads through to the bathroom. She notices he's limping as he goes, and also that he looks around the room, taking in its dishevelled state. The mix of clean and dirty clothes piled on the sofa, hanging over the arm of a chair. The ironing board set up in front of the window. A couple of takeaway pizza boxes piled up next to the bin, patiently waiting to be taken out on a collection day, now weeks gone by since they first took up residency.

"If I knew I was gonna have a visitor," she says, "I still wouldn't have cleaned up. I'm a busy woman, and I've got more important things to do."

Tom laughs, then enters the bathroom and closes the door after himself.

Sally hears the water begin to run, then leaves him to it. Exits her room, checks the lobby. No one there, no one waiting. She goes to the open doorway, looks out onto the street. She's casual about it. Just a curious glance up and down the road. It's quiet. No cop cars. None of the McQuade dealers, that she can see at least. Darby is sitting in his usual spot on the bench out front of the hotel, sucking on a cigarette. He sees her; he's smiling at her. She calls him over.

"What's up?" he says. Sally notices he's missing another tooth, one of his canines.

"I need you to watch the hotel for a while," she says.

"Sure," Darby says, quickly finishing his cigarette and stubbing the butt out under his sneaker.

"I'll knock some money off your bill."

"Appreciate that. But y'know, Sally, one day I'm gonna come good, land myself in a big old pile of money, and first thing I'll do is pay off my tab." He winks at her.

"I long for that day," she says. "I'm counting on it for my retirement." She turns and heads to the stairwell.

"You going out?" Darby says, following her in, taking up her usual position behind the counter.

"Not yet," she says, pausing in the stairwell. "I've just gotta deal with some personal stuff." She heads up the stairs, to Tom's room. She makes sure to stay away from his window, in case, as he suspects, it is being watched. Ducking low, she grabs his bag, then goes back down. By the time she makes it back to her own room, the shower has finished running. Tom is still in the bathroom. She knocks on the door.

"I've got your bag," she says.

Tom opens the door a crack, reaches out with an arm dripping water. "Thanks," he says, pulls the bag into the bathroom, closes the door again.

Sally stands by the door a moment, waiting, then moves away, gives him some privacy. She moves some clothes off her sofa, pushes them to one side, then takes a seat. Tom doesn't take much longer. He steps out from the bathroom, in fresh clothes, his hair slicked back and his beard still dripping, not looking as bad as he did before.

"The shower's done you a world of good," she says.

"Glad to hear it," Tom says. He has his bag in one hand, sets it down on the chair opposite her. He opens it, pulls out his Beretta, checks it's loaded, then tucks it into the waistband of his jeans at the back, clips the KA-BAR's holster to his belt.

"We need to get help," Sally says.

"From who?" Tom says. "Who can we trust?"

"I've been thinking about that."

Tom zips up his bag, leaves it on the chair. He straightens up. "And what conclusion you come to?"

"That we go through to Kirkwood, to the *Culling-worth County Times*. You tell them everything you've told me. They can get the word out, they'll have contacts. They can tell the mayor – he'll likely have contacts too. He's about to become the governor of Texas. He ain't gonna let this stand."

Tom considers this.

"Or we can call the FBI," Sally says. "A larger organization, they can come in and –" Sally stops talking when she realizes Tom is shaking his head.

"We're not calling the FBI," he says. He delivers the statement simply, blankly, with no change to his expression.

"Why not?"

"We just ain't."

Sally frowns. "You had some run-ins with them you care to share with me, let me know exactly why you don't wanna call them? They could be the answer to all our problems right now."

Tom doesn't explain, just repeats, "We're not calling the FBI."

Sally is surprised by his steadfast refusal to contact the feds, figures there must be more to this story than he wants to share. She doesn't push it. She sees a lot of herself in Tom, and she understands that if he doesn't want to talk about something, then he just won't.

"Then we go to the newspaper," she says. "That's our only option. But I can't guarantee they're not just going to call the FBI soon as you finish telling your story."

"Fine," Tom says. "They can tell it, but I'm not. Once they're on their way, I'll go get my things from Earl, and then I'll be gone."

"You know where the ranch is now?"

"No, but I reckon by now, you might be willing to tell me where it is."

"Fine. Now let's get moving. If Daniel's still alive, we're wasting his time standing round here and talking about how we're gonna help him."

Tom nods, and Sally gets to her feet, grabs her car keys. They leave the hotel by the back door, same way Tom came in. Sally is nonplussed to see that he has broken the lock.

"I'll have to owe you a new one," he says.

They go to her car, and Sally gets in the driver's seat. Tom gets in the back, ducks low. "Should be a jacket back there," Sally says. "Pull it over yourself. It'll be hot, but it's better than getting seen."

Tom finds the jacket, pulls it over himself without complaint. Sally pulls out of the parking lot, checks the road, then points her car toward Kirkwood.

36

The car slows as they reach Kirkwood. Tom peers out the window, keeping the jacket over his head. Sees a lot of people walking round, some of them carrying banners. "What's going on?" he says.

"Shit, I forgot," Sally says. "The election is tonight. The mayor's probably having a rally in the town square right now. We ain't gonna get the car through all these people."

Tom ducks back down. "He gonna win?"

"It's looking that way," Sally says. Tom notes the bitterness in her tone as she says this.

"Not a fan?"

"He's running for governor on the back of how pretty Cullingworth County looks, how low the crime rate is under his leadership, but he ain't gonna mention Brenton, not at all. Everyone turns a blind eye to Brenton. It's the forgotten town of Cullingworth County, left to rot."

"Sounds like you got a reason to be resentful."

"I sure feel like I do. So long as his numbers are

good, he's just as happy as everyone else to forget about us."

The car has almost stopped moving. They're inching along. Tom can hear people passing close by, the sounds of their voices, snippets of their conversations. "There somewhere to park?"

"It's round this corner," Sally says. "I just gotta reach it first."

She crawls forward until finally Tom feels the front of the car begin to swing round. Off the main stretch, they're finally able to speed up.

"Any spaces?" Tom says.

"There's a few," Sally says. "It's busy out there, but I reckon most people at the rally already live here in Kirk-wood. They've probably come here on foot."

She slides into a space, tells him to stay low while she gets out of the car, looks around, checks to make sure there's no one to see him emerge from the backseat, hidden under a jacket. There's not, and she opens the door.

Tom steps out, pops his spine. He looks around. "Which way?" He's only been in Kirkwood once before, and he was so desperate to leave, he didn't bother taking a good look at the place.

"Just follow me," Sally says. "We're gonna have to go through the crowd. The newspaper's building is on the other side of it, so stick close."

"Like glue," Tom says.

He stays by Sally's side as she leads him from the back of the main street, where the parking is, to the front, where all the people are. He can see the stage built up in the town square, where everyone is heading, a good number of them already gathered around it. The stage is empty. The people hold up banners of support, or they wave small American flags on sticks.

"That one," Sally says, pointing at the building on the other side of the throng.

They pass by the sheriff's station, and Tom keeps his head down. They reach the back of the crowd, start making their way through. They have to shoulder a number of people out of their way.

Then the crowd comes alive. They start cheering, clapping, waving their arms. A small group starts chanting, "USA! USA!"

Tom looks. The mayor has taken to the stage. There is a large screen behind his podium, surrounded by red, white, and blue bunting. The mayor appears on the screen, waving at the people, giving them all two thumbs up.

Tom stops. Watches. Someone on the stage has caught his eye.

Sally realizes he's not following. She stops and fights her way back through to him. Has to put her mouth close to his ear and shout to be heard. "What're you doing?"

Tom holds up a hand. "Just wait," he says.

The mayor hasn't said a single word into the microphones yet. While the people continue to chant and cheer, he confers with a man to his side. A young man, with a slim build. He wears a suit. He whispers into the mayor's ear. This is the man who has caught Tom's eye, though the last time he saw him was in darkness, his face mostly concealed by shadow. Tom turns to Sally, points at the man. "Who is that?"

Sally strains her eyes to look. "I dunno," she says. "Why? What does it matter?"

Tom turns to a lady beside him, waving a flag on a stick in each hand. He gets her attention, points at the man again, repeats his question. She answers, but Tom can't hear what she says. She has to repeat herself.

"That's Brian Roberts!" she says. "He's the mayor's aide!"

Brian Roberts was at the meth exchange. He was with the McQuades and the Forever Road Dogs.

Then the mayor steps up to the microphone. He starts talking, but Tom doesn't hear a word he says. His face is enlarged on the screen behind him. Tom gets a good look at him finally. Familiar from all the posters he has seen of him in both Brenton and Kirkwood.

But a different kind of familiarity, too.

A familial resemblance.

Tom sees a flash of Brad Smithson, up close, his hand clutching at Tom's face. Disguised with a beard and longer hair and more flesh on his bones. But it's there, in the eyes, the nose, the mouth. In the smile.

The election posters have the mayor's name on them, but Tom did not commit it to memory. It meant nothing to him. He turns to Sally. "What's the mayor's name?"

"What's the matter with you?" she says. "We're not here to listen to his speech. We need to keep moving! We're nowhere near the newspaper yet!"

"What's his name?"

"Lyle."

"His full name!"

"Smithson, Lyle Smithson."

Tom looks back at the screen. Smithson could be a common name, just like Smith. That's why Tom uses it. People hear it, they don't bat an eye. Smiths are everywhere.

Tom thinks. The connection that the deputy mentioned. The man who put the McQuades and the sheriff in touch with the Forever Road Dogs. With Brad Smithson, Sergeant At Arms. It was the mayor.

And now he stands, there on the stage, soon to be the

governor of Texas, wearing his sociopathic politician smile, knowing that a relative of his – brother? Cousin? Uncle? – has been killed, smiling and speaking like he doesn't have a care in the world beyond today, tonight, what comes next for his political career.

Tom thinks of the powers the governorship will grant him. The ability to spread the McQuades' meth with greater ease, to open up the state to them completely, without fear of the Forever Road Dogs being stopped on the road. The potential to start up more labs in places where no one ever goes, because the governor says no one can go there anymore.

Tom grabs Sally by the arm, pulls her out of the crowd back the way they came. "What're you doing?"

Tom doesn't answer until they're out of the crowd, then he tells her what he now knows, still holding her arm, still dragging her back to her car.

Sally pulls out of his grip. "So what? We still go to the newspaper. We tell them *this* now, too."

"No," Tom says. "Do you think in his position of power, with more power to come, that he doesn't already have someone working in the paper? Someone who can quash any story about him or what's really going on here?"

Sally is silent. She understands.

"They can't help us," Tom says. "No one can. We're on our own."

37

L arry sits outside the mayor's office with his hat on his knee, waiting for the secretary to tell him he can go through. The office is filled with newscasters and reporters, asking questions, seeking sound bites. The mayor, the most likely future governor, is shaking hands, all smiles. The rally was a success.

Larry folds his arms, stares straight ahead. Feels like he might have a long wait ahead of him. He's not looking forward to sharing the news of recent happenings and discoveries with Lyle, especially not when it's going to bring him down from the high he is surely riding.

People run up and down the hallway. It's a busy day. Larry gets the secretary's attention. "You told him I was here, darlin', didn't you?"

The secretary is a young woman, more than likely hired to give Lyle something to look at during his long days in office. Employed more for her appearance than her brains. She looks at Larry with her big doe eyes and nods earnestly. "Sure did, Sheriff Collins."

"Think you could tell him again?" Larry isn't

looking forward to the meeting, but he'd rather get it over and done with.

"Lot of people in there with him, Sheriff," the secretary says. "He ain't gonna be happy if I keep buzzing through."

"I'll take the heat on that, darlin'. You just go right on ahead and give him another buzz for me."

She looks nervous, but she does as he says. When she looks back over to tell him it's done, Larry winks at her, and she giggles.

A couple of minutes later, the door to the mayor's office opens. A rush of sound escapes from the gaggle of people packed inside. Brian Roberts slips out. He adjusts his suit, straightens his tie, nods at another employee passing by in the hall. His eyes settle on Larry, and he walks over, motioning for the sheriff to follow. Larry gets to his feet, follows him into his office.

"Lyle is very busy right now," Brian says, taking a seat behind his desk. "You can see that for yourself. What're you doing down here trying to hassle him?"

"I got news."

"You really think he's going to want to see you right now? He's still pissed about his cousin."

"Well, it ties into that."

Brian sits back in his chair, runs his hands back over his face, through his hair. He leans forward again, hands clasped on his desk. "Dare I ask?"

"The guy's still alive."

Brian shrugs. "So deal with him. You've already been told to. Under ordinary circumstances, Lyle would've come and killed him with his own two hands for what he did to Brad – you know the two of them were more like brothers than cousins, right?"

"I've heard."

"Yeah, well, you're gonna hear it again, because it's

all I've fucking heard since he got killed. He hides it well, but Lyle is torn up about it. If it weren't for his cousin, he wouldn't be where he is now."

"Correction," Larry says, "if it weren't for me and Reggie, he wouldn't be where he is. We got him into this office, and it's off of our backs and all our hard work he's gonna be the governor."

"I'm sure he'd argue that point."

"I'm happy to argue it 'til the cows come home if the little prick's forgotten who put him where he is."

Brian holds up his hands, closes his eyes. "Have we gotten off track? I feel like we're off track. Where were we? Oh, yes – Lyle himself would have liked nothing more than to come out to the desert with your boys and kill Smith himself *if* these were ordinary circumstances. But they're not ordinary circumstances. You don't have to keep him alive just for Lyle's sake. He isn't gonna thank you for the gift wrapping. Are you using Smith to try to angle your way back into his good graces?"

Larry clenches his jaw. He hates all these politician types. Hates how he has to rely on them, how they're a necessary evil. "I didn't kill his fuckin' cousin. I wasn't anywhere near that. So I don't care if I'm in his good graces or not."

"You say that now, Larry, but we both know it isn't true. The last thing you want is to be *out* of his good graces, so don't go saying things now that you're gonna regret later."

"I don't regret a fuckin' thing. You need to start listening to me, you little punk – we ain't keeping the guy as a present. He's *escaped*."

Brian's face falls. He doesn't look as smug as he did a few moments ago. He blinks. "So you haven't killed him?"

"Yeah, sure, a fuckin' walking corpse has dug

himself up and gone on the run. What kinda stupid fuckin' question is that?"

Brian shakes his head, like he realizes what he just said. "How did this happen?"

"How should I know? I wasn't there. All I know is he killed the two were supposed to do for him, and he's killed another two out in the desert and taken their car. He could be anywhere right now."

Brian rests his face in his hands, elbows on the desk. He takes deep breaths. "This is the worst fucking time," he says. "I should've just let you talk to Lyle. I don't deserve to be the one has to tell him this." He drops his hands, lets them hang. "I don't suppose it's too much to hope that he's just going to go away? That none of this really concerns him, and he'll be on his way?"

Larry thinks about the car stolen by Earl. "I'm not so sure about that. I think this has gotten personal for him. And there's another thing. His name ain't Smith. It's Rollins."

Brian looks at him. "What?"

"Tom Rollins. That's his name."

"Should that mean anything to me?"

"Could do. You remember that attempted terrorist attack in Dallas couple of months back? He was the one stopped it."

"You're shitting me, right?"

"I wish I were."

Brian's eyes flit left to right. "So who exactly is this Rollins guy?"

"Ex-army, ex-CIA – he's gonna be a bigger handful than we originally thought. Not to mention the fact he's wanted by the US government, so if it gets out that he's here, that's gonna bring us a whole lot more unwanted attention." Larry doesn't mention the call from the FBI. There's already enough going on; he doesn't need to raise any more issues, not right now. That problem can wait. If they're lucky, it won't ever become anything serious.

Brian collapses back in his chair, the magnitude of what Larry is telling him sinking in. "I need a fucking drink…" He reaches into the lower drawer of his desk, pulls out a bottle of bourbon, swigs it straight from the neck. His lips pull back from his teeth, and he gasps. He puts the bottle back, sits up straight. "We need to think," he says.

"I know that," Larry says. "The hell you think I've been doing all this time, sitting with my thumb up my ass?"

"I don't need to know how you spend your private time."

"I ain't interested in your jokes – not right now, not ever."

"Well, humor is how I process things."

"I don't give a shit how you process. I wanna –"

Brian interrupts him. "What about the deputy you've got? The one with Smith – with *Rollins* at the shoot-out?"

"Daniel? What about him?"

Brian's eyes have narrowed. He looks off into space, following a thread only he can see. "You said he was looking into what happened to Deputy Aynsley, didn't you? You were already keeping an eye on him when the shoot-out happened – am I thinking about the right guy?"

"That's him."

"You ever had any trouble like that with him before? Looking into things he shouldn't be, sticking his nose where it doesn't belong?"

"I know he ain't a big fan of the McQuades, but he never stepped out of line, so far as I'm aware."

"He definitely didn't know what Aynsley knew? The connection between Lyle and the Forever Road Dogs?"

"If he did before now, he's done a damn good job of hiding it."

"Can you be sure of that, though? He never talked to the reporter?" Brian starts clicking his fingers. "Ike, that was his name. He never spoke with Ike?"

"I already told you – I don't think so. My answer ain't gonna change just because you keep asking the same question a different way."

Brian finally turns away from the invisible thread, back to the sheriff. "Did he know Rollins before all of this?"

"I don't think so."

"But you aren't *sure*."

"I ain't sure about any of this. Frankly, I think if Daniel has suddenly sprouted some balls, it's a combination of his buddy Frank going missing, and going steady with that Blevins girl. She probably got inside his head."

"What Blevins girl? I thought she was with Earl? Jesus Christ, I can't keep up with this all…"

"The other one. Her sister. The one that's as big a bitch as her father was a bastard. He was always an uptight, overly moral asshole, too."

"I don't know who any of these fucking people are, Larry," Brian says. "And to be honest, I don't really care. What I *do* care about is trying to figure out how we can snuff this Rollins asshole out, once and for all. If we can use the deputy against him, then we've gotta do it."

"I already said I don't think they knew each other."

"He's already helped him at the shoot-out. And you said he was in the army, right? The way I hear it, a bond develops between two guys when they're under fire like that. You think that kind of bond might be enough to draw Rollins out if he thinks his new buddy is in danger?"

"It might work."

Brian looks at his watch. "In a few short hours, Lyle Smithson is going to be the new governor of Texas. He takes that office, and you know what that means? You can run as much meth as you like. And beyond that? Beyond that come bigger things. Things you don't have to do under cover of dark, sneaking around the state down back roads no one ever uses. The fracking contracts. Don't you want some of that fracking money?"

"It's those fracking contracts that got Ike Thoreau looking into Lyle in the first place, got him making connections."

"And now he's dead, so we ain't gotta worry about him. Now we only gotta worry about the future – provided you can tidy up the messes here in the present."

"I know what the stakes are, Brian."

"Good, then I shouldn't have to explain them to you like a child, but it feels like you need a reminder. Get this guy before the results come in, Larry. I don't care how you do it, but catch him, kill him, and if it's all taken care of clean enough, then *neither* of us will have to run this fucking mess by Lyle. We can just make like it never happened. Like it was all just smooth sailing. That sound good to you?"

Larry grunts.

"Great, because it sure sounds good to me."

38

D aniel gets visitors. It's Earl and Dean. He hadn't expected anyone else. Maybe Reggie or Chris. It's not a deep pool of people to pick from on the ranch.

They carry a brown, greasy bag. It looks like take-out food. Earl takes a seat on the back of the stolen car. "Feed him," he says to Dean.

"Why've I gotta feed him?" Dean says.

"'Cause I fuckin' said so, that's why."

Dean hesitates.

"What you think he's gonna do – bite your fingers off?" Earl laughs.

"Naw, it ain't that…"

"I don't care what it is – just feed him already. Sooner he's fed, sooner we can get outta here."

Dean still hesitates. "What's it even matter?" he says. "Ain't like he's gonna, y'know…"

Earl raises his eyebrows, waits for him to finish what he was going to say. "What? You too polite to say it just 'cause he's right there? *Not gonna be with us much longer* – that what you were gonna say?"

Dean shifts his weight from foot to foot, scuffs the toe of his sneaker in the dirt. "Pretty much, yeah."

Earl shrugs. "'Cause my dad told us to feed him, that's why. I dunno, maybe they're holding out they won't have to waste old Danny boy here; maybe he'll see sense and come around, join up with us. But I think it's a little too late for that, don't you?"

Dean nods. Daniel notices how Dean avoids looking directly at him.

"Besides, we know Daniel a little better'n that, don't we?"

"He's always been an asshole," Dean says.

"Exactly," Earl says. "And assholes stink. So hurry up and get that burger in his mouth so we can get the fuck out."

Reluctantly, Dean gets down to a knee, opens up the bag, and pulls out a burger. He pulls the gag from Daniel's mouth, snatches his hand back like he really does worry Daniel will try to bite him.

If Daniel thought it would do any good, he would. Instead, he's just grateful for the food. Opens his mouth for Dean to feed him, takes big bites and chews quickly, trying to ignore the pain from his broken back teeth.

Earl studies his nails, picks dirt out from them, flicks it on the floor. "Enjoy it," he says. "Could be your last meal."

Daniel doesn't respond. The burger is dry and tasteless, and he desperately needs a drink to wash it all down, but he keeps eating, because he knows they're not going to bring him anything else.

Earl starts laughing. "Look at you, man," he says. "Sitting there, pathetic. Needing to be fed like a fuckin' baby. Y'know, for a long damn time now you've thought you were somethin' special, thought you were better than the likes of all of us, just because you wear that uniform. But you're nothing. You're just a moron in a uniform. You don't even have a clue what's happening here."

"I got a better idea than you think," Daniel says.

Earl leans forward from the car. "We're gonna be *kings*, Daniel. If you're lucky, you'll be alive long enough to witness the coronation, but I wouldn't bank on it. You're gonna have a visitor later tonight."

Daniel has to clear the bread and meat from his throat before he can say, "Who?"

"Your boss. Ex-boss? The sheriff, anyway. He wants to come by and ask you a few questions."

"About what?"

"Owner of this." Earl pats the top of the car. "Or should that be *ex*-owner? Wants to know everything you know about our friend Tom Rollins."

Daniel frowns. "Who's that? Guy owns that car goes by the name of Smith."

"You really think that's his name? Sheriff found it out. Knew he recognized him from somewhere else."

"What the hell you talkin' about? Knew him from where?"

"Sheriff'll be along later. You can ask him yourself."

"If I don't even know the guy's real name, why's he think I know anything more than the rest of you?"

Earl shrugs. "Just saying, everything seems to have gone wild and turned to shit since he turned up, and you've got yourself caught up in the middle of it, right next to him. Could be you know him better than you want the rest of us to think, that you've known him longer than that, too." Earl shrugs again. "Sheriff's being thorough. Making sure to cover all his bases."

Earl pushes himself off the car, crouches down in front of Daniel now that Dean has finished feeding him.

"How's it feel, Daniel?" he says. "How's it feel to know so many of your buddies are working for *us*?"

Daniel runs his tongue round the inside of his mouth, doesn't answer. Earl is grinning, mocking him, enjoying himself.

"Like I said," Earl says, "you're just a moron in a uniform. And once the sheriff realizes you ain't any use to him, you're gonna be a dead moron. Don't worry, man, we'll be sure to bury you in it." He pats his shoulder.

"I need to piss," Daniel says.

Earl shrugs, shoves the gag back into his mouth. "Guess you'll just have to go in your pants," he says, then he and Dean leave the barn.

39

Anna is in the bedroom when she hears Earl's and Dean's voices outside, passing by. She goes to the window, watches them. They're carrying a bag of food. They go to the barn. Close the door after themselves.

She sits back on the bed, scratches her head, wonders why they're taking food in there. A picnic? Are they going to eat burgers and admire the car? Are they going to eat burgers inside it, make a mess, leave a greasy insult?

She goes back to the window, watches until they come back out. It's a while before they do so. Earl is laughing. Dean looks perturbed. He carries the empty bag of food, crushes it together in his hands, scrunches it up into a ball. They come back toward the house.

Anna sits down, away from the window. Listens, hears them come indoors. They go straight through into the sitting room. She doesn't hear them start up their video game, but she does hear them start to cough, like they're passing a joint back and forth.

Anna waits a few more minutes, then opens the door

as quietly as she's able. She peers out. Neither of them are looking her way. She creeps on bare feet, slips out the front door. Stands on the porch a moment longer to make sure she's not being followed.

Before she goes, she looks around. Checks the main house; checks Chris's house. Remembers how he saw her from the porch the other day, was looking right at her through the window. He's nowhere to be seen. She makes sure to check the windows, too, but there's no sign of him.

She steps down off the porch, takes her time going to the barn so as not to arouse suspicion. She stops by the dog kennels, says hello to Jojo and Georgie. Strokes their noses through the mesh, the sides of their mouths.

"Feel like you two are the only friends I got out here," she says.

The dogs don't answer, just look back at her with deep, soulful eyes.

Subtly, she checks again to make sure no one is watching, then slips down the back of the kennels, makes her way over to the barn.

She's worried about what she will find. The car was one thing – the car was pretty bad – but they're not going to take food to a car, so that can only really mean one thing. She bites her lip as she gets closer. If she finds a person inside, held captive, what's she supposed to do about that? She can't just leave them in there, but at the same time she can't go against Earl, and especially not against Reggie.

She reaches the barn, though does not enter it through the door. She goes down the side, to the cracks in the boards through which she first spotted the car. Looks back to make sure no one is watching her. Reaching the gap, she peers in. The sun is shining, but it's dark inside. She has to blink a few times.

She sees the car. Looks round. Is about to give up, walk away, tell herself she was just overthinking things, they were just eating in the barn for whatever reason – when she sees the outline. It's at the back of the car, sitting at the bottom of one of the barn's support poles. The person's head is hanging, defeated. Then they sit up, shift around like they're trying to get comfortable. The back of their head rests against the pole.

Anna can see it is a man. She presses the side of her face up against the wood, as close as she can get. Makes out the clothes the man is wearing – it's a uniform. A deputy's uniform.

Anna almost gasps. She holds it in. She looks at his face. Stares at it for a long time until it finally comes into focus and she is sure.

It's Daniel.

40

S ally is silent on the drive back to Brenton. Tom gives her time to process. Her eyes are unblinking; the skin around her mouth is pinched.

Tom doesn't bother to duck down in the back this time. He's in the front now, leaning into the passenger door and looking out the window. He probes at the scab under his eye where he had to puncture it to get all the blood out. It's throbbing. He doesn't pick it.

Sally is the first to break the silence. She clears her throat. "I really think we should –"

"We're not calling the FBI," Tom says.

"Are you at least going to tell me why not?"

Tom looks at her.

Sally throws up her hands, then quickly puts them back down on the steering wheel. "So, *what*? You're gonna take all these guys on by yourself?"

"You're welcome to help. You're pretty handy with that rifle of yours."

Sally stares straight ahead, at the road. They're not far from Brenton now. They can see it in the distance. "What's our next move?" she says.

"If Daniel's still alive, he's likely out at the ranch. Even if he's not, they might know where he is."

"And that's where your car likely is, too."

"Exactly. You want Daniel, I want my car – both points converge on the ranch. So that's where we go next."

Tom sees the tendons twitching in Sally's jaw. "My sister's out there," she says. "I don't want to put her in danger like this."

"How long's she been living out at that ranch? Whose side do you think she'll be on if it comes down to it – yours or Earl's?"

"I don't know."

"If you get her out of there, do you think she'll thank you for it?"

"I don't know."

Sally slows the car before they enter Brenton.

"Are we going straight there?" she says.

"You need your rifle."

"I've never fired it at a person before."

"Ever pointed it at one?"

"Yeah."

"More than once?"

"A lot more than once."

"And in that moment were you prepared to pull the trigger?"

"I guess. If it came down to that."

"There's not much distance between intent and doing. Besides, maybe I'll need to use it. And way I figure it, if we're gonna head out to the ranch, we're gonna need for it to get darker first."

"That's still a couple of hours away."

"I know. We'll have to be patient."

Sally pulls around the back of the hotel. Parks. Neither of them get out of the car.

Tom studies her. She looks straight ahead, at the tree where her target is pinned. "You don't have to come," Tom says. "All you need to do is tell me the way."

She sets her face then. Shakes her head. "No," she says. "I'm coming. How else would you get out there? On foot? It'd take you more than a couple of hours."

"You wouldn't loan me your car?"

"Hell no. I heard you 'borrowed' – and I use that term loosely – a car from Lonnie, and he's never seen it since."

"I doubt he ever will."

"So I don't trust you to take care of mine."

"Fair enough."

They get out of the car, take the broken back door into the hotel. From there, they can see Darby at the front, in the open doorway, smoking a cigarette and looking up and down the road. Sally goes to him. "You okay, Darby? How's it been?"

He gives a start, not expecting them to come from behind him. He flicks his cigarette and turns. He looks concerned. "Your sister called, Sally," he says.

"She did? What'd she want?"

"She wouldn't say. I offered to take a message, but she said she'd call back in an hour." He checks his watch. From where he leans in the doorway, Tom can see that its face is shattered. "That was more than an hour ago now. Oh! She said you shouldn't call her back."

"What's that mean?" Tom says.

"It means she doesn't want me to call her when she's in the middle of dinner with Earl," Sally says. "Means she's got something to say to me that she doesn't want him to hear about." She turns back to Darby. "How'd she sound?"

Darby shrugs.

"Well, was she worried, concerned, excited – what?"

"I don't know," Darby says. "She just sounded... well, like she was whispering. But other than that, she sounded normal."

Tom watches Sally. She goes behind her desk, chews her bottom lip. "Thanks, Darby," she says. "Stay close, though, will you? I'll need to go out again later."

"Sure. Uh..."

She looks at him, waiting.

"You think, maybe, instead of taking money off my bill, you could...uh...maybe see your way to, uh... paying me? In cash? I only need a little."

Sally doesn't lower her gaze. Her face doesn't change. She stares at Darby until he starts to shift uncomfortably, expecting her to say no. "Fine," she says, surprising him. "But after, not before."

"Yeah, yeah, sure, that's great, thank you." He starts backing up to the door, like he's eager to leave before she can change her mind. "I'll just be outside when you need me, on the bench."

Tom remains in the doorway. When Darby is gone, he says, "Any idea what your sister might want?"

"No," Sally says. "But Darby said she's late calling back."

"I heard him." Tom leaves the doorway, but stays away from the main door and the window. Goes into the corner of the room, next to Sally's counter. He has a good view of outside. He keeps one eye on it while he talks to her. "You worried?"

"I'm always worried about her. Right now, not more so than usual."

"She didn't try your cell?"

"No. Either because Darby told her I was busy, or because she didn't have time enough to call a second number."

"She gotta keep her calls a secret from Earl?"

"For the most part."

"Surprised he lets her have a phone of her own, in that case. Be easier to monitor her from a landline, wouldn't it?"

"It creates an illusion of freedom, I guess," Sally says, sighing. "No, you can't go out and see your sister or your friends whenever you want, but here's a cell phone, so don't say I never give you anything. It's probably only got two numbers in it – mine and his. And he can always check the call history, see if there are any numbers he don't recognize, or ask her why she's been talking to me for an hour, everything we've discussed."

They wait. Tom keeps an eye on the road. Sally keeps an eye on the phone.

Ten minutes pass by. The hotel phone begins to ring. Sally grabs it. "Hello?"

She listens, silent. Tom can't hear the responding voice, can only watch as Sally's face begins to drop. Then, as abruptly as it began, the call ends. She puts the phone down.

Tom waits for her to speak.

Sally looks at him. "That was Anna," she says.

"Sounds like she didn't have long to talk."

"Daniel's at the ranch," she says. "Tied up in the barn. With your car."

Tom nods.

"She said he looked beat up. That was all she could get out, said she couldn't talk long. We need to go."

"We're going to."

"No, we need to go *now*."

"That's the worst thing we can do," Tom says. "She tell you how many people are out there?"

"No."

"Then we don't go rushing in headlong. How many people do you *think* are there?"

Sally starts counting off on her fingers. "Earl, Dean, Reggie, Chris, my sister – Anna's told me in the past there's sometimes other guys there, with guns, looking over the place. Like guards."

"How many guards?"

"I don't know. I never asked."

Tom grunts. "So, not including your sister, that's four, and with guards it could be any amount. We're not gonna charge straight out there with no idea of numbers."

"Then what do you suggest? We wait 'til dark? What difference is the dark going to make?" Sally sounds exasperated. She's getting worked up, the volume of her voice rising. Everything that is happening, all the revelations, the knowledge of Daniel being held captive by the same people who have her sister…it's all getting to her.

"The dark will make a big difference, especially if they don't know we're coming," Tom says. "How much do you trust your sister? I asked you earlier, and you said you didn't know."

"You didn't ask me that."

"I asked you something close enough to it."

"What's your point?"

"My point is, do you trust what she just told you? Or is there a chance she's been told to make that call?"

Sally opens her mouth to respond, something adamant, but then she stops herself. Thinks about what he is suggesting. Her shoulders sag. "I don't know," she says.

Tom can see the sadness in her face. The realization – perhaps long understood but buried deep and swallowed down, ignored – that she doesn't know who her sister is anymore. That the trust that perhaps once came so easily must now be questioned.

Tom is thinking. Pondering the unknown numbers out at the ranch. "Get your rifle," Tom says. "We're going out now."

"It's not dark."

"The time we get where we're going, it'll be dark enough."

"Where are we going?"

"To make a distraction."

41

Sally drives. Tom directs. From memory, he leads her out of Brenton, back along the road where he followed Earl and Dean, thinking they were taking him to the ranch. Tom checks his Beretta. He checks Sally's rifle in his lap, then puts it on the backseat.

He's told Sally where they're going. Out to where he saw the exchange take place with the Forever Road Dogs. To where the lab is.

Tom watches the fence until they reach the gate. He gets her to pull over. He jumps out of the car, opens the gate; she pulls through. He leaves the gate open, gets back in the car.

"It's not far from here," he says. "Kill the lights."

Sally does so, then crawls along the uneven road. Tom notices the car he took from Lon is gone. They've moved it. He's not surprised. It was filled with bullet holes. They've probably scrapped it.

"Stop," he says. "You wait here. Maybe keep hold of your rifle. You see anyone other than me approach, shoot them."

"It's dark. How'll I know if it's you or not?"

"I'm trusting your judgment, Sally. I'm trusting you to actually check the face of the man you're going to shoot before you shoot him."

"That's an uncomfortable level of trust," Sally says. "Especially when it's getting dark."

"My life is literally in your hands. I'll be sure to give you a sign, let you know it's me." Tom gets out of the car, surveys the land around the factory, checking for guards. He waits, watches until he's sure. There doesn't appear to be any.

Tom stays low, makes his way down to the factory. Presses himself against the wall next to the broken window through which he pulled the guard the last time. He listens, can't hear any voices, any footsteps. He climbs in through the window, pulls his knife. Holds it low at his side, the hilt pointing upward in his grip, the tip of the blade pointing down.

He makes his way through the abandoned building, listening. Halfway through, he starts to hear voices. They're coming from outside. He gets closer, slides up next to a window that is still intact. There are two guards. They're both armed with AR-15s. They stand close together, smoking and talking. One of them cracks a joke, the other laughs. They stand between the back door of the factory and the side door that leads down, underneath the factory, where the superlab is.

Tom puts his knife away, pulls out his gun. The door next to him is not locked. It sits ajar. He kicks it wide open, steps outside, catches the two guards by surprise. He fires twice, puts a bullet through each of their heads. They crumple, hit the ground.

Tom keeps his gun raised, listens, looks around. No one comes running. There are no other guards. Just these two, dead.

He goes to their bodies. Takes the guns from them, straps one to his back and takes the clip from the other, tucks it into the back of his waistband. He pats the bodies down, finds a crumpled pack of cigarettes, a lighter, and an open packet of beef jerky. He takes the lighter, slides it into his pocket, next to the one he took from the dead man in the desert. He goes to the factory's side door, leading downstairs.

The stairwell is empty. At the bottom, there is an open doorway. He steps through, takes in the lab.

The basement level of the factory is as wide and long below as it is above ground. There are four men working in it, each of them clothed in protective gear and safety masks. Spare PPE hangs from hooks to Tom's left. He picks up one of the masks, rests it on top of his head. Each of the men occupies a different corner of the room, busy with their own thing. None of them notice his arrival.

Tom looks the lab over. The shiny equipment. The vats and bottles of chemicals. The stack of finished product boxed and waiting, close to where he stands.

Tom clears his throat. The four turn as one, look his way. They all freeze. "Take off the masks," he says, holding up his gun. "Wanna get a good look at you all."

They all do as he says. They look terrified of him, staring at his weapons, the gun in his hand and the one strapped to his back.

Tom looks them over. None of them are familiar to him. None of them are armed. There is a table with plastic bottles lined up atop it. The way they stand, Tom cannot see the names of what is inside them. He can see the warning labels, though. The chemicals within are flammable. He points at the cook nearest to them with the gun. The man flinches. "You," he says. "Open those bottles, all of them, and pour the liquid out. You can all put your masks back on."

The cook looks at the others.

"Don't look at them. Look at me," Tom says. "I'm the one telling you what to do. The four of you want to make it out of here alive, do as I say."

The cook lowers his mask, does as Tom tells him. Tom pulls down the mask resting atop his head, covers his face. The three others lower their own as chemicals spill to the floor, splash the bottom of the cook's protective pants and boots.

The liquid spreads out, under the tables. There's a lot of it. Tom takes a step back. It's already reached the length and breadth of the room before the cook is finished opening them all.

"Just drop the rest," Tom says.

The cook does as he says.

Tom pulls one of the lighters from his pocket, sees how the men involuntarily take a step back, hears how they gasp. He steps out of the doorway. "Get out," he says.

They hurry past him. Tom watches them go, keeps the gun on them as they pass and head up the stairs, makes sure they don't try to jam the door closed and trap him below. When they're gone, he flicks the lighter, lays it on its side on the ground out of reach of the spreading, encroaching liquid.

Tom races to the top of the stairs, keeps running when he's outside, pulls the mask from his face, throws it aside. He can see the four cooks scattering, running over the hill, presumably to where they have hidden their cars. Tom makes his way back to Sally. Behind him, he hears a small explosion. The back of the factory begins to crumble.

Sally sees him coming. "I didn't shoot you," she says.

"I'm grateful."

She looks beyond him, to the burning factory. The fire is spreading. Already, smoke is beginning to belch into the sky.

"Let's go," Tom says.

42

I t's hard to tell time inside the barn. It's always dark. Daniel has to turn his head, look through the slats, to make out whether it's day or night. Right now, it looks like it's getting dark. Earl told him the sheriff was on his way. Daniel is counting down the seconds. He's not looking forward to Larry's arrival. When he gets here, it's done. It's over.

Daniel probes his broken teeth with his tongue. The pain keeps him sharp, keeps him alert, when all his weary bones want to do is slump and sleep. He tries to work his hands free, but the ropes are too tight. All his efforts accomplish is making him bleed. He can feel it trickle down his wrists, under the rope, to the tips of his fingers. The rope feels no looser. The blood does not lubricate him, does not make it easier for him to slip his hands free.

He hears vehicles outside the barn. Hears doors opening and closing, the engines cut off. He hears voices.

He listens, recognizes most of them. Larry, for definite. The moment Daniel has been dreading. He hears Jake King, too.

Daniel holds his breath. Takes his tongue out of his sharp teeth. Bites down on the gag.

The barn door opens. A crowd of men comes in. They stroll down the side of the car. Daniel watches them. Larry, Jake, Reggie, Chris, Earl, Dean. Earl is grinning, but everyone else looks deadly serious.

"Take the gag out," Larry says.

Earl nudges Dean. Dean comes forward, unties the gag at the back of Daniel's head, pulls it loose.

Daniel's mouth is dry. He stretches it out, runs his tongue over his lips. They're cracked. He can taste blood.

The six men all remain standing, look down on him. Larry steps forward, folds his arms. Daniel won't allow them to make him feel subjugated. He doesn't bother turning his face up.

"Face me when I'm talking to you, boy," Larry says.

"You ain't talking yet," Daniel says, looking at his shoes.

"I'm talking now."

"Then you better get down to my level, 'cause it hurts my neck to crane it that high. Course, y'all could always just cut me loose, let me stand. No? Naw, didn't think so. What're you so scared of? A beaten man, spent the last God knows how many days tied up in a barn, and you're too scared to cut him loose?"

Larry stands on Daniel's ankle, puts pressure on it until he cries out and looks up. "Did you know Tom before he came to town?"

Daniel was expecting a lot, but he wasn't expecting this question. "What? No."

"Make me believe you."

"I don't care what you believe."

"You *should* fuckin' care, boy."

"*Make* him care," Earl says.

Larry and Reggie both shoot him a look, then turn their attention back to Daniel. "The boy's an asshole," Larry says, referring to Earl. "But he makes a good suggestion. I *will* make you care if you don't start talking of your own volition."

"Why would I know him before?" Daniel says. "Shit, from what I've heard, I didn't even know his real name. And even if I did, what difference would that make? Hell, I was with Dean when he first got into town."

They turn to Dean. Dean looks like he doesn't want brought into this at all. "That's right," Dean says. "But you did go and help him, too. Maybe you were making it look good for my benefit, like you didn't already know him, I don't know."

"Coulda been playacting, Daniel," Earl says. "We see right through your little tricks."

Larry turns on Earl. "You gonna keep talking? Huh? You reckon you could shut the fuck up for maybe five fuckin' minutes?"

"Just keep your mouth shut, will ya?" Reggie says to his son.

Earl isn't grinning anymore. "What, am I embarrassing you in front of your friend the sheriff? The fuckin' lot of you leave me alone with this asshole for ten minutes and I'll get your damn answers."

Reggie glares. "Don't make me tell you again."

Larry gets down to a knee now, leans in close to Daniel. Grabs him by the front of his shirt. "Did you already know him?"

"No," Daniel says.

"Are you lying to me?" He starts to shake Daniel, to bang his back and his head against the support pole.

Daniel starts to laugh at the absurdity of it all.

Larry lets go of him, rears back like he's lost his mind, and like he's afraid it might be catching.

"That why you won't cut me loose, huh?" Daniel says. "'Cause you already fucked up against a beaten man, haven't you? Tom got free. Is that what this is all about? You're trying to find him, ain't you? You think I might know where he is." He laughs again. "God *damn*, you're clutching at straws now, boys."

Larry strikes Daniel across the face.

It doesn't shut Daniel up. He keeps laughing.

Larry gets back to his feet. "Untie this son of a bitch," he says, his usually composed demeanor looking strained, looking like he's about to explode.

"Sure that's a good idea?" Reggie says. "You already lost one man who was untied."

"Shut your damn mouth!" Larry says, roaring, turning on Reggie and showing more cracks in his solid foundations.

"He doesn't know the guy," Reggie says. "We're wasting time here."

"What else do you suggest we do?" Larry says. "Where do you think we look?"

Before Reggie can respond, the barn door opens again. The six men standing turn, look at the new arrival.

A man hurries over. One of the McQuades' boys. He looks panicked, sweating. Nervous to speak.

Chris steps aside, gives him more room to approach Reggie. The man is hesitant to do so.

"The hell's the matter with you?" Reggie says. "Spit it out."

"It's the lab," the man says. He's breathless as he speaks.

"What about the lab?"

"It's blown up," the man says, then braces himself, expecting to be struck, expecting Reggie to explode.

"What the fuck do you mean, it's blown up?" Reggie demands.

"It's been attacked – the chefs were chased out. I asked them for a description. It sounds like this Rollins guy."

Reggie's entire head has turned red.

Daniel can't help himself. He starts laughing again.

Larry kicks him in the leg. "Shut up."

"How long ago was this?" Reggie says.

"The call just came in," the man says. "I asked them the same question. They said it was about twenty minutes ago."

Reggie looks at Larry. "Reckon we could cut him off on the way?"

"We gotta try," Larry says. "But I reckon the next place he's coming is right here. This is where he is" – he points at Daniel – "and where that is." He points at the car.

"Get the cars ready. Fire them up," Reggie says to the bearer of bad news. "*Now!* Get moving, go, go, go!" The man hurries out of the barn, running. "Earl, Dean, you stay here, get armed and watch the ranch. How many of the boys we got here right now?" He turns to Chris.

Chris counts off on his fingers. "Including him gone to the car? Three."

"That it?" Reggie says. "All right, those three stay here with Earl and Dean. The rest of us get out to the lab, cut this motherfucker off, waste him on the road. Get this dealt with once and for all."

"Jake, you're staying here with them," Larry says to his deputy. "Keep an eye on our boy Daniel here."

"Sure thing, Chief," Jake says.

"Whatever," Reggie says. "Let's just move already."

Five of the six men leave the barn. Jake stays behind. The barn door closes. Jake leans against the car. He looks back at Daniel. "Looks like it's just the two of us," he says.

"Don't fuckin' talk to me," Daniel says.

Jake snorts. "Suit yourself."

43

Tom would rather have had a chance to scout the ranch first, get a good look at it, the layout, the number of people present. But there's no time, and he has to make do with what he has.

Before they'd set off to the factory, the superlab, Tom had asked, "Is there a long way around to the ranch?"

"What do you mean?" Sally said.

"Once we blow it up, they're gonna head out to investigate. Probably hoping they'll catch us on the way. That's the point of the distraction. Is there a back road, so we don't run into them on our way to the ranch?"

Sally thought. "Yeah," she said. "It takes us off the main road, and we'll have to go *off* road for a while, but we can get around there that way."

"You know anything about the layout?"

"No. Never been to the ranch itself, just know where it is. Ain't ever been high on my list of destinations I wanna visit. Anna's told me about it before, but I didn't wanna hear, so I didn't really listen."

"That's a shame."

"Yeah, I'm regretting it now. But I never thought we'd get to where we are, so…"

Now, as they draw close to the rear of the ranch, Sally parks the car as close as she's able, and they continue on foot. She carries the rifle. Tom holds his Beretta, straps the AR-15 onto his back again. They reach the top of a hill. They can see the rear of the ranch. Two cars are leaving it, roaring out. One of them is a truck, the other a police cruiser.

"They're looking for us," Tom says.

"I got here fast," Sally says.

"I noticed."

"Don't think I've ever put my foot down that hard before."

They watch the ranch. Tom makes out four men, each of them armed, patrolling the grounds. Tom sees Earl. He stands on a porch, looking around. "Reckon that's his house?" he says.

"Could be."

"So Anna's probably in there."

"That's what I'm banking on."

Tom sees the barn. No one is watching it. His car is likely inside. Daniel is in there.

"You wait here," Tom says. "I'm going down."

"No," Sally says. "My sister's down there. I doubt she was in one of those cars. And Daniel's down there. I'm not staying up here, out the way. I'm coming with you."

Tom doesn't attempt to dissuade her. "Then stay low and stick close. We'll hit the barn first."

They reach the back of the barn, press themselves up against it. They head down the side. Tom finds a gap in the boards to look through. Spots his car. Sees Daniel. Sees a deputy watching over him. Tom gets Sally to stay hidden by the side of the barn, then goes to the back of the nearest house. He ducks low in the shadows, waits for one of the patrolling guards to pass by.

The guard approaches. Tom plucks him from the darkness, cuts his throat, deep. Drops him into the dark. Tom cleans the knife off, then goes to the barn door. He pushes it open a little, then deepens his voice and calls in, "Hey – we need you out here!" Tom keeps his voice low enough so as not to alert the other guard.

He braces himself by the side of the door. Hears the deputy come running. "The hell's the matter with y'all?" he's saying as he reaches the door.

Tom spins, sinks the knife into his gut, clamps a hand over his mouth. Pushes him back into the barn until he hits the front of Tom's car. Tom pulls him off it, shoves him down to the ground, pulls the knife out, sticks it in his chest, holds it there until he stops moving.

Tom summons Sally into the barn, then they cut Daniel free. Daniel puts his arms around Sally, squeezes her.

"Don't suppose you know where my car keys are?" Tom says.

"Probably in Earl's pocket or in his home," Daniel says. "They'll be on him, same as the necklace. Jesus Christ, I'm not imagining this, am I? I ain't drank anything in a long time. I'm not hallucinating, am I?"

"We're here," Sally says, kissing him. "We're right here."

"And this is where you stay," Tom says. "I'll go take out the rest of them."

"I told you, I'm not holding back," Sally says.

"I move faster on my own. And Daniel's not in any state to move at all."

"I want my sister," Sally says.

"And I'll get her. Just wait."

Sally doesn't respond, but he can tell she's not

pleased about doing as he says. Tom leaves the barn, checks the area. He goes back to the house, next to the guard he's already killed. He moves to the corner, peers out. There are kennels in his way. He can hear dogs moving around inside. He leans out further, to where Earl was earlier standing. He's not there anymore.

Tom goes around the other side of the house, to the next guard. Creeps up on him, takes him from behind same as the last one. Stabs him in the back, up through the rib cage, into the heart. Dumps him in the shadows of the nearest house.

Two left.

The darkness helps, keeps him hidden. He makes it to the next guard, takes him out the same way.

One left, then Earl.

The one guard left isn't patrolling. He's standing in front of the house Earl is inside. It's Dean. He's clutching a gun, and he looks nervous.

Earl comes out onto the porch then. He stretches his arms over his head, looks around. He jolts, startled, cries out in a panic. "Over there!" he shouts, getting Dean's attention. "Over there!" He's pointing, but it's not toward Tom. "Shoot her, damn it!"

Tom looks. Sally is down on one knee, the M14 pressed into her shoulder, taking aim at Earl.

Dean starts shooting. Fortunately for Sally, he doesn't look like he's had much practice with the automatic rifle. His shots hit the ground, kick up dirt. The ones that aren't low go too high, go wide. Sally dives for cover. The dogs in the kennel start howling.

Tom looks to the house, to Earl. He sees Anna emerge behind him, rushing out. Earl shoves her back inside. She goes down.

Dean has stopped firing, trying to get the gun under

better control. He takes aim again, the spot down the side of the house where Sally is hidden.

"Blast her!" Earl says.

Tom pulls out his gun, fires. His bullet tears through the base of Dean's skull. Dean drops to the ground.

Earl's face falls. *"Dean!"* His voice breaks as he screams his fallen friend's name, tears threatening to break through.

Earl pulls out his handgun. He starts firing in Tom's direction. Tom hits the ground, rolls. Earl cries out. Tom looks back at the house to see Earl stumble back inside, a hand pressed to the side of his bleeding head. He looks back. Sally has the rifle pressed into her shoulder. She's clipped him, but, just like that day behind the hotel, she's missed the bull's-eye.

Earl doesn't stay inside the house long. Tom hears a woman's scream. He re-emerges, blood streaming down the side of his face, with Anna in front of him, his gun pressed to the side of her head. "Drop the fucking guns!" he says.

Tom doesn't. Sally hesitates, looks into the eyes of her sister. She bites her lip. She drops the rifle, raises her hands.

Earl watches. He sees Tom, gun still raised. Earl crouches behind Anna. "Sally!" he says. "Get your ass over here – now! Right now!"

Sally looks at Tom, but Tom only has eyes for Earl. She raises her hands, steps forward. "All right," she says. "But let Anna go. Don't hurt her."

"Faster you get here, faster she's free," Earl says. His eyes are wild. Even without the blood on his face, he would look maniacal.

Sally reaches the porch. She steps up, closer to Earl. He backhands her across the mouth, then throws Anna to the ground and grabs Sally in her place, holds her to him, his new shield. While he's distracted, while his hands are busy, Tom starts running, gun still raised.

Earl spins on him, gun pressed into Sally's temple now. "Get back!" he says. "Get the fuck back!"

On the ground, Anna crawls back into the house. Earl doesn't notice her go.

Tom stops running. He's close to the porch now, only six paces away. He keeps his gun up.

"Put the fucking guns down!" Earl says. "Both of them – I see that one on your back! I'll waste you both, swear to God!"

Daniel stumbles out of the barn, sees what's happening. Earl sees him, too.

"*Motherfuckers!*" he says. "I'll kill you all, I'll kill every last fuckin' one of you, and I'll feed your bones to my dogs! Put the fucking gun *down!*"

Tom looks past him, into the house. He sees Anna. She's standing now. He sees the look on her face as she realizes Earl is holding her sister hostage. That he'd held her as a shield, too. She disappears from view.

Tom buys her time. "All right," he says. "I'll put the guns down. You're surrounded, Earl. Just be cool, okay?"

"I *am* fucking cool! I don't care if I'm surrounded. None of you are going anywhere! You're all staying right fuckin' here!"

"All right," Tom says. "That's what we'll do."

Anna comes back into view. She has a knife from the kitchen. "I'm putting the gun down, okay, Earl? Watch me. I'm putting it down."

Anna drives the knife into Earl's back, right between the shoulder blades. He screams, releases Sally, starts to turn. Sally throws herself to the ground. Tom starts running. Earl turns, realizes it is Anna who has stabbed him. "You goddamn *bitch* –" He raises the gun, points it at her.

Tom tackles him from the porch, drives him to the ground. He lands on the hilt of the knife. "*Fuck!*"

Tom gets off him. Earl's back arches; he twists in the dirt. Tom reaches into his pockets, searches for his car keys. Finds two pairs. Pulls them both out. Doesn't recognize the first, throws them to one side. The second pair belong to him. He pockets them, then reaches down again.

The pendant is not in Earl's pockets. It's around his neck. Tom takes it from him, holds it in front of Earl's face. "Should've left it well enough alone," he says.

The look in Earl's eyes says he knows this, he understands this now, but he also understands it's too late.

Tom presses down on him, the tip of the knife bursts through his chest, and he's still.

44

L   arry looks the area over. There's no sign of Tom. No sign of him on the way here, either. One of the chefs has hung around. He sits to one side, watching the lab and the factory burn.

Reggie is watching, too. His hands are on top of his head.

They won't call the fire department. They can't. Have to hope no one else sees the billowing clouds of smoke and calls it for them. The factory is set so far back from the road and any of the nearby towns that they shouldn't have to worry about this happening.

Chris stands by Reggie's side, his arms folded. Larry leaves them to it, goes to the sitting chef. "Where are the others?" he says.

The chef doesn't look at him. Stares at the factory. "They ran," he says. "Went home, I guess."

"You're the only one hung around?"

The chef nods.

"Rollins made you burn it down?"

He nods again.

"See where he went?"

"No. I wasn't looking. I was running in the other direction, from his gun. You can see what he did to the guards. I wasn't expecting him to do any less to us. All I know now is he ain't around here anymore. I checked while I was waiting for y'all to get here."

Larry leaves the chef where he sits, goes over to Reggie and Chris. "He ain't here," he says. "We've missed him. We need to head back to the ranch. It's the only other place he might go."

"The lab…" Reggie says.

"Forget about the fucking lab," Larry says. "After tonight, once Lyle is the governor, you can build as many more labs as you fuckin' like. Those fracking contracts come through, you'll be making more money from that than you do the meth, anyway."

Reggie doesn't move. Larry is about to step up to him, do or say something to motivate him, but Chris holds up a hand. He steps in front of Reggie, slaps him across the face.

Reggie blinks, comes back to himself.

"We can either stay here and keep staring at this mess," Chris says, "or we can head back to the ranch and deal with the motherfucker responsible. He's hitting us, and there ain't anywhere left for him to hit. The ranch is the only place."

Reggie runs his hand across his mouth. Some of the fire Larry is more familiar with returns to his eyes. He looks at Larry. "I'm gonna call Earl." He pulls out his phone, punches in his son's number. Larry is already going back to his cruiser.

"There's no answer," Reggie says.

Larry turns back. They look at each other. They both understand. Best-case scenario, Earl is trying to be the big man. He won't call, won't answer, because he wants to deal with it all himself.

Worst-case scenario, Rollins is already there.

They run to their cars, turn them around, and race back to the road, leaving the chef sitting alone to watch his former workplace burn to the ground.

45

Tom has moved the bodies. He's dragged them to the barn, piled them in there, out of view. Now he sits at the window in the main house, the one with the best view of the road that leads into the ranch, and he waits.

He's sent Daniel, Sally, and Anna away. Watched them go off back over the hill at the rear of the ranch, the two sisters standing on either side of Daniel, supporting him.

The dogs were howling. In the main house Tom found them a can of food, opened it, threw it to them through the mesh. It shut them up. They haven't barked since. Fed, they are satiated. They prowl their kennel or else lie down on the floor.

Tom sits by the window, the AR-15 nestled into his shoulder. He eyes along the sight. He can hear cars approaching, the distant and approaching rumble of their engines. The two vehicles come into view. The truck and the cruiser. The same two he earlier saw leave the ranch before he made his move and killed everyone still here.

Tom doesn't open fire yet. He waits. The truck comes to a stop. The cruiser follows it in, pulls up alongside it. The engines stop, but no one gets out, not right away. Inside, they're likely surveying the scene, wondering where their men are, where Earl is.

The doors open. Reggie and Chris get out of the truck. Larry gets out of his cruiser. He has his hand on his holster, remains behind his open door. He pulls his gun loose. The three men are looking around.

Tom fires, looses a tight burst. One-eyed, Chris goes down, a spray of blood erupting out the back of his head.

Larry ducks back into his car. Reggie roars, starts firing toward the house. The dogs are howling again.

Tom fires, hits the front of the truck, cripples it. Blows out the tires, buckles the hood, and blows out the windshield, peppers the radiator. He ducks below the window. It shatters, Reggie returning gunfire. Tom starts moving; then he hears a car roaring forward, getting closer, toward the front door next to which he stands.

Tom runs to the back of the house. The porch takes the worst of the damage, but the sheriff is still able to ram it through the front door. He leans out his open window, starts shooting.

Tom dives for cover behind a wall, hears bullets pepper it from the other side. They start to tear through. Tom gets down low, drops the rifle, pulls out his handgun. He's in a bedroom; he guesses it's Reggie's. He rolls across the floor, under the bed.

The window at the back of the house shatters. Tom is at the edge of the bed. He can see up to where the window is. See a gun poke through, start waving around. Reggie starts climbing in after it. Tom inches back, deeper into the darkness.

"You see him?" Reggie calls.

"He went back there!" Larry shouts.

Tom raises his gun from under the bed just as Reggie looks down. Tom fires; the bullet catches Reggie in the lower face, tears his jaw off. He stumbles back, hits the nearest wall. It holds him up. Tom fires twice more, into his torso.

As he rolls out from under the bed, Larry comes charging into the room. He stamps on the bed, leaps over it, tackles Tom against the wall. He isn't armed. Tom assumes he's used up all his bullets shooting at the wall.

The two men grapple. Larry slams Tom's arm against the wall, desperate to loosen his grip on the gun. He punches Tom across the face. Tom sees stars, drops the gun. On instinct he headbutts the sheriff, sends him back across the bed.

Larry rises, empty hands raised, as Tom picks his gun back up. Larry smirks. "Come on, then," he says. "You damn punk. Shoot me."

Tom lowers the gun, puts it down on the bedside table. He pulls the knife from its holster.

Larry raises an eyebrow. "That's how you wanna do it, huh? Wanna try and carve me up like some kinda butcher? Too scared to fight man on man, that it, *Rollins*?"

Tom raises an eyebrow, then he smiles. He stabs the knife into the wooden wall, steps out from behind the bed.

Larry lowers his submissive arms. "You really wanna do this?"

Tom raises his fists.

"It's your fuckin' funeral, kid," Larry says, matching his stance. "You ain't gonna ask how I found out who you are?"

"I don't care," Tom says.

Larry swings first. Tom easily avoids it, then moves through and delivers two lefts of his own, right into the sheriff's ribs. The two men have switched positions, Tom now occupying the space Larry previously stood.

Larry rubs his ribs with an elbow, rolls his shoulders. "So you tagged me," he says. "A couple of cheap shots. Good for you."

Larry comes in again, but this time he feigns a left. As Tom goes to duck it, Larry brings up his right, catches him in the center of his face. Larry presses his advantage, throws fists, keeps moving forward. Tom keeps his arms up, defensive, lets Larry get closer, then lashes out with a kick, knocks his right leg out from under him. Larry goes down, takes a knee. His arms falter. Tom drives an elbow across his face, smashes it into his cheekbone.

Larry lies facedown on the ground, spits. Tom steps back, gives him a chance to stand.

Larry laughs, using the wall for support. "You're letting me get up? How do you think this ends, boy?"

"One of two ways," Tom says. "Either you make a confession, or you die."

"You really think I'm gonna confess?" He laughs. "And you really think you can kill me, you punk?"

Tom smiles again. "No," he says. "I don't think you'll confess at all."

Larry charges in, keeps his head low, tackles Tom around the waist and pushes him back. Tom drives the point of his elbow into Larry's back, until they land on the bed. Larry rolls. He's reaching for the gun. Tom keeps hold of him, keeps him close. Larry gets the gun, turns with it. Tom grabs his wrist, keeps the gun high, out of his face. He gets a grip on Larry's thumb, wrenches it back, hears it snap. Larry lets go of the gun. He grimaces, but he doesn't scream. Tom forces him off the side of the bed, down to his knees in the space between the bed and the wall.

Tom takes him by the back of the head, slams his face into the wall, again, again, until he's limp. Tom slips an arm around his neck.

"Do it, boy," Larry says through busted lips, shattered teeth, the sound of his voice muffled by Tom's arm. "I ain't saying shit."

Tom snaps his neck.

46

D aniel listens as Sally tells him everything they have found out while she drives them away from the ranch. She tells him about the mayor, about Tom seeing the aide at the exchange, and about the family resemblance – and last names – of the mayor and the Forever Road Dog.

"Where are we going?" Daniel says.

Sally looks at him. "Back to the hotel. We'll wait for Tom there. That's what he said."

Daniel checks the time on the dashboard clock. "No," he says, "we're going to Kirkwood."

"Why do we wanna go to Kirkwood?" Anna says. She's in the back and for the most part has been silent this journey. Daniel imagines she's been thinking about what she did to Earl, stabbing him in the back both literally and metaphorically.

"Because the results are in," Daniel says, "the election's over, and whether or not the mayor is now the governor, we have an aide to arrest."

"What about the mayor?" Sally says.

"Not enough against him right now," Daniel says.

"But taking his aide will be enough to spook him. Then I'll get him to roll over on his boss. I'll build a case, then we'll take Lyle Smithson."

"You're gonna do this on your own?" Anna says.

"No." Daniel has been thinking. "Give me a phone."

Sally reaches into her pocket, hands hers over.

Daniel takes a moment to remember the number, then calls Mark Colt. He trusts Mark. He *has* to trust Mark. If they've got to Mark too, they may as well have gotten the whole department.

Mark listens in disbelief while Daniel explains to him what has happened, and what he's going to do.

"He told us you were sick," Mark says, his voice low.

"Yeah, as sick as Frank Aynsley," Daniel says. "Will you meet us there?"

"I'll be there."

"Don't tell anyone else, Mark. Not a soul. You're the only one I trust."

"Got it."

"I hope you're right about him," Sally says when he's off the phone and hands it back to her.

"Me too," Daniel says.

When they reach Kirkwood, the results are in. Mayor Lyle Smithson is now the governor of Texas. He stands upon his stage in the center of the town, giving a victory speech to a large and cheering gathering of townspeople and journalists. There are cameras.

Mark waves them down. He looks nervous, but angry, too. Daniel knows the look. He feels it. The deep sense of betrayal they have been subjected to. "We gonna fuckin' do this?" Mark says. His hand rests on his holster.

Daniel winces getting out of the car. "Let's go."

Mark looks him over, sees the swelling in his face, in his jaw. "You sure you can manage? You're all beat up."

"If it ain't me, and it ain't you, who else is gonna do it?"

They push their way through the crowd, to the side of the stage. Security tries to stop them ascending the steps. Daniel shoves them roughly aside. At the top, he sees the aide. Brian Roberts. Beaming by the mayor's side. Daniel takes a deep breath, looks at Mark. They nod at each other, then stride out across the stage, hand-cuffs ready.

47

T om lies low in Sally's hotel for a few days, recovering. The FBI are all over the county, and Tom doesn't want to bump into them.

It has been a busy time in Cullingworth County. Judging by the news that Sally has brought him, it's been a busy time in Texas. Lyle Smithson's new governorship has been suspended pending a federal investigation into his suspected illegal activities and connections to the Forever Road Dogs.

"How's your sister?" Tom says.

"She's sick, but she'll get better," Sally says, sitting on the end of his bed. "She's agreed to go to rehab. I think, more than anything else, she feels relieved. She's free of Earl now, of the McQuades, and she took that step herself when she stuck the knife in his back. No one tried to make the choice for her, no one tried to drag her away, and I think that's made all the difference."

"She made a choice between you and him," Tom says.

"Yeah. And I'm real glad she made the right one."

Tom sits in the chair at the desk, leans back in it a

little, arms folded. He itches, desperate to get back on the road, to continue his journey to Mexico. Knowing that he can't, not yet, makes it worse. When things calm down, he will slip out on a back road, put on his sunglasses and his hat, keep his head down as he goes. "How's Daniel?"

"He's sore, but he's busy," Sally says. "He's acting as interim sheriff until things calm down enough to have another election, but to be honest, after everything he's done lately, I don't see why people won't vote for him. He's hoping to come by and see you when he has a chance. You'll still be here?"

"Guess that depends on when he comes."

Sally grins, gets to her feet. "I better get back to work," she says.

"Check on my car," Tom says. It's parked around the back, right next to Sally's.

"Always do," Sally says, leaving.

She's brought him a handful of paperbacks to pass the time. They're piled on the desk. Tom turns back to them, resumes reading. In his hand, he holds the Santa Muerte pendant, holds it tight.

Daniel comes to see him that night. Tom is still in the chair, still reading. Daniel knocks, pokes his head through the door. "You got a minute?" he says.

"Sure." Tom slips the pendant into his pocket, turns the chair round. "Come on in. Take a seat. I understand congratulations are in order."

Daniel waves his hands, looking sheepish. He looks better than the last time Tom saw him, but then Tom probably looks better himself. They've had enough time to heal. And, in Daniel's case, anything would be an improvement on being tied up in a barn.

Daniel takes a seat, the same spot on the bed earlier occupied by Sally. "How you doing?" he says.

"Ready to leave."

"So soon? What's the rush?"

"I got somewhere I need to be."

"This sure has been a long detour."

"Mm. I'll be more careful next time I have to pull off the road to go around a crash scene."

"I'd assume that was a given."

"Yeah, well, me too. How's it going with the mayor?"

"Brian Roberts broke, told us everything. The feds have Lyle now. They're working him over."

"And what about in the department? You flushed out all the bad apples?"

"Well, to be honest with you, Tom, I think most of them are dead." Daniel raises his eyebrows. "And any who might be left over, they're keeping their mouths tightly closed. They see which way the wind is blowing. Still, I'll find them. I don't care how long it takes, they can't stay hidden from me forever. There's always a trail of some kind."

Tom grunts. "Sally tells me you spun some story regarding the sheriff."

"Had to," Daniel says. "Since you don't wanna talk to anyone. How else was I gonna explain away all those bodies?"

The story, as Sally had told it to Tom, was that Daniel and Mark, along with the sheriff and all the other dead deputies, received an anonymous tip-off as to the whereabouts of the McQuades' superlab. The McQuades destroyed the lab in response and attempted to shoot their way to freedom, making their last stand at the ranch, where the only survivors were Daniel and Mark. This was also where they discovered the involvement of the mayor's aide in the running of the meth.

"How'd you explain his broken neck?"

"Left his car plowed into the house like it was, sat him behind the wheel. Said he charged the house to subdue the shooters, must've broke his neck in the crash. He was an old man, but always thought he was younger."

"I appreciate what you did, but the sheriff was no hero."

"Yeah, well, unless you wanna tell your part in the story, that's how it's gotta be," Daniel says. "We know the truth. It might kill me that that's how he'll be remembered, but I owe you a bigger debt than how much my feelings hurt."

"What if the mayor starts talking about Larry's part in things?"

Daniel shrugs. "It'll sound like he's trying to shift blame. But by then you'll be gone, right? So it won't matter to you, and it won't matter what stories get told. And if the truth about him eventually comes out, good. Mark and I have plausible deniability. There's no one can contradict our story."

Tom nods. "Sounds like you got it figured out."

"I sure as hell hope so. I need to thank you, Tom."

"No, you don't." Tom has never taken gratitude well. In this instance, he's just a man who got caught up in something he wanted no part of.

"I do," Daniel says. "It wasn't for you, the McQuades would still be running things, Larry would still be offing good deputies who did their job a little too well, and Lyle Smithson would be the governor of Texas, and Christ only knows what kinda further shit-storm that would've brought down around us."

"Well," Tom says, shifting in his seat, not sure how to respond, "glad I could help, I guess."

Daniel gets to his feet, holds out his hand. Tom stands, takes it. They shake.

"Wherever it is you're going," Daniel says, "good luck getting there. I sure hope the rest of your journey is a smooth one."

Tom nods, and Daniel leaves. Tom doesn't sit down, doesn't pick his book back up. Instead, he gets onto the bed, lies flat on his back, looks up at the ceiling. It's starting to get dark outside.

Tomorrow, he will get back on his journey. Two weeks has been enough time to wait. The feds will be thinned on the road. They'll be busy with the mayor, with his aide, with everything else that has been going on around here.

Tomorrow, he will continue on to Mexico.

48

Tom intends to leave the hotel out the back door, but Sally has changed the lock. It looks more secure than the last one.

"Hey, Tom," Darby says. He's in the lobby, leans out from behind the desk to look into the stairwell. "You leaving?"

Tom steps out. "Trying to," he says.

"Sally asked me to keep an eye out for you."

"That so?"

Darby nods.

Tom looks around. "So where is she?"

"In her room."

"You reckon you can just let me slide?"

Darby grins. "I would, but Sally's a friend."

"I get that. How you doing, Darby? I understand things are changing round here, but you're looking well."

"For now," Darby says. "Sally says if I get clean, she'll give me a job. A real one."

"That what you want?"

Darby shrugs. "It's better than the alternative. I

dunno. I usedta live for the present, I knew what I wanted, and I knew how to get it, but now I gotta think about the future, and the future's unclear. I don't know what I'm supposed to do. So I guess if Sally wants to give me some kind of idea, then I'm gonna follow that."

"You afford to go to rehab?"

"Deputy Murphy's gonna try and get some kind of center set up for us."

Tom knows how easy it can be to cook meth if the desire is there. He looks at Darby, at his haggard face and his missing teeth. The way he itches the inside of his arms. He doesn't have the look of someone who works on the desk of a hotel, the first person people see. Maybe if the people who come in look like him, but if Deputy Murphy is going to clean up Brenton the way he says he is, they aren't the kind of people Sally will be looking to draw in anymore.

"Well, good luck to you, Darby," Tom says.

Sally's door opens. Behind her, in her apartment, he hears the two dogs taken from the ranch. They live with her now until Anna is out of rehab. She steps through into the lobby. "Thought I heard your voice," she says to Tom.

"I was about to come get you," Darby says.

Sally smiles at him, then, to Tom, "This is you leaving?"

"It is."

"Like the new lock on the back?"

"Admired it."

"I'll look upon it as a memento of your brief but memorable stay here."

"Usually I try to pass through places as anonymously as I can."

"Then consider this a colossal failure. Come on, I'll walk you out."

"You don't need to do that."

"I ain't gonna say goodbye here, Tom."

"All right, then. Let's go. Goodbye, Darby. I hope that'll be enough for you, and you don't feel like you gotta follow me out, too."

Darby takes his seat behind the desk again. "Naw," he says. "That's good enough for me. Goodbye, Tom."

Tom and Sally step out of the hotel, into the midday heat. They go around the back, to his car. "So where you going next?" Sally says.

"I got a place to be."

"That place have a name, or are you determined to be a man of mystery?"

Tom opens the passenger door, puts his bag on the seat. Closes the door and takes his time going around to the driver's side. "It's south," he says.

"Suit yourself," Sally says, holding up her hands. "You keep its name a secret. You know it ain't like I'm gonna try to come follow you, right? I've got enough on my hands here."

"I know that. It's just…"

"You're a private guy."

"You could say that."

"I do. A frustratingly private guy, Mr. Rollins." She winks.

Tom grins, opens the driver's door.

"One question, though," Sally says.

"All right," Tom says, one leg inside the car, his arms leaning atop the door. "One question."

"It's the girl, right?"

Tom cocks his head, raises an eyebrow.

"The one in the picture. The one you had in the mirror in your room, that you got all worked up about when you thought it was missing."

Alejandra. She's talking about Alejandra. "No," Tom says. "Not her. Not yet."

"You upset her or something? I'm sure you can make it up. You're a tenacious guy."

Tom smiles at her. He can feel the sadness that tinges it, that tugs at the corners, and he can see in Sally's face that she notices it, too. "She's dead," he says.

Sally looks like she doesn't know what to say. She clears her throat. "The pendant," she manages to say. "I couldn't understand why you did all of this just for that. Was it hers?"

"It was a gift," Tom says. "From her."

"The urn…" Sally realizes.

Tom nods. "Goodbye, Sally," he says, getting into the car. He winds the window down. "I hope your sister gets better. Good luck with everything here."

"Bye, Tom," Sally says, her voice not as bright and lively as it earlier was, escorting him out of the hotel and to his car. "Good luck in Mexico. Whatever else you might go looking for, I hope you find it."

Tom pulls the Santa Muerte pendant from his pocket, hangs it back in its place from the rearview mirror. "I will," he says.

He reverses the car, raises his hand to Sally in a goodbye wave, then pulls out of the parking lot, and out of Brenton.

49

Senator Seth Goldberg still goes to synagogue with his family every Saturday morning. The close call they had a couple of months ago, the bombing that was very likely aimed at him – and, by extension, his family – admittedly put them off from going to Shabbat for a couple of weeks. They didn't feel safe. The security they had at the house was ramped up. Seth acquired a couple more bodyguards to transport him to and from work.

Mostly, though, he and Abigail worried about their children. About how what had happened would affect them. The fact there had been a threat to them, that they'd had a near-death experience. That they'd seen a man killed right in front of them, despite how their parents tried to shield their eyes.

It was Abigail who said they needed to go back to synagogue. "Sooner rather than later," she said. "The longer we leave it, the worse it will be for them. We can't live like this, Seth. If we cower, they win. They failed; we can't let them claim our lives this way instead."

She was right. Of course she was right. They could not be bowed, could not be forced to live in fear. The next Saturday, they went back to synagogue. It was quiet that weekend. Others still shared their concerns, clearly. But as the weeks and months have gone by, the numbers have returned. Increased, even.

Today is not Saturday, however. Today is Sunday. The one day of the week Seth does not have to get up early, either for work or for synagogue.

He is awake, though. He lies in bed, wrapped up in the warmth of the sheets and the blanket, listening to his daughters watching television downstairs. He stares at the ceiling and thinks about what lies ahead for him in the coming week. His clean energy bill has passed, more than likely buoyed by the wave of public support that engulfed him after the foiled domestic terrorism attack, but there is still much to do on it. The bill was just one battle in an ongoing war. There are still many battles ahead.

He hears footsteps coming up the stairs, too heavy to be either of the girls. A moment later, there's a knock on the door. Abigail pokes her head through. "Are you awake?" she says.

"I'm awake," Seth says, raising his head to see her.

Abigail comes into the room, something in her hand. A newspaper, one of her fingers inside it, keeping her place. She bounces to the bed, looks excited about something. "Sit up," she says, sitting down next to him. "Look at this." She opens up the paper, spreads it out.

Seth rubs his eyes, pushes himself up. He scans the paper. "What are you showing me?" he says. He sees nothing pertinent, nothing that catches his eye.

Abigail points to the page on the right. There is a small article, no pictures. Seth reads it. It tells of the recently elected, and just as quickly shamed, governor of Texas Lyle Smithson, how his entire political career had been buoyed by a family of meth cooks and his contacts in a biker gang.

Seth shrugs. "I never met him," he says. "They arrested him before I ever had the misfortune."

Abigail looks at him expectantly. "You haven't reached the end, have you?"

"I get the gist."

"Read to the end."

Seth does. A name catches his eye. He rereads the sentence. He sits up straighter. The newspaper had been told, confidentially, of the involvement of one Tom Rollins in recent events, a name familiar for, it is believed, foiling the recent attempted bombing in Dallas. Interim sheriff Daniel Murphy has denied any knowledge of Tom Rollins, but seemed interested to know where the paper heard such a name.

The newspaper is quick to point out, however, that it is skeptical of Tom Rollins's involvement. *We find it hard to believe the same man who saved Dallas has been involved in what has transpired in the town of Brenton. Indeed, the bearded and long-haired mystery man that we're told of does not exactly bear a striking resemblance to the stubbled and shaven-headed mystery man of a few months ago. Perhaps our informant – a resident of a town still early in its recovery from a meth epidemic – merely remembered the name Rollins from all the recent coverage? Perhaps they conflated two separate events, two separate men, and brought them together to create a hero of almost folkloric proportions? We may never know.*

The article ends there.

Seth looks at Abigail. She looks back, raises her eyebrows. "See, I knew you hadn't gotten to the end," she says.

"They say they don't think it's him."

"They say they're *skeptical*. And it's a lead, right?"

"Why haven't we heard about this already?" Seth says. "I'd think someone would have mentioned something."

"This is today's paper. Presumably the story has only just broken. It says they were told confidentially. They could be the only ones who know about it yet, no one else."

Seth reads the article over again. "So if it *is* him – and that's a big if – that's where he is," he says.

"That's where he's *been*," Abigail says.

Seth looks at her. "Then we need to find out where he's going."

EPILOGUE

Eric Thompson pulls into Brenton, looks up and down the main road, searching for the hotel. He passes a group of three junkies on a street corner. They look like they're hurting. He rolls down his window. "I'm looking for the hotel in this town," he says. "I was told there's only one."

One of the three steps forward, points. "It's the big building there," he says. "Hey, man, you got a buck?"

Eric looks the man over. He's so desperate and pitiful Eric almost wants to say no just to see if he'll cry. He doesn't have time for this, though. He reaches into his pocket, pulls out a ten, hands it over. "I appreciate the directions," he says.

The man's face lights up. "Oh, hey, no problem – oh, by the way, if you see that asshole Darby, you tell him from us –"

Eric holds up his hand, silences him, uninterested. He drives on, pulls to a stop in front of the hotel. A man sits on the bench in front, smoking a cigarette with shaking hands. He nods at Eric as he sees him approach.

This man looks as rough as the three he's just spoken to. "Is this the hotel?" Eric says.

"Sure is," the man says, nodding enthusiastically. "You looking for a room?"

"Not exactly. The owner home? Miss Blevins, I believe?"

"Sure, she's in there, at the desk. Can't miss her."

"Thank you. Say, are you Darby, by any chance?"

The man looks confused. Eric can see that he is who he's assumed. He smiles at him, then heads inside.

There is one person in the lobby, the woman behind the counter. She's on the phone. Eric leans on the counter, smiles at her, waits for her to finish her call.

"I'm glad to hear that," she says, looking Eric over, paying close attention to his black jacket, black tie, white shirt. A familiar uniform from a hundred different movies and TV shows. "Okay, I got a customer. I gotta go. Yes, Jojo and Georgie are very happy. I walk them all the time. Anna, I have to go. I'll see you soon. I love you too." Sally puts the phone down, looks up at Eric expectantly. "You after a room?"

"Not this time," Eric says, taking out his ID and flipping it open so she can get a good look. "I was just wondering if you could answer a few questions for me, Miss Blevins. I'll make them quick."

"Sure," she says. "But call me Sally."

"Will do, Sally." He smiles at her, wide, but keeps his teeth hidden. "So, I'll give you a little background first. About a month ago, I placed a call through to one Sheriff Larry Collins regarding some files he'd been paying close attention to in the online database, files belonging to one Tom Rollins."

He watches her face for traces of recognition, but nothing changes. "Now, when I spoke to the sheriff, he said he'd looked up the wrong Tom Rollins. Of course, look up the wrong guy once, I can believe that, but then to look into the background of his family? That got me to thinking.

"Anyway, I've been busy, and this is the first chance I've had to come out here, so imagine my surprise as I roll into Kirkwood and find that a whole bunch of my colleagues have already been there, and Sheriff Larry Collins himself is dead. And then I'm talking to the interim sheriff, Daniel Murphy – who I've been told is very close to you, Sally – and he starts telling me about a shoot-out with some family called the McQuades, and how they destroyed their own superlab in a blaze of glory, how they had connections to the Forever Road Dogs, and how the mayor was tied up in it all, too. How your former mayor, disgraced and already scrubbed from the gubernatorial records, was having inquisitive deputies and journalists executed out in the desert. Sounds like a real piece of work, am I right in thinking?"

When Sally realizes he is waiting for a response, she says, "Yeah, I'd say so."

"Mm, most certainly. I can't imagine what it was like to live under the local rule of such a man. Anyway, I start telling interim Sheriff Daniel Murphy about the reason I've come to town, and that is one Tom Rollins. Except Murphy tells me that he's unfamiliar with any Tom Rollins." Eric starts to stroke his chin. "He's an elusive bugger, isn't he?"

Sally listens to him, watches him with unblinking eyes. Her face is like stone.

"Anyway, I'm thinking to myself, oh well, maybe it's all a dead end. Maybe old Larry wasn't lying when he said he'd looked into the wrong Tom Rollins's files, maybe he was telling the truth when he said he found them to be such an interesting read." Eric holds out his hands, shrugs. "But one thing about being in the FBI,

Sally, you don't become an agent by believing every-thing a person tells you the first time around, even if that person *is* a lawman. So I started asking around in Kirkwood – talking to the deputies, talking to the people, talking to a few of the McQuade family's former employees. And you know what they told me?"

"No. What?"

"Well, they told me they'd heard the name. A couple of them told me he'd rolled into Brenton here just over a month back, shortly before I called up old Larry. They said he was staying right here, in this hotel." Eric taps the counter, as if to drive his point home. "So, after all that, I'm sure you can guess what I've come here to ask you about, right?"

Sally regards him for a moment, then slowly says, "I don't know any Tom Rollins. That isn't to say he wasn't here. I don't always ask for names, and people don't always give their real ones."

Eric nods along. "Sure," he says. "I can understand that." He stands where he is, continues to smile at Sally, doesn't make any move to indicate he is about to leave. He reaches into his pocket, pulls out a photograph. It's an old picture, taken from Rollins's time in the army. He holds it in front of her. "Luckily, I brought along a visual aid, too."

Sally looks at him. "I don't recognize him."

"Try adding a beard, perhaps, and some hair."

Sally frowns, looks back at the picture. "Sorry, no. Maybe I just don't have the imagination."

"Maybe not." Eric puts the photo back in his pocket. "I find it strange you haven't asked me who he is."

Sally shrugs. "So who is he? Why's he so important you've gotta come all the way out here to try to track him down?"

"Oh, just an old friend," Eric says. "I've been missing him. Was hoping to catch up."

"That sounds like a gross misuse of federal time."

Eric laughs. "Well, maybe I'm just being coy, and maybe there's a little more to it than that."

"You want to arrest him?"

"Not exactly."

"What, then?"

Eric taps the side of his nose. He can see how Sally is growing flustered with him and his behavior.

"Is he dangerous?" she says.

Eric lets his smile fade. "Oh, yes," he says. "Very."

"Y'know, you're being very secretive about all this. People would be more inclined to help you if you were a little more straight-talking."

"I ask straightforward questions, Sally," Eric says, smiling again. "Do you know, or have you ever known, a Tom Rollins?"

"I already told you, no."

"So if he came through here, stayed in this hotel, you wouldn't have any idea where he was going next?"

"No."

She's good. He doesn't entirely believe her, but she covers herself well. Even if it's not true what she said, and no one by that name checked in here, he's sure she at least has an idea whom he's talking about. But she shows no hesitations, no tics. Maintains eye contact all the way through. A cool customer if he's ever seen one.

"Okay, then," Eric says in an exhalation of air, patting the palms of both hands on the top of the counter. "Thank you for your time, Sally. You ever do happen to come into contact with this Tom Rollins, you just call our field offices in Houston, ask for me. That's Senior Special Agent Eric Thompson. You got that? Easy enough to remember, right? Maybe write it down, though – everyone thinks they'll remember it, but they don't. All righty, then, you have a great day, Sally."

He steps out of the hotel, stands on the sidewalk in front of it, looks up and down. The man smoking on the bench, Darby, is still there. Eric takes a step toward him. "Say, I don't suppose you've ever heard the name Tom Rollins, have you? Lately?"

Darby flicks what's left of his cigarette, gets to his feet. "Sorry, mister," he says. "Can't say that I have." He heads into the hotel, off the street.

Eric watches him go, then gets back into his car. He drives out of Brenton, shakes his head as he goes, starts laughing.

"You're a slippery one, all right, Tom," he says, turning the radio on and tapping his hands on the steering wheel in time to 'You Can't Hurry Love' by The Supremes. "But I'll find you one day."

He turns up the music. It's a beautiful day, and he has a long drive ahead of him. He takes his time.

ABOUT THE AUTHOR

Did you enjoy *Wrong Turn*? Please consider leaving a review on Amazon to help other readers discover the book.

Paul Heatley left school at sixteen, and since then has held a variety of jobs including mechanic, carpet fitter, and bookshop assistant, but his passion has always been for writing. He writes mostly in the genres of crime fiction and thriller, and links to his other titles can be found on his website. He lives in the north east of England.

Want to connect with Paul? Visit him at his website or on any of these social media channels.

www.PaulHeatley.com

Published by Inkubator Books
www.inkubatorbooks.com

Printed in Great Britain
by Amazon

25628499R00179